DOLPH
THE UNICORN KILLER & OTHER STORIES

I0592753

MARTIN LASTRAPES

Also by Martin Lastrapes

Inside the Outside
The Vampire, the Hunter, and the Girl
The Vampire, the Hunter, and the Witch
The Vampire, the Hunter, and Frank

Praise for insidetheoutside

"This may be one of the most disturbing, well-written, amazing, and mind-blowing novels I've read in ages."
    –Miya Kressin, author of *The Asylum Saga* **and** *No Expectations*

"If you want a grisly page-turner, this book will more than deliver. Get beneath the skin and subcutaneous fat though and, as with the human body, what you'll find with *Inside The Outside* is a complex and impressive structure, not of veins and capillaries but themes, ideas and commentary."
    –Andy Elliott, author of *Composition*

"I can tell you that I haven't had a book call me back as much as *Inside the Outside* in some time. The characters are unconventional, flawed, and as real as the world Martin's made for them."
    –Belinda Frisch, author of *Cure* **and** *Afterbirth*

Praise for THE VAMPIRE AND THE HUNTER TRILOGY

"*The Vampire and the Hunter Trilogy* sucks you in (pun fully intended) and doesn't let go. Is there anything new to say about vampires? Martin Lastrapes proves there is and it is creepy and sexy and definitely full of fresh blood."
    –Diana Wagman, author of *Life #6* **and**
    The Care and Feeding of Exotic Pets

"Martin Lastrapes' knack for storytelling stands up easily alongside such stalwarts as Stephen King and Chuck Palahniuk and *The Vampire and the Hunter Trilogy* is no exception. I don't simply enjoy his stories, I crave them."
    –Gianna Perada, author of *Blood Life*

"Martin Lastrapes' storytelling is addictive—the superlative narration, the excitement and intensity of the words, the relatable characters and the nuances of their lives. Lastrapes' meticulous presentation and techniques are masterful; his style is reminiscent of Tim O'Brien."
    –Jake Aurelian, author of *The Life & Mimes*
    (& Zombie Apocalypse) of Ripper the Clown:
    The Autobiography of an Unconventional Zombie

For Kay and Jim

CONTENTS

"Vegas is purposefully constructed as a self-enclosed and isolated biosphere, sort of what a recreational colony built on the moon might be like."
–Marc Cooper, *The Last Honest Place in America*

"Las Vegas is sort of like how God would do it if he had money."
–Steve Wynn

The Vampire and the Madman

L as Vegas is a desert.

And I'm a vampire.

We're a match made in Heaven, friend, and until recently I never wanted to be anywhere else in the world. Locals know Las Vegas is a desert, as do a few tourists. But, if everything you know about Las Vegas comes from movies and television, then you probably think the entirety of my city is the Strip. Bright lights, resort hotels, celebrity chefs, gambling, casinos, sex, and more. More, more, more. If you've only seen Las Vegas in sweeping aerial shots during boxing pay-per-views or UFC fights, then you've been given the illusion of a metropolitan city rivaling other illusions, such as Los Angeles or Paris. The full length of the Strip is less than five miles, but you'd hardly know it seeing previews for the latest Jason Bourne movie or waxing nostalgic over *The Hangover*. You can easily spend days or even weeks on the Strip without ever needing to go anywhere else, leading you to believe that the whole city really is encompassed within that 4.2 mile stretch of bright lights and swimming pools, night clubs and showgirls, black jacks and snake eyes.

When you're a vampire, you have the time and energy to travel far and wide. Certainly, you need money, but any vampire worth his salt can get cash anytime he needs it. I've set foot on at least half the globe, seen the Leaning Tower and the Great Wall. I've swum amongst the phytoplankton in the Indian Ocean and soaked up moonlight at the peak of the Himalayas, but I've never loved any place in the world like I love Las Vegas—at least, not since I've been a vampire. I hardly recall how long I've been a vampire, though there was a time when I could've told you down to the minute. I can comfortably say it's been over a century—and probably longer than that. But, the time frame isn't important. Only that I ended up in Las Vegas, that's the part that matters to this story. Las Vegas is where I've lived my best and happiest years. And now it's where I will likely meet my end, imprisoned inside some madman's mansion.

I don't know how long I've been here. I sit inside a glass cell, hardly bigger than a phone booth. My cell sits in a long row of other cells, some of which also contain vampires. The madman fancies himself a vampire hunter, which I suppose he is, but I also imagine a vampire hunter would have the integrity to kill you where he found you—or greet death honorably should you have him outmatched. Instead, I got kidnapped and thrown into this cell. He hasn't yet explained the purpose of our imprisonment, nor has he given any indication that we should expect an explanation. I'm not an idiot, however, so it's not been too difficult to work out at least part of the purpose. The madman is using us for experiments like immortal guinea pigs. At any given time of the day, I'll see men and women buzzing about in white lab coats concocting liquids and weapons and smoking beakers. I have no idea what they are exactly doing, but I do know the end goal is to help the madman kill vampires. Even if the madman doesn't kill me himself, I'm sure I'll die in here of starvation.

Yes, vampires can starve to death. We're immortal, but not unconditionally. We can't survive stakes to the heart. Silver burns like scorching hot metal. Fire hurts, too, and it'll kill me just as effectively as it'll kill you. Garlic won't necessarily kill a vampire, but it's very painful to the touch—and, perhaps as evolution's cruel joke, vampires can't smell it. Sunlight, however, is the most dangerous and persistent killer of vampires. Imagine spending half the day inside your home, knowing there's a serial killer just waiting for you to step outside. If I go outside while the sun is overhead, I'm as good as toast.

And there's plenty of sun in Las Vegas, especially during the summer when the sun rises by five in the morning and stays up until nearly eight in the evening. I used to feel like I was in prison during the summers in Las Vegas because the nighttime hours were so limited. I had less time to roam the streets, hitting up feeding posts, gambling, and generally getting into trouble. I wasn't in Las Vegas long as a vampire before learning about a network of underground tunnels where we could hang out and socialize during the daytime hours. Thousands of Las Vegas' homeless residents populate these tunnels, many of whom find themselves chained up in feeding posts where vampires drink from them until they're good and empty. I've never snatched a human myself, though. I leave that to the hunters who keep the inventory of our feeding posts in stock.

Steel grates, concrete, graffiti, makeshift tents and beds, coffee tables made of wooden crates, roofs made of cardboard—such are the tunnels beneath Las Vegas. At any given time of the day while you're playing a hand of poker in Caesar's Palace or taking in a show at the MGM Grand, immediately below you men and women are getting high or catching sleep, while vampires are drinking blood and waiting for sunset. A lot of vampires live in the tunnels, but not me. I prefer something a little more civilized, so I've always kept a room in North Las Vegas, which is generally the rougher part of town. The Las Vegas Strip runs north and south. South takes you in the direction of pure desert, nothing but dirt and rocks until you're flushed out into California. North takes you into the urban decay of Las Vegas, the remnants of the older city, near Downtown, where you can still find old-fashioned peepshows, dive bars, and cheap motels.

I've kept the same room at the same motel for a few decades now.

The owners usually change over the years, sometimes over a legitimate sell, other times because of a gambling debt or worse. Nobody pays much mind to the guy in Room 21, the one who never goes out during the day, never eats solid food, and never ages. I pay my rent, mind my own business, and nobody bothers me. People mostly use the rooms to fuck, mainly johns and prostitutes, but, once in a while, there'll be a marital affair that needs the anonymity of Downtown. Most other times the rooms are occupied by naïve tourists looking to save money by not staying on the Strip. If you don't know any better, here's a word of warning: Wander into Downtown at your own risk.

And I'm not talking about Fremont Street or the bright lights and kitschy hotels of old time Vegas, where gangsters and lounge singers hung out in the same company. I'm talking about the Downtown beyond the bright lights and general safety. If you're a tourist, your safest bet—literally—is to stick to the tourist traps. Unless you're a vampire, in which case you can wander anywhere you like. At least, that's what I used to think before the madman kidnapped me.

Would you believe I actually had a job before I found myself in the madman's prison? I was working at a call center called Kwipz. Call centers are abundant in Las Vegas, employing much of the city's workforce as they'll take pretty much anybody willing to talk to grumpy consumers all day. Before I got hired, I assumed all call centers were in India somewhere with customer service agents doing their best impersonation of an American accent. Most every person you meet in Vegas has likely worked in at least one call center in their life—and it's very likely that place was Kwipz. At Kwipz, you didn't need the requisite motivation of a paycheck to get hired, you simply needed a heartbeat and a social security number (of which I had both, thank you very much).

I worked at Kwipz for the money, but also for the hours. I showed up for the opening shift five days a week, which was an ideal way to earn a buck while avoiding the sun. My shift started at 4 o'clock in the morning, all but guaranteeing I'd avoid the sun on my way in.

Of course, I had to stay indoors until sunset, but that was no big deal. The call center was inside of a big building with several empty and purposeless rooms, so there was never a shortage of places to catch a nap before taking in the night. Or, if I felt like it, I'd just put in overtime on the phones. Kwipz granted overtime to reliable agents who received good surveys and kept their metrics above goal, which described me to a tee. Kwipz employees mostly didn't notice me, with the exception of Bentley and Isaiah, a pair of homoerotic best friends who call me Whitey when they think I can't hear them. I only know their names because I fantasize about saying them out loud, over and over again, as I murder them slowly and painfully. It's just a fantasy, though, as I'm not a murderer myself.

Incidentally, money had nothing to do with why I worked at Kwipz. Like I mentioned earlier, any vampire worth his salt can get cash anytime he needs it. I've robbed liquor stores, mugged tourists, panhandled on Las Vegas Boulevard, sold drugs, and gone silver mining in every hotel in Las Vegas. Given a choice, I always preferred non-violent means of earning money. Even when I mugged people, I was mostly polite and left them physically unharmed, if not in fear of their lives. Silver mining was the best combination of non-violent and entertaining when it came to earning money. There's not much to it, really. You just go into a casino and wander around the slot machines looking for unused credits. Once upon a time, such a scheme would've been impossible when all slot machines were coin operated and little old women walked around smoky casinos with plastic cups full of nickels and dimes. But now that they're all computerized it's fairly common for a gambler—whether they're too drunk to realize it or too careless to mind—to leave credit on a slot machine. It might be a dollar here or twenty there, but whatever it is you simply spit out the receipt and take it to the cashier. Once, not all that long ago, I found $212 of credit in a single slot machine.

You won't get rich silver-mining and you can hardly put together a good haul without being patient, but I'm nothing if not patient.

Barring a sunbath or an altercation with a wealthy madman, I've got all the time in the world. If you've got time and patience, you can make a half-decent living silver-mining. At least you can make enough to cover rent in a cheap motel in North Las Vegas. I started working in Kwipz just to do something different, change up my routine a bit. I had a cubicle, privacy, and something to keep my mind occupied. And it kept my nights free, which is sort of a big deal when you're a vampire.

Here's the problem with vampire hunters: They're mythological figures, figments of some fictional tale, until the day you meet one. Up until that day, vampire hunters are as real as the Bogeyman. Sure, you hear the occasional story of the vampire who crossed paths with a vampire hunter and lived to tell the tale, but you're never quite sure how reliable the source is. It was probably just some vampire shining himself up at the feeding post, trying to make himself feel good. Generally speaking, vampires are solitary creatures. We scarcely travel in groups at all, so, if a vampire hunter did cross your path, you almost definitely wouldn't have any sort of backup. Then again, you would have super speed and strength on your side. When I say "super," I mean as compared to humans. We're not comic book heroes, like Dolph the Unicorn Killer, but we're still very impressive. Though, as I think about it, Dolph doesn't have super speed or strength. I suppose Courageous Man is a better example, but that's neither here nor there.

It occurs to me that I haven't explained feeding posts to you yet. I suspect you can work out what they are, but perhaps not why they exist. Especially given the fact that vampires have super speed and strength, why would we need a one-stop feeding shop? It comes down to this— vampires aren't allowed to hunt. I mean, vampires *can* hunt, but they can't go freelancing for themselves. You can only hunt if the purpose is for providing inventory for a feeding post. There are several feeding posts all around the world, so hunters are always in demand. I've never been too terribly interested in hunting myself on account of the whole non-violence thing. My feeding post of choice was underground in the tunnels and that's exactly where I was headed when the madman snatched me.

I'd just finished watching *Jersey Boys* at the Paris, which is a wonderful musical. One of the great perks of living in Las Vegas is never being at a loss for things to do. There's always a way to entertain yourself and, for me, I love a good stage show. On this particular weekend I decided to treat myself to dinner *and* a show, just not in that order. It wasn't my first time seeing *Jersey Boys*, but I enjoyed it like it was the first time. As much as I enjoy the show, I love to see people in the audience enjoying themselves, especially when it's clearly their first time because *Jersey Boys* washes over you like a religious experience. After the show I walked out with the rest of the herd, some folks heading to the casino, while others went into Mon Ami Gabi for some French cuisine. I headed out onto Las Vegas Boulevard and began walking north, taking in a few moments of the Bellagio's elegant water show across the street.

I moved quickly, anxious to enter Downtown, but not so fast as to make anybody take notice. While I may be superior to humans, I don't want any of them to know that I'm a vampire. One of the most important rules about being a vampire is not letting humans know you exist. Yes, I know, between the hunting and keeping ourselves secret from humans, it seems there are a lot of rules governing vampires—and there are. It's just part of our culture. While there are no vampire police out there enforcing the rules, we're all generally respectful of the boundaries placed upon us. Plus, there are stories of vampires who've broken the rules and were never heard from again. So, you know, why take chances?

I walked up Las Vegas Boulevard, past the Flamingo Hilton and Harrah's, past the Venetian and Wynn, past the Encore and Trump International, past the Fashion Show Mall, the Sands Expo, Circus Circus, the Stratosphere, Gold & Silver Pawn Shop, Showgirl Video, and

Graceland Wedding Chapel, until the lights became less bright and the buildings less inviting, until the tourists faded away and the only people around were those naïve enough, careless enough, or brave enough to travel by foot through the mangled edges of this wonderful city.

This next part is embarrassing, as it involves the scuffle that ended with me being kidnapped by the madman. I was heading to the entrance of the tunnels to get dinner, the dense aroma of fear in the air already properly stirring my appetite. The night was relatively silent, save for the ambient sound of cars and passersby. Then out of nowhere, a high-pitched squeal sliced through the air. I'd never heard anything like it. It wasn't so much loud as it was painful—extremely painful. I brought my hands to my ears, but there was no amount of pressure I could apply to fully drown out the pain. I dropped to my knees, looking around, expecting to see everyone around me covering their ears, but nobody else seemed bothered—just me and a stray dog barking his discomfort across the street.

I was still holding my ears when a hoop dropped over my head, sizzling as it touched my hands and wrists. I knew immediately the hoop was made of silver, so I pulled my hands away from my head and, as I did, the hoop cinched around my neck, leaving little-to-no room to move. Connected to the hoop was a pole and holding the pole was the madman. He had long gray hair and a thick mustache. With him was a younger man pointing a gun at me—at least it looked like a gun—his finger squeezing the trigger. Attached to the end of the gun was something that looked like a small satellite dish. When the younger man took his finger off of the trigger, the high-pitch noise went away.

The madman yanked on the pole, burning the silver hoop against my neck.

"Move it," he said, "you fucking vampire."

I walked in the direction he pulled me until I found myself in the back of a van. He attached the pole to the wall of the van, before shutting the doors, leaving me alone and trapped.

And that was that.

That was the whole struggle. Hell, there *was* no struggle. I never even had a chance to put up a fight. That's what makes it so embarrassing. You always imagine that, should the day come when a vampire hunter confronts you, you'll fight and claw, protecting yourself and the culture you represent. You'll make him regret his misguided plans of murder or, should things go awry, you'll take pride in knowing you didn't go out without a fight. But, for me, there were none of those things. Just a horrible sound, a silver hoop, and the inside of a van.

Pathetic.

"Who're you talking to?"

"Pardon?"

"Leave him alone."

"No, I want to know who he's calling pathetic."

Sorry, about this, friend. The other imprisoned vampires have decided to chime in. There are four of us in all, not that we know one another. At least, we didn't know each other before being co-inhabitants in the madman's basement. Three boys and a girl. The girl's name is Sandy.

"He's just talking to himself," Sandy says. "Leave him alone."

Sandy is kind. I like her.

The other is not so kind. His name is Cliff. Some days he leaves me be, while other days he just can't help himself. Cliff, unfortunately, is in the cell beside mine. He's staring at me now, nose pressed to the glass.

"Seriously," he says, "who're you talking to?"

Sigh.

All I want is for Cliff to stop talking. I'd gladly spend one hundred more years in this prison if he'd just leave me alone. I wish he were more like Eddie. That's Sandy's brother. He's quiet and reserved, keeps to himself unless he's talking to Sandy. I like him, too. We've never exchanged a word with one another, good or bad. I like it just fine that way.

"Well?" Cliff asks. "Who're you talking to?"

"I'm talking to them."

"Them who?"

I point at you, friend, my fingertip pressed to the glass.

"Nobody's there you whack job."

He can't see you. Consider yourself lucky.

"Leave him alone."

"He won't stop talking!"

Sandy looks at me, smiling.

"Maybe you can talk inside your head," she says. "Will you do that?"

"But, they need to hear," I say. "They need to know my story."

"They can hear you," she says. "I promise."

She smiles and I believe her. I'll stay inside my head and have faith you can still hear me, friend, faith that you're still listening. I don't know how long I've been in here. I've seen several vampires come and go, often murdered before my eyes. I've been poked and prodded by men and women in white lab coats and sometimes by the madman himself. I'm so hungry. He doesn't feed us. I'd drink my own blood if I thought it'd make the hunger go away. Maybe it's been months. Or years. I really don't know. Most days I wish I'd die. Not all days, though. Some days there is hope.

Hope.

Hope.

Hope.

The madman comes down into the basement with a Hispanic guy I've never seen before. Also with him are the pretty witch and the younger hunter, both of whom are all too familiar. The madman is giving the Hispanic guy a tour, showing him the equipment, the men and women in the white lab coats, and eventually he shows him us. I'm sitting cross-legged inside my cell, choosing to look uninterested in hopes they won't bother me. Sandy gives them her full attention, pressing her nose against the glass and watching as they approach.

"Now, you might be wondering why I've got these vampires here," the madman says. "They serve a whole host of purposes from testing out weapons to experimentation."

It's the first time I've heard him admit out loud what he does with us. I'm not shocked by the revelation, but it's still a bit jarring to know for certain what my role is in this prison.

"When the lab monkeys come up with something new," the madman says, "such as the high-pitch air horn that Nick showed you, we test it out on these here vampires to make sure it works."

Asshole.

"Well, maybe not these vampires exactly," the madman says. "I suppose you can say we have a high turnover rate where it concerns our bloodsucking guests."

The Hispanic guy looks us over, curious, but not afraid. He doesn't seem surprised to learn vampires are real. Sandy continues to stare, focusing her attention on the Hispanic guy, her palms pressed against the glass.

"Don't mind her," the madman says. "She looks like a nice gal, but you take her out of that box and she's a monster just like the rest of them."

The madman walks the Hispanic guy to a chair, where the white coats poked him with a needle, extracting a blood sample. The sight of that delicious crimson nectar filling the tube makes me salivate to an almost embarrassing degree. They pay us no more attention and within a few minutes they're all gone, but for the white coats and the madman. One of the white coats sucks a portion of the blood up into an eyedropper, handing it to the madman. He walks with the eyedropper, heading directly for my cell. My eyes lock onto that blood, my stomach aching as I watch it ebb and flow.

He opens up the middle portion of my cell, letting one of the white coats slide the silver hoop inside. I'd learned my lesson several weeks (or months or years) earlier that if you obey the silver hoop, they don't necessarily hurt you. I let the lab coat bring the hoop over my head, closing it just tight enough so that I won't move. The madman motions for me to get down on my knees, so I do. He reaches into the cell, holding the eyedropper over my mouth. I'm so excited that I inadvertently burn my neck against the silver hoop. The pain doesn't take my focus from the eyedropper. I open my mouth, fangs exposed, and let the madman drop three delicious crimson pearls onto my tongue.

He looks at the white coat.

"Yank the hoop."

Before I know what's happening, the white coat pulls back the pole, pressing the silver hoop hard against the back of my neck. I nearly yelp in anticipation of the pain—only there is no pain. The madman lifts a silver needle from one of the countertops and reaches his arm into the cell, poking me with it. The prick of the needle didn't feel good, but the silver has no effect whatsoever. It's a miracle. One of the white coats approaches with a bundle of garlic, handing it to the madman. He presses the garlic to my cheek and, again, I feel nothing more than the force of his hand. The madman snaps his fingers and points at the counter, prompting one of the white coats to bring him an X-Acto knife. The madman reaches his hand into the cell, quickly swiping the knife against my cheek—this time, I felt tremendous pain. I scream, bringing my fingers to my cheek, feeling blood run down my knuckles.

"I'll be goddamned," the madman says. "This son of a bitch is human."

What?

How could this be?

I don't want to be human.

Not again.

A sizzling sounds, followed by searing pain against my neck. It's the silver hoop. In my confusion, I'd become careless and let the hoop touch my skin. But, if I was human, it shouldn't have hurt. Only it *did* hurt. I scream again, before beginning to cry. I hate being treated this way, like some sort of animal not worthy of sympathy or affection. The madman pokes me again with the silver pin and presses the garlic to my cheek, both of which hurt like hell.

"Alright," the madman says, "I've seen enough."

The white coat removes the hoop from my neck and closes the cell. I sit again, cross-legged, crying to myself. I touch my fingers to my cheek and find the knife wound has completely healed. I wasn't human after all. At least, not anymore.

The madman exits the basement and the white coats go to work on the Hispanic guy's blood. I hadn't a clue what they were doing with it, but it all seemed awfully wasteful of perfectly good blood. They pour it into various beakers, diluting it, shaking it, and watching it. They add other liquids and powders, scribbling notes and conversing in hushed tones.

"Hey," Sandy says, "you okay?"

"Yes," I say. "Thank you."

"What happened?"

"I don't know," I say. "For a few minutes there, silver and garlic didn't hurt."

"But that knife did, huh?"

"Yes."

"Strange."

One of the white coats makes a phone call and a few minutes later the madman is back in the basement, along with the young hunter. The white coats tell them about the Hispanic guy's blood and the tests they've run and what they learned. They tell him the Hispanic guy has anabolic steroids in his blood and they believe that's what affected me. They open up the middle portion of my cell once again, only this time it's the young hunter who slips the silver hoop over my head. I am obedient as usual, as I don't care to feel any more pain. One of the white coats hands the madman another eyedropper, but this one didn't have blood in it. He holds it over my mouth and I obediently open, letting him drop the relatively flavorless liquid on my tongue.

"Yank it," the madman says.

The young hunter yanks the hoop, touching the silver to my neck. It doesn't hurt.

"Hold it there," the madman said. "I want to time this."

The young hunter pulls so hard on the hoop, my cheek presses against the glass of my cell. The madman eyes his watch, looking up when he hears me scream.

"The silver hurts again," he says. "That was about three minutes."

The young hunter removes the hoop, before closing the cell. I collapse in pain, holding my neck where the skin burns like it was about to fall off. The madman and the young hunter exit the basement, leaving the white coats to do whatever they were doing. I curl up into myself and cry. I hear Sandy calling for my attention, but I don't feel like talking. I just want the pain to go away, so I lay like this until I fell asleep.

I wake up to the sound of the madman and the young hunter walking towards our cells. The pretty witch and the Hispanic guy are with them. The madman explains to the Hispanic guy what he'd been doing to me earlier, as they walk over to my cell and knock on the glass. I sit up, giving the humans my attention. The memory of what he'd done boiled over inside of me, causing me to jump to my feet and pound my fists against the glass.

"This one here is who got to taste it," the madman says.

"Fuck you!" I scream.

"As you can tell," the madman says, "he's none too happy about it."

I can feel Sandy's eyes on me. I look over to her, seeing her palms pressed to the glass, quietly imploring me to settle down. I sit down on the floor, hugging my knees to my chest.

"As best as I could tell," the madman says, "that vampire was temporarily human."

He tells the Hispanic guy it was the steroids that did it.

"You mean, like, the steroids in *conjunction* with my blood?" the Hispanic guy asks.

"No," the madman says. "Turns out, the steroids alone will do the trick. Once the lab monkeys figured out it was the steroids, we tested it on another vampire, injecting him with a silver-needled syringe. He got weak, just like the first one. Then we tested it on the other two and the same thing happened."

I look over at the other vampires, extending my silent sympathy. I must've slept through their torture. The madman and the Hispanic guy talk about whatever—missiles and steroids and someone named Frank. None of it seems to involve me or the other vampires and, so long as they aren't torturing us anymore, I don't care. They walk across the basement and open a small door, pulling out a glass sphere about the size of a bowling ball. A light glows inside of the glass ball, right at the center. The madman calls it a sunlight bomb, because the pretty witch concocted some sort of spell that infused the glass ball with sunlight.

"How does it work?" the Hispanic guy asks.

"Well, *if* it works," the pretty witch says, "all you have to do is throw the sunlight bomb on the ground as close to your target as possible. When the glass shatters, it should release a burst of sunlight. The sunlight won't harm a human any more than high noon, but it should be potent enough to scorch a vampire to death."

My stomach drops.

"If you think it's ready to go," the madman says, "I say we give it a try."

He grabs the pole with the silver hoop and tells the young hunter to open one of the cells.

"Which one?"

"The one on the end is fine."

I'm on the end, which means I'm about to be tested on again. But, Eddie is on the *other* end and that's the cell the young hunter approaches. He opens the top section of the cell and Eddie immediately jumps towards the opening, trying to push his head through. The madman pushes him back with the silver hoop and Eddie screams, bringing his hands to his forehead where the silver burned him. The madman slips the hoop over Eddie's head, cinching it up just enough to make sure he doesn't try any more sudden moves.

"Go ahead and open the rest of the door," the madman says.

The young hunter opens the cell fully and the madman leads Eddie out with the silver hoop, guiding him to the middle of the floor. The madman tells the pretty witch to get the sunlight bomb, so she does.

"Whenever you're ready," the madman says, "let her rip."

"No!" Eddie screams. "Please don't do this."

The madman smiles.

"Please don't do what?"

"Please don't kill me."

My heart breaks as Sandy slaps her palms against the glass, watching her brother beg for his life.

"Looking for mercy?" the madman says. "How many people did you take mercy on before killing them?"

"I never killed anybody."

"Bullshit," the madman says, tugging on the silver hoop. "You think I'm stupid?"

Eddie falls to his knees, screaming in pain.

"Please," he says, crying. "Don't do this."

The madman waits for the pretty witch to use the sunlight bomb, but she tells him she can't do it. Maybe I'm looking for hope where it doesn't exist, but I think she's actually taking pity on Eddie. The madman tells her to give the sunlight bomb to the young hunter, so she does.

"All I have to do is smash it on the floor?" the young hunter asks.

"Yes," says the pretty witch.

The madman tells him to smash it when he's ready.

Sandy pounds her fists against her cell.

"Please, no!" she screams.

The young hunter already has the sunlight bomb over his head, bringing it down hard against the floor, smashing the glass beside Eddie. Upon its impact, a dome of bright sunlight expands up and out, swallowing Eddie completely, before engulfing him in flames. Within moments the dome of sunlight disappears, but the damage is already done. We can only watch in horror as Eddie burns to death in front of us, his body collapsing into a pile of black ash.

Sandy cries for several days, but the madman isn't here to see it. Neither is the pretty witch, the young hunter, or the Hispanic guy. Even the white coats haven't been around. The basement is completely empty. I don't know how long it's been. I wish more than anything I could hug her. Even Cliff was being kind, though I had my doubts as to just how upset he was about Eddie's death. I had a little brother who died when we were kids in 1899 or thereabouts. Tuberculosis took him away. They've got a vaccine for it now, which is nice for all those big brothers who don't have to watch their little brothers die.

It's funny the things you see when you're immortal, the view of the world you become privy to. I wonder what my family would've been like—my mom and dad, my brothers and sister—if we'd been born now, today, in a world with advanced medicine, plentiful food, the Internet, and cable news. I love being a vampire, but I sometimes feel guilty for the blessing, especially since my family will never have the opportunity to see the things I've seen or do the things I've done. I envy Sandy and Eddie for the time they enjoyed as vampires together. Such a rare opportunity to share immortality with a sibling. But, even for vampires, life can be startlingly fragile. Sometimes forever simply means a very long time.

"Are you still talking to them?" Sandy asks.

"Pardon?"

"You're audience," she says. "Are you still talking to them?"

My god, can she see you? No, of course not. That would be silly.

"Yes," I say.

"You're still telling them your story?"

"Yes."

"Have you told them about this place?"

"I have, yes," I say. "I've told them about the glass cells and the madman and I've just finished telling them about your brother. He was very kind and didn't deserve the end he got."

"Thank you," she says. "How do you think it will end?"

"How what will end?"

"The story."

"I don't know."

"Do you think it will end inside of this prison?"

Between you and I, friend, the answer is yes. I *do* believe my story will end here.

"No," I say. "No, I don't."

Sandy smiles.

Hope.

Time is fluid in this prison. It passes with speed and sloth, furious and monotonous all at once, so it's never clear when the day has begun or a new week has passed. There is a clock in the basement, but no windows. I only know it's a clock based on its general shape and place-ment in the room, but I can't actually see the time on it. So, when the elevator doors open and the pretty witch turns up in the basement, I have no real idea as to how much time has passed since I saw her last. I'd grown accustomed to the basement's silence, so the sound of the elevator opening was startling.

Sandy calls out to the pretty witch as she walks past our cells. She turns and looks at Sandy, but doesn't respond.

"Can you help us?"

"With what?"

"We're hungry," Sandy says. "We need to get out of here."

"I can't do that," says the pretty witch. "I'm sorry."

"Nobody's been around," Sandy says. "The white coats usually feed us, but it's been empty. We're starving."

"You all would kill me if I let you out."

Cliff responds to this before Sandy can.

"She's the witch," he says. "She made that fucking glass ball that killed Eddie."

"I know who she is," Sandy says. "What's your name?"

"Whisper."

"My name's Sandy," she says. "Eddie was my brother."

Sandy's voice is calm and measured, like a politician. I know she's hurting, but you'd never know it in that moment.

"I watched him die," Sandy says. "Do you know what that's like?"

"I'm sorry."

"I don't need you to be sorry," Sandy says. "I just need you to let us out of here."

"Even if I wanted to," Whisper says, "I don't know how."

"She's lying," I say, punching the glass. "She's fucking lying!"

I don't know why I said that. I think it's just all the anger and sadness that's been boiling up inside of me. Sandy quiets me with her eyes, letting me know in her silent way that she has things under control.

"We know what you do here," Sandy says. "We've seen you all working around the clock before it went empty. We'll die in here if you don't let us out. And it won't be fast. It would take years, maybe decades. Possibly centuries. I wouldn't wish that death on anybody."

Whisper is quiet for a few moments and, on her face, I can see a flash of the same sympathy she'd shown Eddie.

"There's nothing I can do," she says.

"But you want to."

Whisper is silent again.

"I can smell it in your fear," Sandy says. "You want to help us, but you're afraid we'll turn on you. I can assure you, we won't do anything to harm you. We just want a chance to fend for ourselves back on the outside."

"Somebody's going to get hurt, though," Whisper says. "That's the price of what you do."

"We have to eat," Sandy says. "That's just how it is. We won't eat you, though. I have to believe that's worth something."

Silence.

"I listened to my brother beg for his life," Sandy says. "He begged, then your friend killed him."

This makes Whisper cry.

"You're not evil," Sandy says. "I know that. Neither are we."

Silence.

The next sound we hear isn't a voice, but rather the elevator doors opening. All of us—Sandy, Cliff, Whisper, and me—turn our heads to see who will come out. It's a woman. She's wearing blue jeans and a T-shirt. I recognize her face. She's one of the white coats. She walks towards Whisper, smiling. They share greetings and hellos. The white coat says her name is Janice. Still crying, Whisper tries to compose herself.

"Is George here?" Janice asks.

"No."

"It's been about a week," Janice says. "Will he be back soon?"

A week? Is that really how much time has passed? I'd have sooner believed seven years before I believed only seven days have come and gone.

"George is dead."

I wish I were better at remembering names, which is why I'm not 100% certain as to who George is. But, I think George is the name of the madman—at least I hope it is.

"Oh my god," Janice says. "What happened?"

"A vampire killed him."

"Where was Nick?"

"Nick was there, too."

"Is he okay?"

Whisper shakes her head, no.

"Is he—?"

More silence.

"What about the new guy," Janice asks, "Jesus?"

"He survived," Whisper says, "but he's in bad shape."

Okay, if I'm putting things together properly, Nick is the young hunter and Jesus is the Hispanic guy who toured the basement last week. I don't know all that much about Jesus, but I'm sure as hell happy to hear Nick is dead. Whisper and Janice speak some more, mostly about California and vengeance. Janice cautions her against going after the vampire that killed her friends, but Whisper tells her it's complicated. Janice leaves the basement, going up the elevator for a drink.

"I'll be right up," Whisper tells her. "I just need to collect a few things down here."

She walks past our cells to the other end of the basement.

"I'm sorry for your loss," Sandy says.

Whisper stops.

"I know he wasn't a friend to vampires," Sandy says, "but I also know what it is to lose someone."

"Thank you."

Sandy says nothing else, so Whisper continues walking until she reaches the end of the basement. She opens a small door in the wall, removing some contents, before walking back to the elevator.

"Are you coming back?" Sandy asks.

"I don't know."

"Please don't leave us here."

"I don't want you to suffer," Whisper says. "I really don't. But, I don't know what to do."

"I understand your position," Sandy says. "But, I promise you can trust us. We won't harm you."

Silence.

"Will you do me one favor?" Sandy asks. "Whatever you decide, just come back and let us know face to face?"

Whisper and Janice return to the basement. Janice leads her towards our cells, stopping at a keypad on the wall.

"Over here," she says. "You'll just have to punch in the code, which I'll give you in a second. Following that, you'll press the pound key followed by the number for the cell you want to open. They're in cells one, two, and three."

"Do I have to put in the code for each cell?"

"No," Janice says. "Just hit pound one, pound two, and pound three immediately after inputting the code. All three doors will open at once."

My god, is this happening? Is Whisper's sympathy shining through? Oh please, let it be so.

"You sure you want to do this?"

"Yeah," Whisper says, "I think so."

"Just promise you'll give me time to get out," Janice says. "At least ten minutes."

"I promise."

They shake hands before Whisper watches Janice get into the elevator, waving goodbye as the doors slide shut. All three of us vampires are on our feet at this point, anticipating what is about to happen. As Whisper turns to face us, Sandy speaks.

"I knew you were decent," she says. "Thank you."

"I hope you won't make me regret this."

"You have my word."

It all feels too good to be true, but it's happening. Whisper stands quietly, looking at the clock on the wall, presumably waiting the ten minutes she'd promised Janice. For whatever time has passed since my capture, for all the agony and grief, none of it can compare to the ten minutes I stand here in my cell hoping against hope that Whisper won't change her mind.

Cliff sniffs the air, smelling the same thing Sandy and I can smell: Fear. It's like the aroma of freshly baked bread or the char of sweet barbecue, the snapping of fresh produce or perfume of a candy shop. It's an unnamable smell, but the joy is universal. It's the smell of a delicious meal floating beneath the nostrils of a starving man. Sandy gives Cliff a hard look. The last thing we need is for him to ruin our release before it actually happens. My stomach drops with Whisper's next movement, as I assume the worst, but she repays my hope and moves to the keypad. Once she's punched in all of the codes, our prison cells open simultaneously.

I'm free.

I want to thank Whisper, maybe even give her a hug. But, before I can, Cliff bursts out of his cell and attacks her. Whisper screams as Cliff tackles her to the floor, his lips already pressed to her neck. If it were just me in here, I'd have been too dumbstruck to react at all. Luckily, Sandy is here. She responds immediately, throwing Cliff off of Whisper. As he gets back to his feet, he charges at Whisper again—and again Sandy intercepts him, wrestling him to the concrete.

I exit my cell, the glorious moment of freedom lost on me as I focus on the struggle between Sandy and Cliff. I step closer to the struggle, watching without getting involved. I stand behind Whisper, who remains sitting on the concrete, each of us watching the struggle unfold. Sandy overpowers Cliff, pinning his shoulders to the concrete.

Her head snaps up, staring me.

"Help!"

I'm not used to such drama, nor am I used to being the one

someone calls on for help. The heightened sense of urgency in the air causes a fresh wave of fear to lift from Whisper's pores, right beneath my nose. I look down at her, scarcely able to ignore my hunger.

"Help me!" Sandy screams again.

I rush to Sandy's side and help hold Cliff down.

"Grab his head!"

I have a feeling I know exactly what she has planned for Cliff and, to be honest, I'm not terribly comfortable taking part in it.

"Do it!" Sandy yells. "Now!"

I kneel over Cliff, gripping his head between my hands, squeezing like a vice. Sandy hugs her arms tight around his waist. He struggles against us, but there is little else he can do.

"Don't do this!" Cliff screams. "Please!"

Sandy looks at me.

"Now!"

Still holding Cliff's head between my hands, I leverage my knees against his shoulders and pull as hard as I can, while Sandy pulls him in the opposite direction. Cliff screams against our efforts, his neck stretching to its breaking point until it finally snaps. I tumble backward with Cliff's head in my hands, his spine still attached. His body remains exactly where Sandy has pinned him down, melting into a crimson puddle on the concrete. His head does the same, leaving my hands a bloody mess. Sandy stands to her feet, wiping her hands on her jeans, before helping Whisper up.

"I'm sorry about that."

"Thank you."

"No," Sandy says, "thank you. I never liked him much anyway. So, what now?"

"The elevator will take you up into the mansion," Whisper says. "I'm sure you'll be able to find your way out from there."

"Any idea what time it is?"

"It's still light out," Whisper says. "You should be okay to leave in a few hours."

"Okay."

Whisper backs up into the elevator, keeping her eyes on Sandy and me the whole way. Her fear nearly fills the basement and, even after the elevator doors closed, her delicious aroma remains in the air. Sandy looks down at the puddle that used to be Cliff, before looking at me. She walks over and gives me a hug, crying into my shoulder. Her body quivers, nearly collapsing, so I make sure to hold her tight. We'd never known each outside of our glass cells, but as we hold each other—both of us now crying—it feels like we've known each other our whole lives.

We wait only twenty minutes or so, before getting into the elevator. As it goes up, the thought occurs to me that the doors could open to the outside world and a wave of sunlight could kill us before we have a chance to truly claim our freedom. But, truthfully, I wouldn't want to stay in that basement a moment longer and I know Sandy feels the same. When the doors open, we step out into the biggest mansion I've ever seen. It's the sort of mansion you see on TV, the sort of place movie stars live. I would never have guessed a vampire hunter could live like this. Sandy and I walk around, staying clear of the windows until we find the front of the mansion. We wait until the sun has fully set before opening the door and stepping outside. The cool desert air hits my skin and I'm home again.

Sandy and I eventually find a gate that leads to the street. We walk together, making our way towards the bright lights of the Strip out in the distance.

"Where're you headed?" I ask.

"I don't know," she says. "I'm not from around here."

"You're a tourist?"

Sandy laughs.

"I guess so," she says. "Eddie and I were passing through on our way to wherever."

"Well, I'm a local," I say, "and I love it here."

"That good, huh?"

"Oh, yeah," I say. "You should give it a try."

"Maybe I will."

"You should watch *Jersey Boys*," I say. "It's a wonderful musical about Frankie Valli and The Four Seasons. I had no idea how many of their songs I loved until I saw the play. I can take you if you like."

"That sounds nice," she says. "Any place good to eat around here?"

I tell her about the feeding post and the tunnels underneath Las Vegas. I tell her about the motel I live in and my job at Kwipz. I tell her about my brother who died of tuberculosis and someday I'll even tell her all about you, friend. But, not tonight. For now, I want to keep you all to myself and simply say thank you.

Thank you for your time.

Thank you for my sanity.

Thank you for the hope.

Invisible
Cosmic Fingers

I cheated on Riley once. That part matters, but I don't want to tell you about it just yet. For now, I'm sitting across from Riley at a small table in our favorite Mexican restaurant. Riley: My college sweetheart, the love of my barely-two-decades-old life, and my soon-to-be bride. Our wedding is two weeks away, but, before we get married, I'll be leaving the country for seven days with my best friend, Zachary. I know what you're probably thinking, that my future wife should *also* be my best friend. Believe me, I've thought about this more than once and I haven't ruled out the possibility that Riley might one day seize Zachary's best friend crown. But, for now, he simply has too much ground on her, given how he and I have known each since grade school, bonding over comic books, video games, and softcore pornography. The more likely scenario is that Zachary will remain my best friend even after the wedding.

I mentioned that Riley and I are college sweethearts, which is true, but we're also still technically in college. We're a young couple, each of us twenty-three years old, though she's older than me by two months—a fact I'm always happy to brag about when I talk about my hot older woman. We're each a few weeks away from graduating with our teaching credentials from UNLV and, believe it or not, we already have jobs waiting for us in the fall. I'll be teaching kindergarten and Riley will be teaching eighth-grade science. We don't have a house yet, but that's going to be our focus just as soon as the wedding is over and we officially begin our life together.

But, before the wedding and the house and the future, there's the matter of me leaving the country for seven days with Zachary. He's the only real friend I have outside of Riley, so he's throwing me a two-man bachelor party. And by "throwing," I mean he came up with the idea of going on a seven-day cruise to the Mexican Riviera, each of us paying our own way (though he promises to buy me a drink). The night before Zachary and I hit the Pacific Ocean together, Riley and I are having dinner at our favorite Mexican restaurant. It's a small restaurant, with good food and a pleasant staff. The menu caters nicely to our vegetarianism, as the beans aren't cooked in lard or chicken stock, which matters a great deal to Riley.

I only became a vegetarian after meeting Riley, while she's been one her whole life. She hates meat, hates seeing it cooked, hates walking by the deli aisle in Smith's, and she especially hates seeing people eat it. This made going on dinner dates particularly awkward in the beginning, which is largely why I became a vegetarian. A few times early on, I would eat meat when she wasn't around, but she's so sensitive to it, she could actually smell it on me. So, I stopped eating meat altogether, even when I was alone.

Despite its better qualities, this restaurant is rarely busy, which, as much as anything else, is why we love it. We can talk about anything here without having to censor ourselves too much. Most often we talk about our relationship, our families, our sex life, and our friends' sex lives, and nobody—save for the ear of a bored busboy or wandering waitress—will ever hear a word of what we say. It was here that I told her about my sexual indiscretion, which occurred roughly two years before tonight and, by the way, it was hardly my fault. I mean, listen, I messed around with another girl, but Riley and I had a fight—a *bad* one—and, maybe I read too much into it, but I assumed we'd broken up afterward. Well, okay, I knew we hadn't *actually* broken up, but it *felt* like we were going to break up the very next time we saw each other, so, when the messing around went down, it didn't really feel like I was cheating. Whatever, there're more details and I'm sure I'll spill my guts to you later, but for now I'm here with Riley and it's the night before I leave the country with Zachary and my bride-to-be wants to talk about only one thing.

Fidelity.

She obviously remembers the time I cheated on her and she has every right to bring it up, regardless of how uncomfortable it makes me. It's not like I enjoy feeling like an asshole, but she ultimately took me back and part of the unspoken agreement with that is she can remind me that I cheated on her whenever she likes. Tonight, however, is less about me being an asshole, and more about my best friend Zachary, who she's never liked all that much and thinks is a terrible influence on me. While I don't necessarily think Zachary is a bad influence, he was sort of instrumental in the whole cheating thing, so given that he and I will be on a seven-day cruise without her, I can see how she might be a bit uneasy about the whole thing.

In Riley's estimation, the cruise ship will be teaming with thousands of beautiful women, all of whom will spend their vacation attempting to seduce me into the sort of sexual acts usually hidden in the dusky margins of the Internet. And, while I appreciate the high value she's placing on my desirability, the truth is I've never been the sort of guy that women throw themselves at. Zachary, on the other hand, *is* that kind of guy, and before Riley and I were together I benefited more than once from his leftovers (sorry, that last part sounded more crass than I meant for it to be, but I think you get my point). As much of a poon hound as Zachary is, he's actually settled down a bit since meeting his girlfriend, Nicole. Riley likes Nicole quite a bit, which is the only reason she's letting me go on this cruise alone with Zachary.

"I really wish you weren't going on this cruise alone with Zachary."

"What? I thought you were okay with it?"

She rolls her eyes.

"I would be fine with it if Zachary weren't going with you."

"C'mon," I say, "he'll be fine."

"He's fine around Nicole," she says, "but when you put him alone on a cruise ship for a week, I know he'll be looking for the first hole he can stick his dick in."

"Where's all this coming from?" I ask. "I thought we were good."

"No, we're not good," she says. "I never liked this idea, but we're getting married and I know how important 'bachelor parties' are" (by the way, she actually threw finger quotes around "bachelor parties") "and I don't want to be the kind of wife who doesn't trust her husband to go out without her, so I've been trying to be okay with it. But, the truth is I'm not."

"But, the trip is tomorrow," I say, "and it's paid for and—"

"I'm not asking you not to go," she says. "I'm just saying I don't trust him. So, be careful."

"Be careful of what?"

"You know exactly what I want you to be careful of."

"It's going to be fine," I say. "We'll tan by the pool, enjoy some drinks, and do tourist stuff at the ports."

"Tourist stuff at the ports is exactly the sort of thing I'm worried about," she says. "There are brothels in Mexico, you know. And they cater to tourists."

"How do you know?"

"I Googled it."

"Well, lucky for you," I say, "I wouldn't know how to find a brothel in Mexico even if I wanted to. And, more than that, I *don't* want to."

That last part was mostly true. Truthfully, I've been fascinated with prostitutes ever since I was a kid and I watched *Pretty Woman* with my mom. When, as a teenager, I learned about brothels, my fascination was only heightened. As of yet, I've never been to a brothel, but I've seen every documentary HBO ever produced about prostitutes, including *Hookers at the Point, Downtown Girls: The Hookers of Honolulu*, and *Cathouse*.

Cathouse was really the one that captured my imagination because I live in Las Vegas and it seemed to me like the brothel featured in the show, the Moonlite BunnyRanch, was *also* in Las Vegas. Turns out it's not. It's definitely in Nevada, but it's actually located in a town called Mound House, which is about eight hours from where I live. Not that I've ever been there, mind you, but I have looked up the directions on Google Maps. There is, however, Sheri's Ranch, which is about an hour west of Las Vegas, just outside of Clark County in a small desert town called Pahrump. They've got a population of 36,000 in Pahrump, so you could comfortably fit the whole town into Caesar's Palace, Treasure Island, and the Bellagio combined. By the way, I've also never been to Sheri's Ranch, but Zachary has tried to talk me into it more than once.

Riley expressed very early on in our relationship a disdain for prostitution and I've always gone along with it, so as not to rock the boat, but, really, I don't have a problem with it myself. I don't think it's a bad thing and, if I'm being honest, I'll feel sort of like I missed out on something if I never have sex in a brothel. That said, I'm totally committed to Riley and I'm mostly ready to get married and I'm truly not looking for any reasons to sabotage our relationship.

"I know *you're* not interested in going to a brothel," Riley says, "but that doesn't mean Zachary isn't."

"I can assure you that he's not."

"I guess I'm just going to miss you," she says. "I don't like the idea of being apart for so long."

"It's only a week," I say. "Nothing's going to happen. Probably the most exciting thing that'll happen on the trip is me parasailing."

"You are absolutely *not* parasailing!"

I laugh.

Riley doesn't.

"I'm serious," she says. "You better not go parasailing."

"Fine, fine."

"Tell me you won't go parasailing."

"I won't go parasailing."

"Look me in the eyes and say it."

I look her in the eyes.

"I won't go parasailing."

"Thank you."

I smile and she seems happy.

Besides, she only asked me to *say* it. She didn't say I had to *mean* it. That's not lying, is it?

My name's Bentley, by the way. I only just now realized we'd come this far and you didn't even know what to call me. Dinner with Riley went well for the most part. We ate enchiladas and drank horchata, before going back to my apartment where we didn't have farewell sex like we'd planned earlier in the week. I guess we were tired and the food was sitting sort of heavy, so we just went to sleep. Riley stays with me most nights, though we don't live together. She still lives at home with her mom, who doesn't want her to move in with me until we're married. Riley's going to housesit my apartment for me while I'm gone, not that it needs any tending to or watching over. It's mostly an excuse to have her own space for a week, which she's happy about.

Riley and Nicole drive Zachary and me to McCarran Airport for our short flight to LAX. The cruise sets sail out of San Pedro, California, so we'll only be in the air for about 50 minutes or so. I try to tell Riley we can take an Uber to save her the trip, but she insists on driving us. It seems sweet, but I can't help feeling like she doesn't trust me to even go to the airport with Zachary without cheating on her. Nicole seems a lot cooler and way more trusting. Like, when they drop us off, Nicole says, "You boys be good," but it's cute, like "Don't get too drunk" or "Don't go streaking on the first night." Then Riley follows up with, "Yeah, be good," but there was nothing cute about it. She meant that shit.

"Why does Riley have to be such a fucking buzz kill?" Zachary asks.

We're inside the airport at this point, walking to our terminal, so Riley isn't around to hear him.

"It's your fucking fault."

"What the hell did I do?"

"You know what you did?"

"Oh, that again," he says. "I'm not sorry I helped you get lucky and, besides, Riley should know I didn't actually put your dick in that girl. That part's on you."

"Yeah, well, whatever," I say. "I know that and you know that, but Riley doesn't give a shit."

"I don't know why you're getting married."

"Hey, man, this is my bachelor party," I say. "How about some support."

"You already know I don't support this marriage," he says. "I'm in this for the vacation and to hang with my best friend. You'll be lucky if I show up to the wedding at all."

"But, you're my best man."

"Exactly."

Zachary and Riley have never really gotten along, which sucks for me, because Zachary and I are pretty much inseparable. From the day we met, we did pretty much everything together. But, after I met Riley, we didn't hang out as much. I was nineteen and we were enjoying our first year of college—or, in Zachary's case, his *only* year of college. That summer he got hired at Kwipz, which is a call center where he eventually helped get me a job. The money wasn't awesome, but it paid more than being a college student, so when the fall came around he dropped out of school by never going back.

"I heard Whitey came back," Zachary says.

"Really?"

Whitey's this quiet guy who works at Kwipz. He's pale as the moon like he hasn't seen the sun in a hundred years, which is why we gave him his nickname. For as much as Whitey doesn't talk to anyone—besides the customers who call in—he's a pretty reliable customer service agent. He shows up on time and never misses a shift, so it was strange when one day he just stopped coming in to work. Our manager hadn't heard from him and he wasn't returning any calls. Employees not showing up to work in a call center isn't the most unusual thing in the world, given there's a lot of turnover, but Whitey didn't seem like the type to do that. After a few weeks, we all just assumed he'd quit or died or something.

"Yeah," Zachary says, "he showed up and wanted to know if he still had a job."

"That's crazy," I say. "Where was he?"

"How should I know?"

"Well, you knew he turned up."

"That's just what I heard," he says. "Anyway, it's Kwipz, so of course they'll let him come back. It's either him or some other asshole off the street."

Kwipz isn't an amazing job, but it pays enough to ensure I don't starve, which is particularly important when you're a college student. It also pays enough that I can go on a seven-day cruise and while I'm at it I can go parasailing for the first time since I was thirteen.

The first and only time I parasailed was during a vacation with my family and, along with my dad, I'd entrusted my parasailing experience to two men who ran their business along the sand of Cabo San Lucas. They walked us out to a motorboat floating at the lip of the Pacific Ocean. The driver took the boat's wheel and drove us out and away from the beach. The other man, the parasailing expert—or "expert"—proceeded to wrap me up in some straps and buckles, all of them attaching in some form or fashion to the large parachute that would lift me up into the air like a human kite. Because I was a kid, slight in frame and weight, the expert hooked me up to a smaller parachute as a safety precaution. So, right away he'd demonstrated his expertise.

As they drove us out into the ocean, both the driver and the expert decided the winds were too strong for me to go up alone. But, to ensure they didn't have to give us a refund, the expert decided we'd go up in tandem, so he attached himself to me with an extra set of straps and buckles. The expectation was that we'd go up together, allowing for the expert to navigate the strong winds. In making this last minute adjustment, the expert forgot to change the small parachute—the very same parachute designed for a smaller person of slight frame and weight. This smaller parachute wasn't meant to carry a full-grown man up in the air, let alone a full-grown man with a kid attached to his belly. This lapse in execution didn't become apparent until the expert and I were dragged through the unforgiving Pacific Ocean, parachute in tow, for a good five minutes or so.

After it had become clear that the expert and I weren't going to become airborne, the driver stopped the boat and reeled us in. But, in his haste, he forgot to turn off the propeller, which I—wholly unaware—was being pulled straight towards. In the home video my dad recorded, you can see the driver jump towards the button that turns off the propeller at just the last moment, preventing me from getting chopped up. He then helped pull the expert and me back onto the boat, before driving us back to the beach. For our trouble, they gave us a full refund. I haven't been parasailing since, a fact I intend to change sometime in the next seen days.

It's an overcast Sunday morning in San Pedro as Zachary and I begin the tedious task of navigating through the Port of Los Angeles. We wait, along with several hundred other people, in an impossibly long line to get through customs and eventually aboard the ship. The reason it takes so long for us to get on the ship is that there's a hierarchy that the passengers fall into based on how much money they've spent for their cabins and, based on that hierarchy, Zachary and I are only slightly more important than stowaways. For those folks who don't work in call centers and can actually afford the bigger, nicer rooms up on the higher decks, they'll have king sized beds, balconies, and the respect of their peers.

The cabin Zachary and I get is about the size of a large bathroom, which is ironic because our bathroom is about the size of a large shower, which is also ironic because our shower is in the corner, designated only by a plastic curtain. The two beds in the cabin take up half the room, while a small couch, a small dresser, and a small television occupy the rest. All in all, it feels like more of a gesture than anything else, a hypothetical of what a real cabin might look like on a bigger ship, with regular sized people occupying it. But, it's okay, because if we're doing this vacation right, then we should be in our cabin as little as possible.

The cruise will eventually make three stops: Cabo San Lucas, Puerto Vallarta, and Mazatlán. Until we reach those ports, however, we'll spend two full days at sea. After we get settled in our cabin, Zachary and I—along with the rest of the passengers—run through some safety drills, before figuring out where we can eat (Spoiler Alert: Everywhere).

Pretty much as soon as we wake up the next morning, we get into our bathing suits and secure a couple of chairs by the pool. The ship has three pools in total, each with an accompanying hot tub. Of the three pools, Zachary and I plant our flags at the main one at the center of the ship with the hopes that we'll maximize our view of bikinied women. I have an aerosol can of sunscreen with me, while Zachary, as per usual, is totally unprepared. I let him have some of mine, of course, so he doesn't burn up by the pool.

"Did it even occur to you to bring sunscreen?"

"Why would it?"

"Because we're on vacation and you knew we'd be sunbathing."

"Sure," he says, "and I also knew you'd bring sunscreen."

"What if I wasn't here?"

"If you weren't here, I wouldn't be here."

"What if you went on vacation with Nicole?"

"Then I'd use her sunscreen."

"But, what if she doesn't have any?"

"Why wouldn't she have sunscreen?"

When Zachary and I were in college together, I bought the text-books and he borrowed them. When I cooked dinner, he showed up at the table. When I bought a TV, he was on the couch with the remote control. When I bought a car, he always needed a ride. And it's not that I resent helping him and it's not even that I worry what he would do without me, I just sometimes wish there were a little more balance to our relationship.

"I know what you're thinking?" he says. "You think I never give you anything."

"That's not true."

"Well, I've got something for you."

"Really?" I ask. "What is it?"

He smiles.

"What?"

"It's a surprise."

"C'mon."

"Seriously," he says. "Listen, whether I like it or not, you're marry-ing Riley. So, before you enter a world of misery, I'm going to make sure you go out in style."

"You mean, something more than going on a cruise?"

"Just wait," he says. "You'll see."

I spray on another layer of sunscreen, tracing it up and down my bare skin. I pass it over to Zachary so he can do the same. A server comes by to check on us, so I order a piña colada and Zachary orders a bucket of iced beers. I've got my iPad with me, equipped with several dozen digital comic books. As kids, when we weren't busy watching every movie Arnold Schwarzenegger ever made, Zachary and I obsessed over comic books, arguing all the time about our favorites. Mine is Superman, while his has always been the Flash. For all the amazing things Superman can do, his power of flight is my favorite. I've had countless fantasies—and a few lucid dreams—of flying through the air like Superman, breathing the rarified air, tasting the clouds.

Zachary loves the Flash because he's the fastest man on Earth, which, for him, means he can get away with anything he wants. I always remind him that the Flash doesn't use his powers to get away with stuff, but Zachary says it's because he's not thinking big enough. Currently, I'm reading the latest issue of *Dolph the Unicorn Killer*. In this particular issue, Dolph is hot on the trail of the unicorn who murdered his parents. I consider sharing it with Zachary, as I'm certain he'd love it, but he stopped reading comic books several years ago, right about the time he discovered all girls have pussies and some of them are willing to share.

Zachary loves gambling, particularly—although not exclusively—in casinos. Later in the day, after lunch, Zachary and I go to the ship's casino. It's a nice casino, not unlike what you'd see in most any hotel on the Las Vegas Strip. It's got the same rhythm of bright lights and exciting sounds, mingling together with smoke and alcohol and the hum of desperate optimism. Plus, the dealers are generally nicer and the minimum bets are much cheaper. Black Jack is the only game I even sort of know how to play. Ironically, Zachary doesn't know how to play *any* games, which is what makes his gambling so much more literal. He's attracted to the one game that requires less skill and critical thinking than a slot machine.

Roulette.

It seems a silly game to me, as you can't ever really be good at roulette. You put your chips on the table, the dealer drops a marble into the wheel, gravity and chance mingle for a few thrilling moments, and you do nothing but watch and hope. Most people seem to play the various red and black numbers on the felt table, but not Zachary. He keeps his gambling simple. "Numbers are for suckers," he likes to say. "The only choice worth making is red or black." It's a simple fifty-fifty bet, which is how he likes it. It's the next best thing to a coin toss. The payout is clear with a red or black bet, a one-to-one pay out. Put down five, win five. Put down fifty, win fifty. There is hardly a more seductive or reckless way to double your money or lose it completely.

Zachary and I enter the casino, shirtless and in our swim trunks, our skin still warm from the sun. He circles the roulette table like a shark, slowly taking in his target, making no rush to attack. With hardly a moment of consideration, he moves in and places a ten-dollar bill on the table.

"Red."

The dealer stuffs Zachary's ten into a slot in the table, before placing a ten-dollar chip on the red square. He spins the wheel and, just like that, the ball is bouncing around, leaving Zachary's money in limbo for the next few moments. The anticipation makes me nervous like I've just bet my own money. The wheel begins to slow down and the ball bounces less and less, before settling on red. The dealer places a ten-dollar chip on top of the one Zachary bet. He takes his chips, puts them in his pocket and walks away. Just like that, he's ten dollars richer.

Following two days at sea filled with eating, sunbathing, and alcohol drinking, it's time for our first port: Cabo San Lucas. Because the water by the shore in Cabo San Lucas is shallow, the ship can't dock right against it, so instead it's anchored in the middle of the ocean and the passengers are taxied out to shore on little boats called tenders. The tenders carry ten to fifteen passengers to shore every five or ten minutes and, because the ship has thousands of waiting passengers, this process takes a little while. For this reason, Zachary and I get up bright and early, eating a quick breakfast before heading for the tender queue.

"So," I ask, "things are good with you and Nicole?"

"Sure," he says. "Why?"

"Just making conversation."

"She's not here," he says, "so no need to think about her."

"What's that mean?"

"Am I speaking Chinese all of a sudden?"

"No, I just—"

"Nicole is great," he says. "She's hot and smart and she makes her own money. You can't beat that. But, I'm still me and right now I'm about to step foot in another country with my best friend. So, I've got to keep my mind limber and free, ready to take on whatever fun and adventure presents itself. I can't do that *and* think about Nicole at the same time."

If it's not obvious enough, Zachary is talking about fucking other girls. He's usually not this subtle, though. Normally, he'd come right out and say exactly what he means. It's a notable change, almost mature by his standards. I also didn't realize just how serious he's feeling about Nicole. In the past, I've seen him get blowjobs from girls while talking to future ex-girlfriends on the phone. He never gave a shit. He kept it simple, just like the casino. "I never break up with girls," he's often told me. "I date them and do whatever the fuck I want. If they catch me, fine. They can break up with me or not. That's on them."

Me, on the other hand, I've never had a relationship end smoothly. I don't know why, either. When a relationship has run its course, it usually seems pretty obvious, but I'm generally the one who figures it out first. Even when I know it's done, though, I usually stay with them for a while longer, maybe a few months or so. It's not out of any delusions that something can be salvaged—or even *needs* to be salvaged—I just don't like breaking up with girls. It's not that

I've ever met anybody who enjoys the process of breaking up, but for me it's always excruciatingly uncomfortable. It's much easier to just *not* break up even when I know I should. Of course, when the breakup does finally occur, it always ends with a girl screaming at me. Maybe I should take it as a compliment or something like they're so angry about becoming my ex that they have to express themselves with shrieking volume and obscenities. I don't know, maybe there's something to be said about Zachary's romantic pragmatism.

After a long wait, Zachary and I finally get to board the tender. After a brief five-minute ride to shore, we see some federales on the dock decked out in black combat gear, steel-toed boots, and automatic rifles. Two of them stand like statues, while the others patrol the general vicinity. Zachary and I get off the tender and walk along the short dock, passing the federales who generally ignore us as we officially enter Cabo San Lucas. Almost immediately the local street peddlers shower us with attention, each of them selling trinkets that we have no use for. One woman offers the service of styling hair into cornrows, showing us a photo album filled with faded old photographs of her pervious customers.

Zachary and I walk along the shore, right up against the water, avoiding the many local children who play in the ocean who seem mostly oblivious to the several hundred tourists pouring in. We're not too far into the city when one of the many roaming peddlers approaches us. He's a young man with a strong accent, but his English is good. He carries a green felt-board covered in jewelry and holds it in front of us, asking if we want to buy anything. Zachary takes the liberty of shutting him down as we walk away. When our backs are turned, the peddler whispers something just loud enough to reach our ears.

"Want some weed?"

Zachary and I stop, looking at each other.

"Did he just offer us weed?" I ask.

"You want some?"

"When have you ever known me to smoke weed?"

"Well, doesn't your bachelor party seem like a good time to start?"

Before I can tell him no, Zachary is already walking back to the young peddler, so of course I have to go with him.

"I got what you like," the peddler says. "Weed, chronic, yayo."

I turn to Zachary.

"What's yayo?"

"Cocaine."

And just like that, I don't want to be here anymore.

"You like yayo?" the peddler asks. "I got good shit, man. The best."

"How would we get it back on the ship?" Zachary asks.

"They no check you, man," the peddler says. "I sell to ship's crew all the time. They no catch you."

"What about the federales?"

The peddler laughs.

"They not here for you, man," he says. "They here for me."

"What else you got?"

"What you want?"

"Viagra?"

"No have," he says. "I can get for you. Come back, yeah?"

"Sure."

"I got good Viagra," he says. "Best in world. I got three bitches, man. Their pussies always hot. My dick hard like donkey."

He holds his arm out with a closed fist, punctuating his point.

"Cool," Zachary says, "sounds good."

"Meet me later, yeah?" the peddler says. "I get you Viagra."

"Okay."

"Meet me here, yeah?"

"You got it."

"Right here," the peddler says. "I got good shit, man. The best. They no catch you. I sell all the time."

"I believe you," Zachary says. "We'll find you later."

I'm relieved when he stops talking to the peddler so that we can join the rest of the tourists in the heart of the city. In Downtown Cabo San Lucas, the streets are poorly paved and the shops exist in worn down buildings. Strolling around from block to block, I see mostly smiling faces. From children running down the street chasing the ice cream cart to men and women enjoying fresh tacos under a rusty umbrella, everybody appears content.

"Let's get a taco," I say.

I'm already walking towards a taco cart on the street where the thick aroma of carne asada, grilled onions, and peppers hang heavy in the air. I order four tacos and begin eating the first one just as soon as I pay for them.

Zachary laughs.

"Look at you."

"What?"

"You know what," he says. "Didn't Riley decide you were a vegetarian?"

I smile.

"Riley's not here."

"Atta boy," he says. "This is just the beginning."

"The beginning of what?"

"The best vacation ever."

Zachary and I pop into a few shops, looking over the trinkets to see if we can find souvenirs for Riley and Nicole. The more trinkets I look at, the more I realize I have no idea what Riley would like. I start looking at jewelry—nothing fancy, mind you, just some of the more arts-and-craft looking stuff—when the pretty shop girl approaches me.

"Who are you shopping for?" she asks.

I love her accent—and her face, for that matter. And her caramel skin and her supple lips and her shiny hair and her tastefully presented cleavage and too many other features to be thinking about while shopping for Riley.

"My fiancé."

The shop girl smiles.

"Lucky girl," she says. "What does she like?"

"I'm not sure."

"Maybe a necklace?"

"Okay."

The shop girl leads me to a display of necklaces and, walking behind her, I shamelessly admire the curves beneath her dress. She waves her fingers over the necklaces, presenting them like Vanna White.

"What color does she like?"

"I don't know."

"That's okay," she says. "What color are her eyes?"

I close my eyes, trying to see Riley's face. She's there, just as I remember her—but I can't make out the color of her eyes.

"I don't know."

The shop girl giggles.

"Really?"

"Really."

"Well, my eyes are brown," she says, "in case you need to remember."

This makes me smile, which immediately makes me feel guilty. She's probably not even interested in me. It's more likely she's just trying to ensure a sale. Of course, knowing this doesn't stop me from enjoying a brief fantasy of asking her out to dinner, enjoying a few drinks, walking along the beach, kissing under the moonlight, waking up in her bed, moving to Cabo San Lucas, and getting married barefoot in the sand.

"What color do you like?" she asks.

"Brown."

She smiles.

"Good."

She helps me pick out a necklace, before walking me over to the front counter. She wraps the necklace for me and tells me what I owe. Zachary turns up behind me as I'm counting my money.

"You found something?"

"Yeah," I say. "She helped me."

The shop girl smiles.

"It was my pleasure," she says. "What is your name?"

"Bentley."

"Bent-ley," she says, giving each syllable her full attention. "I like it. I am Isabella."

"Isabella," I say, smiling.

"Can I ask you a question?" Zachary says. "Where's the nearest strip club?"

I'm mortified, of course, but Isabella appears unfazed.

"Not far," she says. "Three blocks."

"And it's a good one?"

"My cousin works there," she says. "She's very pretty."

Riley would never stand for talk of strip clubs in public like this, but Zachary and Isabella make it seem like no big deal. I realize I haven't paid for the necklace yet, having been distracted by their conversation, so I hand Isabella the money. She punches a few keys on the cash register and puts the receipt in the bag, sliding it across the counter. As I grab it, Isabella touches her fingers to mine.

"You are on the ship?"

"Yes."

"Maybe you come back before you leave."

I smile.

"Maybe."

She slowly slides her fingers off of mine, watching me as I back away from the counter with Riley's necklace. I'm sure me walking backward out of the shop looks silly, but I don't want to stop looking at Isabella just yet because I'm pretty certain that once I leave this shop, I'll never see her again. Zachary slaps me on the shoulder on his way to the door, so I turn to follow him. As I exit, I turn to look at Isabella one last time, but she's no longer behind the counter. If I weren't holding the necklace she sold me I'd wonder if Isabella ever existed at all.

"Dude," Zachary says, as we walk away, "that was awesome."

"What?"

"She wanted to fuck you, man!"

"Isabella? No."

"Look at you," he says. "You're already on a first name basis."

"Well, that's her name."

"I sure as fuck didn't know her name," he says. "I'm telling you, that pussy is yours for the taking."

"I'm getting married," I say, "so, even if she *is* interested, I'm not in a position to do anything about it."

Zachary smiles.

"So, you *are* interested."

"Where'd you get that from?"

"You didn't say you *weren't* interested," he says. "All you said was you couldn't do anything about it. That means you want to fuck her, too. And you *should!* Dude, she's fucking hot."

"I'm sure I'll cross paths with many hot women in my life," I say, "but being married means I don't go trying to have sex with them."

"That's exactly why you shouldn't get married."

"But, I *want* to get married."

"I'm not so sure about that."

"Well, *I* am."

"We'll see."

We walk for about twenty minutes before finding the strip club Isabella told Zachary about. It's on the second floor of a dubious-looking shopping center, so we climb a flight of concrete steps to the entrance. At the top of the stairs, we find an open doorway. We don't hear any music and there's nobody standing at the door, so I assume they're closed. I turn to walk away, but Zachary stays put.

"C'mon," he says.

"Let's just get out of here," I say.

He smiles, before walking through the doorway, leaving me little choice but to follow him. It's empty inside, save for two men playing pool. We wait for a minute, thinking one of them will greet us, but neither does. There are two small stages with poles and a couple of beat-up couches, but no girls in sight. The two men playing pool look at as like we don't belong here.

"Hi," Zachary says.

They stop their game and look at us without speaking.

"Where're the girls?" Zachary asks.

One of the men says something to his friend in Spanish while keeping his eye on Zachary. They walk towards us and, as soon as I see one of them reach into his pocket, I run out the door and down the stairs. Zachary is behind me and we run as fast as we can for the next minute or so, before we're both out of breath and have to stop.

Inexplicably, we're both laughing as we catch our breath.

"That was fun," Zachary says. "Wanna grab a beer?"

"You thought that was fun?"

"Hell yeah," he says. "Look, we're alive, unharmed, and you'll be telling this story for the rest of your life."

Here I am thinking we nearly got murdered in Cabo San Lucas and Zachary's wants a beer. I mean, I know he's not a sociopath or anything—at least, I don't think he is—but I sometimes wonder what the hell is wrong with him. Or maybe there's nothing wrong with him. Maybe he's living life exactly the way it's meant to be lived. If that's the case, does it mean there's actually something wrong with me?

We find a beachside bar and sit down for a few beers with chips and salsa, listening to music and enjoying the salty air. I haven't forgotten about parasailing, but, at this point, I don't want to do anything else even remotely crazy in Cabo San Lucas. Maybe I'll do it tomorrow in Mazatlán. We finish our beers and start heading back to the dock. Just as the federales are in sight, I hear somebody whistling behind us. Zachary and I turn at the same time and see the peddler from earlier running our way. He's out of breath when he reaches us, but he's clearly happy to see Zachary.

"I got Viagra, man," he says.

"Great."

I'm waiting for Zachary to tell him he wasn't really interested, which I figure will be followed by some cursing and name-calling. But, instead, Zachary asks how much, then hands over some cash in exchange for a bottle of Viagra before we start walking again to the dock.

"Did you really just buy Viagra from a street peddler?"

"Sure."

"Why?"

"Because it's way cheaper than buying it at home?"

"Why do you even need Viagra?"

"Because we're on vacation."

"What about Nicole."

"I told you not to bring her up," he says. "Besides, if you get lucky, you may decide you want a few blue pills for yourself."

"I don't need Viagra."

"Neither do I," he says, "but it's like putting a jet pack on your cock."

"I don't want a jet pack on my cock."

"I think you do, but you just don't know it yet."

I see no point in discussing it further, so I start walking to the dock where the federales are still standing guard. There's a family—mom, dad, and a little boy—on the dock waiting for the next tender. The little boy is crying, holding his dad's leg. Mom is soothing him and it becomes clear he's scared of the federales and their big guns. Zachary walks over to the family, crouching down so he's eye level with the little boy.

"Hey, buddy," he says, "it's okay. They're not here to hurt us. They're keeping the bad guys away to keep you safe."

Amazingly, the little boy stops crying. The mom smiles, offering a quiet thank you. The dad pats Zachary on the shoulder and says he owes him a drink. We board the next tender with the family and the little boy sits beside Zachary, like he's his favorite uncle. Zachary makes small talk with the parents and they hang on his every word. Back on the ship Zachary and I spend a few hours at the pool, before getting cleaned up for dinner. After dinner we go to the theater for a magic show, then we head over to the casino.

I follow Zachary to the roulette table, where he puts down twenty dollars on red. The marble, of course, lands on red and Zachary immediately puts fifty down on black. After the marble lands on black, Zachary immediately puts a hundred down on red—but, before the dealer spins the wheel, he changes his bet to black. He grabs my arm and closes his eyes, clearly nervous about this last bet. "Tell me what happens," he says. I watch the marble bounce around, flirting with black and then red, back and forth, settling on red for a moment, before teetering into black where it stays put.

And just like that, in the span of about five minutes, Zachary turns $170 into $340. The ease of his winnings is so seductive I decide to put ten dollars down on red and, a few fleeting moments later, the marble lands on black.

I guess I should go ahead and tell you about the time I cheated on Riley. We hadn't quite been together a year, maybe about nine or ten months. We'd celebrated most of the major holidays together, culminating with a New Years Eve party at Zachary's family's house. Riley and I were still relatively young at the time, barely adults, and for me it was my first grown-up relationship. I'd had girlfriends in high school, but none of those relationships lasted more than three or four months—and, frankly, the word "relationship" is a bit of a stretch when describing them. By the time I'd met Riley, I hadn't been with a girl for close to two years. That dry spell was not by choice, either. The closest thing I got to female attention was at the strip club with Zachary and even that attention didn't come as often as I'd have liked, given I was a college student and perpetually incapable of making it rain. It was very likely I was going to fall in love with the first girl who paid attention to me—and that girl turned out to be Riley.

Ironically, given how much they dislike each other, I met Riley because of Zachary. It was the middle of the night and we'd just finished watching a movie, so we went to Denny's to get dinner. The hostess was walking us to our table when Zachary saw Riley and her friend sitting at another table. Zachary sat down beside Riley's friend and put his arm across the seat, just behind her shoulders, and told the hostess he'd found his seat. I, of course, was mortified as Zachary was about to get us kicked out or, worse yet, humiliated in front of a couple of pretty girls. But to my surprise, they laughed. Both of them. Even Riley. They were genuinely charmed by Zachary's bravado.

The hostess looked at the girls, making sure they didn't mind our presence, before walking away. I stood by the table, until Zachary said, "What are you waiting for, weirdo? Sit down." So, I sat beside Riley. Zachary made fast friends with his girl, leaving me to make conversation with Riley. She was much prettier than any other girl I'd ever talked to, so I automatically assumed she wouldn't be interested in me and, for that reason, I ended up treating Riley like a regular person as opposed to a girl I was trying to hook up with. I don't remember much of anything we talked about, but do I remember we talked. A lot. And she smiled and laughed and at the end of the night, while Zachary French-kissed her friend against his car, I got Riley's phone number.

I didn't call her right away, mostly because I was nervous. Like I said, she was much prettier than any girl who'd ever paid me any attention, let alone given me a phone number. In another bout of irony, it was Zachary who finally convinced me to call Riley. "What're you afraid will happen if you call?" he'd asked. I didn't have much of an answer because I didn't know what I was afraid of. I just knew I was afraid. "What you *should* be afraid of is her forgetting who the fuck you are, so when you do finally call it'll be too late." So, I called her and she remembered me and we had a nice chat, which led to dinner and a movie the following weekend.

Things moved pretty fast from there. We held hands in the theater, kissed in the parking lot, and fucked in her apartment. That last part was a first for me, by the way. I'd never had sex with a girl on the first date. Frankly, I'd started believing that sort of thing only happened in the movies. But there I was on Riley's bed, staring at the ceiling as I held her hips, vacillating between joy and disbelief as she rode on top of me. After that, spending time with Riley was about the only thing I cared about. Zachary didn't mind too much at first, given his front row seat to my romantic ineptitude. After a few weeks, though, he started getting antsy—or "jealous" as Riley put it.

When we were kids, Zachary and I were inseparable. Slumber parties on the weekends, hours of playing video games, late nights watching grainy VHS copies of softcore pornography. Not a whole lot changed when we got out of high school, except we were a little bit older, but still doing all the same things. Zachary, of course, was significantly better at meeting girls than I was, though he wasn't much of a wingman. It's not that he didn't want to help me to get laid, he just didn't know how, which left me generally helpless—until the night I met Riley. Even though I wouldn't have met her without him, I also wouldn't have pursued her if she hadn't been kind and talkative, before giving me her number.

You know what—I'm sorry. Here I am giving you all the sweet details of how Riley and I met, while still avoiding the uncomfortable and embarrassing details you're obviously waiting for. Okay, here we go. We had a fight on New Years Day a few months after we'd begun dating. I hardly remember what we fought about, but that part doesn't really matter. The fight might've started over what to have for dinner, but what we were really fighting about was being scared. She didn't know if she wanted to stay in a relationship with me and I didn't want to break up. "What if we're committing too young and too soon," she'd said, "and what if we regret it." And by "we" she meant her.

She said she needed a little time to herself. I asked how long and she'd said, "At least a few days." I called Zachary straight away and told him what was going on. While he isn't much of a romantic himself, he appreciates romance and relationships—and, more than that, he values our friendship, as well as me as a person. So, he took me out to a bar and bought me drinks all night, getting both of us stupid drunk together.

"You're too good for her," he'd said. "I can't believe she thinks she can do better."

"But, she can."

"Fuck you," he'd said. "You're a good man, dude. A good fucking man. If that's not what she's looking for, then fuck her. Seriously, dude. Fuck her."

I'm certain we said more, but that's the part that stuck. It meant a lot to me, especially since those aren't the sort of things Zachary and I generally say to each other. Honestly, I didn't even know he thought so highly of me. We got drunk again the next night and the night after that. I hadn't heard from Riley since New Years and I wasn't sure if I was supposed to call her or wait for her to call me.

"Why does she get to decide?" he'd asked. "She's doing what she wants right now and so should you."

"I don't think it's like that."

"Are you the one who broke up with her?"

"We didn't break up."

"Really? Is she here? Is she with you?"

"But, we never said we were broken up."

"You're putting too much importance on the fucking words," he'd said. "Look around, dude. She's not fucking here!"

Zachary insisted on taking me to Little Darlings, a strip club just off the Las Vegas Strip. It's a fully nude club, which means they can't serve alcohol, but Zachary and I were already sufficiently drunk. We weren't sloppy drunk and I certainly wasn't blackout drunk, so I don't want you to think I'm making any excuses for the events that happened next. We'd spent about an hour or so sitting by the stage, watching the strippers do their thing, while tipping them conservatively. Zachary excused himself to use the bathroom, but, unbeknownst to me, he was really talking to one of the strippers on my behalf. He gave her a sob story about how my fiancé left me at the alter and I was heartbroken and so he wondered if there was there anything she could do to help me feel better.

Soon enough, the stripper walked over and took my hand, telling me she wanted to give me a private dance. I told her I couldn't afford it, but she let me know my friend had already paid. I walked back with her, looking over my shoulder at Zachary who was smiling like a proud father. She took me through a tall red door, sitting me down on a sofa with velvet curtains on either side of us. She stripped off her clothes pretty casually, before straddling my lap. I kept my hands to myself, until she put them on her ass, squeezing her fingers over mine. She grinded on top of me for a minute or so, before asking, "Do you have an extra twenty dollars?"

"No, I'm sorry."

She looked at me a moment, before touching her fingers to my cheek. "It's okay."

She got off my lap and kneeled between my legs, pushing her hands up my thighs until she was unfastening my belt. I hardly knew what was happening, like I was having an out-of-body experience. She unbuttoned my jeans, unzipped my fly, and reached into my underwear. It wasn't until her fingers grabbed my cock that I jolted back into reality. I thought immediately of Riley and how I shouldn't be in the situation I was in. But, the stripper was also so beautiful and kind and, before I knew it, my cock was in her mouth and it felt really good and I saw no good reason to stop her. "Give me a warning before you shoot," she'd said. About a minute later, I tapped her on the shoulder and she finished me off with a handjob. For about five or ten seconds, I was overcome with euphoria. Then the blood rushed back to my head and I looked at the congealed shame on my jeans, while the stripper cleaned her hands and wiped her mouth with a towel I hadn't previously noticed. She kissed me on the cheek and helped fasten my pants, before walking me back out. Zachary was waiting for me, smiling.

"So?"

"Let's go home."

I told him what the stripper did and he told me he'd paid her to do it. I wanted to be mad at him, but, as my best friend, he was just doing what he felt he needed to do. And I wasn't forced to do anything I didn't want to do. The stripper was very attractive and she made me feel good and, quite frankly, I liked the part when she did what Zachary paid her to do. But, on the other hand, I also felt like a real jerk, especially when Riley called the next day. We met for lunch and we talked and she told me she didn't have any more doubts. I'll just skip ahead to a few days later when we were at her apartment, about to make love for the first time since before New Years, and I felt compelled to tell her about the stripper at Little Darlings.

She was every bit as upset as you're probably imagining, yelling and crying and calling me a "typical male asshole" and saying "I thought you were different" and she was threatening to end things for good and I didn't know what to do, so I threw Zachary under the bus. Now before you judge me for that part, you have to know how desperate I was not to lose Riley and, frankly, it was the truth. Plus, Riley already didn't like Zachary all that much, because he never called back her friend after they'd had sex (Riley isn't even friends with her anymore, which probably has something to do with why I don't remember her name), so I figured it wouldn't be a big deal.

Even though Riley was still mad at me, learning about Zachary's participation tempered her anger. It also gave her a fair amount of ammunition to try and split Zachary and me up as friends. She hadn't yet given a him-or-me ultimatum, but I suspected that would follow soon after the wedding. I think maybe Zachary expected the same thing. For the record, I told him that Riley knew about the stripper at Little Darlings and that he'd been the one to initiate it. Zachary, of course, didn't care that I told her and, in fact, said, "Good, I want her to know."

Zachary and I grab a quick breakfast, while the ship ports in Mazatlán. We hurry from the dining room to the ship's exit, hoping to avoid any long lines. Stepping off the ship, we're met by one of the cruise photographers. He's taking pictures of passengers beside a large wreath with "Mazatlán" spelled out in red flowers. We pose beside the wreath, Zachary draping his arm over my shoulders as the photographer snaps his shot. As it was in Cabo San Lucas, the peddlers are waiting in force as we step foot onto shore. Zachary and I move through without much trouble, only to find a new group of entrepreneurs to reckon with.

Drivers.

"We should hire one of these guys," Zachary says.

"That's not necessary," I say, "we can just walk around."

"Yeah, but we don't know where we're going," he says. "These guys are like tour guides."

Before I can say anything else, one of the drivers breaks away from the herd and makes his way towards us. He starts speaking Spanish, but neither Zachary nor I know what he's saying. Of course, it's not hard to deduce that whatever he's saying has something to do with wanting us to pay him to drive us around. He uses his fingers to tell us his price is $20 for the day. We accept the offer and follow him to his car, which looks more like a golf cart. With a strong accent, he tells us in his best English his name is Raul. Zachary and I follow suit, telling him our names. While I'm half-convinced Raul doesn't realize we've just told him our names, he smiles anyway and invites us into his cart. As soon as we sit down Raul starts driving, so, given that we haven't told him where we'd like to go, Zachary and I trust he's taking us somewhere interesting.

"We should do something crazy today," Zachary says.

"Crazier than getting into a stranger's golf cart who doesn't speak our language?"

"Raul knows what he's doing," Zachary says. "I mean we need to do something memorable. If you actually plan on going through with this marriage, then this trip is our last hurrah. We need to make it count."

"I haven't gone parasailing yet."

"Dude, fuck parasailing," he says. "I'm talking about something crazy and exciting and fucking memorable."

"Parasailing checks all those boxes."

"Whatever," he says. "I just want us to make a memory together, that's all."

Raul drives us into the heart of Mazatlán, dropping us off at a corner. He says something to us in Spanish, pointing at the sidewalk as he speaks, so Zachary and I assume he's telling us he'll be here waiting for us. I smile and wave, hoping to communicate his message was received before we walk away. We walk along a cobblestone road, peeking into shops, and admiring any attractive women that pass by. We come across a large old church and without conferring with one another Zachary and I walk inside. I'm not religious, but I've been inside churches before and I've never seen one like this. It's beautiful, filled with culture and history. The walls are lined with intricately designed panes of stained glass and, below them, a row of confessional booths. A janitor approaches me, broom in hand, and makes a gesture of removing an invisible hat from his head. I touch the top of my head and find I'm wearing a baseball cap that I'd forgotten about. I take it off and smile and the janitor just walks away.

"I love this place," I say.

"Of course you do," Zachary says.

"What's that supposed to mean?"

"It means you fall in love way too easily."

"With churches?"

"With everything," he says, "and every*one*."

"That's not true."

"Sure it is," he says. "You fall in love with every girl who gives you attention."

"You're exaggerating."

"You're probably in love with the shop girl from Cabo San Lucas."

"Wrong."

"I'll bet you fantasized about getting married and making babies already."

"No," I say, "you're wrong."

"Am I?"

"I didn't fantasize about babies."

Zachary laughs.

"I stand corrected."

We leave the church and walk around for another fifteen minutes or so before finding ourselves back at the corner where Raul is waiting for us. We get into his cart and he starts driving again. Raul tries his best to mix what little English he knows with his Spanish, so as to make small talk. He talks mainly about all of the beautiful women that live in Mazatlán, holding his hands in front of his chest to pantomime large breasts. This makes Zachary and I laugh.

"Where can we find these women?" Zachary asks

"¿Qué?"

"We want to meet them."

Zachary pantomimes large breasts with his hands and Raul's eyes grow big. Without another word, he begins driving with a purpose that was previously absent, taking us through what appears to be a residential block of buildings. Each building appears empty and dilapidated, perfect for kidnapping and murdering a couple of naïve American tourists, before chopping up their remains and stealing whatever cash they have on them. As Raul accelerates deeper and deeper into this anonymous neighborhood, I want to believe that my imagination is simply getting the best of me, that he doesn't have any devious intent, that Zachary and I will be just fine. I want to believe that, but these streets a getting more and more empty, punctuating the reality that if anybody decided to look for Zachary and me, they'd have very little luck finding us.

Just as quickly as Raul accelerated into action ten minutes prior, he pulls over against a curb, next to one of the anonymous buildings. Getting out, he walks towards a door that looks exactly like all the others. I have no idea what we're supposed to do, so I stay in the cart. Raul stands at the front of the small building, holding the door open and waving for us to join him inside. Zachary gets out of the cart, nearly causing me to panic.

"What're you doing?"

"Going to see where we are."

"What if he plans on murdering us?"

"He's not going to murder us."

"You don't know that."

"That's true," Zachary says, smiling. "If we *were* going to get murdered, however, there's only one way to find out."

He walks to the door and enters the building. I definitely don't want to get murdered, but I also don't want Zachary to be in there alone, so I take a deep breath and jump out the cart, hurrying to join him inside. Raul smiles, patting me on the shoulder as I enter the building. Behind the door is a large room with tall white walls. There's a big wooden desk and a dirty couch near the entrance. Around the corner is a room with a widescreen TV more expensive than every collective brick holding this building together. There are five young women sitting in the TV room watching *The Little Mermaid*, each of them scantily clad in some combination of mini skirt, halter top, tight pants, and high heels.

Beside the room with the TV is a winding iron staircase, which isn't connected to anything except the second floor. Raul stands at the foot of the staircase, calling up to somebody in Spanish and, as he does, the women in the TV room stop watching their cartoon, quickly check themselves in front of a mirror, and come out to where Zachary and I are standing. They stand beside each other, like a police lineup, each one making an effort to look sexier than the next. If it wasn't obvious before, it's clear now that Raul has brought us to a brothel.

A woman comes down the winding stairs in a long black robe that flows behind her with every step. I know without question she's the madam, the one who runs the show. She greets Raul with a familiar nod, before turning her attention to Zachary and me. She's older than the girls lined up before us, but not by much. I imagine she used to be one of these girls, working in this very place or one just like it. I imagine she learned a few lessons the hard way before earning her spot as madam. She takes a seat at the large wooden desk and begins speaking to Zachary and me in Spanish. Raul cuts her off and, as best as I can tell, he tells her we don't speak Spanish.

"My girls give massage, blowjob, sex, whatever you like," she says. "Fifty dollar for thirty minute. Eighty dollar for one hour. Who you like?"

I'm trying to figure out the most tactful way to get out of here, when Zachary asks the madam if she can go any lower on her prices.

"Dude," I say, "quit messing around."

"We're already here," he says, "so why not?"

"You're serious?"

"Fuck yeah," he says, "I popped a Viagra at breakfast just in case. It's kismet."

The madam grows impatient.

"So?"

"Can you go cheaper?" Zachary asks again.

"No," she says. "Which you girl you like?"

"I don't know yet."

She sighs, then looks at me.

"Which girl you like?"

"Oh, I'm not interested," I say. "Thank you, though. I appreciate the consideration."

Zachary finally picks a pretty girl with curly hair and a tight black dress.

"Thirty or sixty minute?" the madam asks.

"Thirty."

He hands over the money to the madam, before the pretty girl with the curly hair takes his hand, leading him up the winding staircase. Once he's out of sight, Raul and I take a seat on the dirty couch. He looks at me for a moment, like he wants to make small talk, only to remember that he'd have better luck communicating with a Martian. The rest of the girls go back to watching *The Little Mermaid*, while the madam stays behind the wooden desk to do what appears to be paperwork. I can't help but think of Riley and what she would think if she knew where I was right now. I think about Nicole, too, and how she'd feel if she knew Zachary was about to fuck a prostitute. I think about love and relationships and people—and I think about how fragile they all are and how quickly and thoughtlessly the most life altering decisions seem to get made.

And then I see one of the scantily clad girls looking at me. When I catch her eye, she looks away, giving her attention back to *The Little Mermaid*. She has long black hair and fair skin. She sits with her feet on the couch, hugging her knees. She looks at me again, this time smiling when she catches my eye, before looking back at the TV. I fully understand where I am and what she's paid to do, but it doesn't stop me from feeling that the attention she's giving me isn't about money. This leads me to think about what she *does* do for money and the startling realization that the only thing stopping me from having sex with this beautiful and exotic woman is me. And, of course, Riley, but, she's not here.

And it's not like we're married yet.

And maybe Zachary's right.

And just like that I'm standing up from the dirty couch.

Raul says something in Spanish, which gets the madam's attention. She lifts her head as I approach the large wooden desk. I hear the words first in my head, then I hear them coming from my mouth, but when I request the pretty girl with the long black hair it feels like someone else's moment, like a softcore sex movie I'm watching in the middle of the night in Zachary's bedroom. And when the madam calls the girls back out and I watch my choice slip her high heels back on, it feels like somebody else's finger pointing at her, somebody else's eyes watching her smile.

Her name is Linda I learn from the madam as I pull out my wallet and retrieve the necessary cash. I can already feel the consequences of this choice setting into motion a series of events within the large cosmic machine. It's as if there's an invisible force moving me around like a chess piece or an author weaving a tale with me at its center, fingers typing at a keyboard, dictating my moves, my words, the very thoughts in my head. And it's these fingers that let Linda take my hand, guiding me up the winding staircase. And it's these fingers that let her walk me down the hall, past a series of closed doors until we stop in front of hers. And when Linda opens the door, it's these invisible fingers and their cosmic keyboard that push me into the room.

But, I know this is just a fiction I'm telling myself, that there are no invisible cosmic fingers nor is there an omniscient author guiding my choices. I'm in this room now because I've chosen to be. This small, dirty room with its massage table in the center and its bed in the corner. Beside the bed is a small sink with a cabinet full of condoms, lube, paper towels, and bottles that I can't quite make out. Just past the sink is a tiny bathroom with a shower. Linda steps into the bathroom and turns on the water. I assume it's for her, which seems really thoughtful until she comes out of the bathroom and hands me a towel. She says something in Spanish, pantomiming washing her armpits and between her thighs.

I point to myself, touching my finger to my chest.

"Me?"

"Sí," she says, "rápido."

I may not speak Spanish, but it's easy enough for me to deduce

Linda wants me to take a fast shower. Makes sense, I guess. The room may be dirty, but that doesn't mean she wants me to stink. I wonder if this is a request she always makes or if it's a special request of me, like she wants our time to be particularly special, untainted by any stink or funk I may be walking around with. I remove my clothes and step into the shower. There's a bar of soap on the wall, but the pubic hair stuck to it convinces me to leave it be. A few minutes under the hot water will suffice, I decide. And, really, it's not like Linda's expecting me to prepare myself for surgery. Plus, she's not even watching, so I'll let her believe I soaped up.

I finish my shower, drying off and wrapping the towel around my waist, before walking back into the room where I find Linda standing beside the massage table. She waves me over, patting her hand on the table. She's already laid a towel down on it. Before I get on the table, Linda stops me and removes the towel from around my waist, leaving me completely naked. I climb onto the massage table and lay flat on my belly, watching Linda remove her clothes. It's a pragmatic affair, nothing sexual or seductive about it.

She squeezes oil on my back and begins rubbing it on my skin. Her fingers are tiny against my flesh, smoothing the oil along my shoulders and spine, ass and hips, thighs and calves. Even this, I find, is absent of the sensuality it's meant to evoke. Linda climbs onto the table and straddles me, settling the warmth between her legs on the small of my back. She puts her weight into the heels of her hands, pushing them up my back and into my shoulders, squeezing and rubbing. I close my eyes and try to enjoy it, but I start thinking of Riley.

I'm imagining her back home, watching her reality shows on DVR and waiting faithfully for my return, completely unaware of where I am and what I'm doing. I also think of Zachary and what he would say, how proud he'd be if he knew where I was. I even think of myself, eighty years from now, an old man with white hair and aching joints, laying in bed and reflecting on my life. I'm wondering what I'll regret more: Fucking Linda or *not* fucking Linda.

She climbs off of me and walks to the cabinet over the sink, retrieving a condom. When she returns to the table, I'm still on my belly, so she motions for me to turn over. She probably expected me to be hard when I turned, but I'm not, so she takes me into her hand and starts massaging. The erection isn't immediate, given how disconnected Linda is from the whole process and how conflicted my own feelings are. As soon as she gets me semi-hard, she removes the condom from its wrapper and rolls it on, before putting me in her mouth in an effort to get me all the way hard.

Until this moment, I never would've imagined how joyless sex could be in the appropriate circumstances. I realize now that whatever I'm doing here isn't worth whatever I may risk losing. I mean, sure, I'm naked in a brothel while a pretty girl sort of blows me, but, honestly, given how much further we could be in the process, I feel like I haven't really done anything too horribly wrong, at least nothing I can't reasonably explain to Riley. So, I gently push Linda's head off my cock and slide off the massage table. She appears confused as I put my clothes back on and starts saying something in Spanish.

"I know you don't understand me," I say, "but I hope you don't take this as a rejection of you. I'm getting married soon and I thought maybe this could be something fun and exciting I did for myself, but the truth is I just wasn't enjoying it. You're beautiful and you look wonderful naked and I'm sure under different circumstances we could've had a great time together. But, the circumstances aren't different. They are as they are, so there's no need to pretend any different. But, thank you, Linda. Thank you for everything."

Linda smiles and says, "Tip?"

I pull a ten-dollar bill from my wallet and hand it to her, hoping that's an appropriate tip for this situation. She seems more than happy with it as she puts her clothes back on and leads me out of the room, through the hallway, and down the winding staircase. She drops me off at the dirty couch, before heading back into the TV room where *The Little Mermaid* is still playing. The madam is no longer sitting behind the large desk, but Raul is still on the couch.

He nudges me with his elbow.

"Eso fue rápido."

I say nothing, mostly because there's nothing to say and, even if there were, I wouldn't know how to say it. Soon enough, Zachary is coming back down the winding staircase. He quickly moves past me and exits without saying a word. Raul and I follow him out, finding him already sitting in the cart. I take a seat beside him and Raul gets into the driver's seat, starting it up and zooming us away.

"Take us back to the ship," I say.

Raul nods and gives his attention to the road.

Zachary still hasn't spoken.

"You okay?"

He shrugs.

"How was it?"

"I don't know what I was thinking," he says, shaking his head. "That was stupid."

"What was?" I ask. "What happened?"

He doesn't say anything else for the rest of the ride. When we get back to the ship, I pay Raul and shake his hand. He smiles and says one last thing in Spanish to us. Zachary is already walking to the ship, so I say goodbye to Raul and leave him mid-sentence. I catch up with Zachary and walk beside him, neither of us speaking, as we get back on the ship. "I need a drink," Zachary says, so we find one of the several bars on the ship and take a seat, ordering a couple beers from the bartender. Zachary also asks for a shot of whiskey. The bartender brings the shot and Zachary throws it back with purpose. He stares ahead, looking at his reflection in the mirror behind the bar.

"I wish I could go back," he says. "I wish I could take it back."

"Take what back?" I ask. "What happened?"

"I cheated," he says. "I cheated on Nicole."

"You've cheated on girls before."

"Yeah, but not Nicole."

"Honestly, I assumed you already had."

"Well, I haven't," he says, "not before today. Fuck, man. This sucks. This feeling really sucks. What is it?"

"I guess it's something to do with caring about someone else other than yourself."

He asks the bartender for another shot.

"Is this how you feel all the time?" he asks.

"Probably, I guess."

"I don't know how you do it," he says. "But, I'm glad *you* didn't do anything over there."

"Well, I didn't exactly do *nothing*."

"What? You fucked somebody? Good for you, man."

"You just said you were glad I didn't."

"That was before I knew you did."

"But, you were turning the corner on the whole cheating thing."

"Yeah, that was about me cheating on Nicole," he says, "not you and Riley. Fuck her."

"You're way too comfortable hating her around me."

"You should try and get used to it," he says. "What'd you do back at the brothel? And with whom?"

"Her name was Linda."

"That doesn't help."

"She had long black hair."

"You're terrible at this," he says. "Just tell me what you did."

"Nothing," I say. "She gave me a massage and blew me a little, but I wasn't into it. I mostly felt bad, so I stopped."

"You just stopped?"

"Yeah."

"That's like some crazy monk shit."

"I have no idea what that means."

"I felt bad the whole time," he says, "like sick-to-my-stomach bad, but I still fucked her."

"It didn't occur to you to stop?"

"I didn't know that was an option."

"Well, at least you felt bad," I say. "That's a good start."

"What do I do now?"

"About what?"

"About these feelings?"

"Just feel them," I say. "There's not much else you can do."

I excuse myself to use the bathroom and when I come back to the bar, Zachary is gone. I walk around the ship looking for him, starting first with the casino. I ask the roulette dealer—who now knows him by name—if Zachary's been around, but she hasn't seen him. I walk by the dormant dance club and a dessert buffet, stopping for an ice cream cone, before walking some more until I end up in the gift shop. There are two whole walls covered top to bottom with pictures taken by the ship's photographers. I browse through the photos until I find the one we posed for earlier in the morning, Zachary and I standing behind the large wreath with "Mazatlán" spelled out in red flowers.

I look at Zachary's arm draped over my shoulder and the baseball cap I forgot I was wearing. We'd taken this picture just a few hours prior, but it feels like a lifetime ago. The two boys in this picture feel like completely different people from the ones who returned to the ship, unburdened by the events they'd soon be experiencing. I pay for the photo at the register, before getting back to the business of finding Zachary. I walk around the ship for another twenty minutes or so, before finally finding him on the lido deck. He's leaning his elbows against the rail, his back to the pool and the handful of half-naked women in it. I lean my elbows beside him, looking out into the ocean, watching as it slowly swallows up the sun for the night.

"I'm gonna tell Nicole," he says.

"I think that's the right thing to do."

"You think she'll break up with me?"

"I don't know."

"Honestly, what do you think she'll do?"

"She'll probably break up with you."

He stares out at the Pacific, nodding in agreement.

"You think if I tell her," he says, "this feeling will go away?"

"I think it'll help," I say. "And, besides, even if she breaks up with you, that doesn't mean you can't try to win her back."

"I guess that's true," he says. "Are you gonna tell Riley?"

"I don't know," I say. "Normally, I would, right?"

"It would totally be the Bentley thing to do."

"But, I worry it would do more harm than good."

"You mean like getting the wedding canceled?"

"Yeah."

"In that case," he says, "I think you should definitely tell her."

I shake my head and stare out at the setting sun.

"No really," he says, laughing, "I think it's the right thing to do."

We spend the rest of the night drinking, though Zachary went harder than me. In the morning when the ship stops at our final port, Zachary opts to sleep off his hangover. I'm not exactly feeling like a million bucks myself, but I feel good enough not to miss out on Puerto Vallarta. I find a driver who speaks good English and offers to give me a great tour of his town. He drives me through a thick green jungle on our way to visiting a tiny village, built around a small tequila distillery. The village has one road with one market, as well as a stray dog that nobody seems to mind.

I take a tour with a small group of fellow tourists through the distillery. Our guide speaks immaculate English and he's the great-grandson of the distillery's matron founder. He explains the process of harvesting blue agave plants and using a knife called a cao to cut the leaves away from the piña. He tells us that the piñas are slowly baked in ovens, then mashed under a large wheel called a tahona. We see a man in a denim shirt and cowboy hat outside the distillery working on the tahona, surrounded by thousands of bees. The guide tells us the bees are attracted to the sweet juice that comes from the agave roots. The man in the cowboy hat is totally unfazed by the bees like he doesn't even know they're around. At the end of the tour, we sample delicious shots of almond, coffee, and mandarin flavored tequila in little plastic cups.

From the distillery, my driver takes me to a small pond with an outdoor restaurant called El Eden. He tells me this is where the Arnold Schwarzenegger movie *Predator* was filmed, which is awesome because Zachary and I have watched *Predator* no less than a hundred times. I'm mostly excited to be here, but also a little sad that Zachary's not with me to enjoy it. I invite the driver to have lunch with me in El Eden, but he politely declines. I take a seat at a small table beneath an umbrella overlooking the pond. When the waitress comes to my table, I order tacos, enchiladas, and a cold beer. The water in the pond is clear with small fish swimming around and a waterfall that spills over a tilt of rocks.

The restaurant is built atop a wooden deck and about ten feet away from my table tourists line up in their swim trunks and take turns swinging off a rope into the pond. It looks like fun and I don't know when—if ever—I'll have an opportunity like this again, so I finish my lunch and quickly remove my clothes down to my swim trunks. I get in line behind a couple of kids and when it's my turn I take the rope in both hands, jump up from the deck, and let the momentum of my weight swing me out over the pond. I'd planned to hold onto the rope until the apex of my swing, but I'm immediately shocked at how difficult it is to support my weight, losing my grip on the rope about halfway through and falling clumsily into the water.

The water is very cold, leaving me breathless. I sink until my feet touch the smooth rocks at the bottom, before pushing myself up to the surface. I swim to the edge of the pond and climb out, shivering as I shuffle back to my table to put on my clothes. I pay my bill, then head back to the car where the driver sits patiently, reading the latest issue of *Dolph the Unicorn Killer*. As we leave El Eden, the driver and I talk about Dolph, each of us wondering if the Super Human Squad will ever accept him and if he'll ever find his parents' murderer. The driver takes me to a beautiful beach, with white sand and clear blue water. There's a long row of resort hotels along the beach, as well as a handful of restaurants and bars. Waiters walk through the sand, carrying trays and taking orders from people lounging in their bathing suits underneath large umbrellas.

It's been a pretty wonderful day in Puerto Vallarta and really, up until now, I haven't thought about Riley or Linda or what very nearly happened yesterday in Mazatlán. I haven't yet decided if it's something I should tell Riley about, but, if I'm being honest, I'll probably keep it to myself—at least until we've been married a few years. Maybe I'll tell her on a mundane Sunday afternoon on the couch while we're watching reruns of *I Love Lucy*. I don't expect she'll be happy about it, but hopefully there'll be enough time removed from the actual occurrence that she can't do much more than be disappointed for a little while. Maybe by then we'll have kids and I'll be able to invest my time with them, while Riley gives me the silent treatment.

Thinking about Riley being upset reminds me that I don't want to finish this trip without having gone parasailing. I tell the driver this is what I want to do and he says he has a friend who works on the beach. He takes me to his friend and speaks to him in Spanish. While I don't understand what they're saying, I hear the word "parasailing" mentioned a few times.

"Twenty dollars," the driver says. "Ten minutes."

"Ten minutes of parasailing?"

"Yes, sir."

"Sounds good."

The driver relays this to his friend.

"Vamonos," the friend says, waving for me to follow him.

He takes me to a group of three men, all of them standing around parasailing equipment. Unlike my first parasailing attempt a decade prior, this one takes off from the sand of the beach. I give the guide twenty dollars, before surrendering myself to the three men who begin wrapping me up in a series of buckles and straps, connecting me to a large parachute laying in the sand. One of the men runs out into the ocean until he's waist deep, holding a long rope that's connected to all of the straps and buckles strapped around me. He whistles and waves in a motorboat that drives towards the man in the water. When the boat is near enough, the man wades towards it and attaches the rope.

Another of the three men begins giving me instructions in broken English on how to control the parachute when I'm in the air and how to land when it's time. He speaks fast and I'm not sure I understand all of it, but I don't interrupt and before I know it the motorboat is starting to accelerate out into the ocean. Two of the men take hold of the rope in front of me, pulling on it like they're having a tug of war with the boat as it drives away. The third man stands behind me, lifting the parachute from the sand. As the motorboat gets further out and the rope pulls taut, I feel the parachute catching air behind me. I grip hard on the straps beside my head, wondering now if I've made a terrible decision.

The men let go of the rope and my feet begin dragging through the sand. I run along with the force, trying to keep from falling face-first. The ocean is approaching fast and I expect to get wet, but before I do the parachute expands behind me, sounding like a giant plastic bird unfurling it's wings and just like that I'm flying. Nothing exists up here: No problems, no anxieties, no troubled best friends or temperamental fiancés. I slice the wind with outstretched arms, closing my eyes and pretending there is no parachute, no buckles or straps, no motorboat racing below. I pretend that there is only me soaring through the sky, flying without wings.

Back on the ship, I find Zachary lounging by the pool. He's got a bucket of iced beer and he's entertaining himself with my iPad. I sit in the lounge chair beside him and he offers me one of his beers. He asks about Puerto Vallarta and I tell him about the tequila and the pond and *Predator* and parasailing. He listens, but I can tell he's still thinking about Nicole and the unfamiliar feelings he's experiencing. While I know it's not any sort of real solution, I tell him about the Flash comic that's on my iPad.

"I love the Flash."

"I know," I say. "That's why I'm telling you."

"What's it about?"

"The Flash wakes up in an alternate universe where he doesn't have any superpowers and everyone around him has changed," I say. "In this universe his mother hasn't been murdered and he's happy about that, but there are also some not so good things happening, including a war between Wonder Woman and Aquaman. It turns out that the Flash himself has affected this universe by traveling back in time to stop Reverse-Flash from killing his mom."

"He went back in time to fix things," Zachary says, "but he messed up other things."

"Yeah," I say. "Want to read it?"

"Yeah."

We spend the rest of the afternoon by the pool, reading comics and drinking beer. Eventually, as evening approaches, we go back to our cabin and clean up for dinner. After dinner, we spend some time in the casino. Throughout the week, Zachary has won five hundred dollars playing roulette. It's an uncanny streak of luck and, for reasons I can't relate to, Zachary decides to push his luck. He places all five hundred dollars on red and a moment later the marble is bouncing across the roulette wheel. Zachary grabs my arm and closes his eyes. I watch the wheel for him, holding my breath as it slows down. The marble makes a few last reluctant bounces, before settling on red.

Some guys have all the luck.

The dealer seems genuinely happy for Zachary as she places his winnings on the table. Zachary takes his chips and cashes out, saying he's done gambling for the rest of the cruise, which will be over in a day.

"What're you going to do with your winnings?"

"I think I'll buy something nice for Nicole," he says. "Maybe some jewelry."

"Before or after you tell her?"

"I was thinking before," he says. "What do you think?"

"I think after might be better," I say. "In case you have to win her back."

"Good thinking."

The cruise is over and we're back home. Riley and Nicole pick us up from the airport in separate cars. I give Zachary a hug and wish him luck, before putting my luggage in Riley's backseat. She asks if I'm hungry, which I am, so, before taking me back to my apartment, she drives us to our favorite Mexican restaurant. The waiter brings us chips and salsa and we each order Horchatas. Riley asks about the trip and I tell her it was really nice.

"You didn't get into any trouble, did you?"

Even as she asks this, I can swear she already knows the answer. But, I know better, so I say nothing incriminating. The wedding is a week away and I don't want to say or do anything to mess that up.

"Nope, no trouble," I say. "We saw an old church in Mazatlán and I found this cool little shop where I bought you a necklace."

"That's sweet."

"And I toured a tequila refinery in Puerto Vallarta and ate lunch in the jungle where *Predator* was filmed."

"What's *Predator*?"

"An Arnold Schwarzenegger movie."

"Neat."

"And after that I went parasailing and that was about it."

"You went parasailing?!"

"It's not a big deal."

"It *is* a big deal," she says. "I very specifically told you *not* to go parasailing and you gave me your word that you wouldn't. You gave me your *word*, Bentley."

"Riley," I say, "nothing happened. It's no big deal. I'll never do it again."

She stands up from the table and I'm not so sure what's happening anymore.

"I can't do this."

"Can't do what?"

"*This*," she says. "Us."

"What are you talking about?""I trusted you," she says, "and you betrayed that trust.""I don't understand."She's already pulled off her engagement ring, setting it on the table.

"Riley, seriously?"

She's walking away.

The waiter comes to take our order and asks if I'd like to wait for my date to return. I get up from the table and follow Riley outside. She's already at her car, removing my luggage from the back seat. I try talking to her, but she's not answering me. Before driving away, she rolls down her window.

"It's over," she says. "I'll take care of canceling the wedding. Don't bother calling me."

She drives away, leaving me with my luggage and no ride home.

Obviously, I called Zachary and, obviously, he dropped everything to come pick me up. He drank with me over the next several days, in between me calling Riley and her not answering. He also helped contact my family and friends, letting them know the wedding had been canceled. It seems they were almost as shocked as I was, especially when Zachary didn't have an answer to the inevitable question, "What happened?" I couldn't believe that after everything we'd been through, parasailing was our undoing. Zachary couldn't believe it either, so he did some investigating—meaning he asked Nicole.

Speaking of Nicole, I almost forgot to tell you that Zachary told Nicole about his indiscretion with the prostitute in Mazatlán. She was upset, of course, but not really as upset as she probably should've been. And she didn't break up with him, which surprised both Zachary and me equally. When he asked her what she knew about Riley calling off the wedding, she didn't crack right way, but she eventually broke down and told him Riley had cheated on me. Actually, Riley *and* Nicole both cheated—and with the same guy, no less.

A stripper named Pierre.

Nicole enjoyed it for the fling that it was, but apparently Riley believed she'd fallen in love or something. As the story goes, while Riley was apartment-sitting for me, Nicole called her and said there was a party at her neighbor's place that involved a very handsome stripper. Whatever the details are between Riley and Pierre fucking don't really matter. It's not that I couldn't forgive Riley for it, but the truth is I'm kind of relieved. I mean, I would've gladly gone through with the wedding, but, after a few days of sitting in the rubble, I realized marrying Riley would've been a huge disaster. I can't help but wonder how many other people end up in my situation, but actually go through with their marriages.

As for Zachary and Nicole, they're doing better than ever. It turns out being in a relationship with the right girl has opened up a whole new world for Zachary. For one, he'd never been with a girl who cheated on him before. He assumed, as most anybody would, that such a scenario would be upsetting. But, when he was faced with the reality of Nicole fucking another man, Zachary was apparently turned on. "Dude," he told me, "I'm just as shocked as you." After mining Nicole for as many graphic details as she could recall, Zachary was ready for the next step in their relationship. He wanted to bring another man into their bedroom so he could watch Nicole get fucked in front of him. "It's not gay or anything," he tells me, "I just love watching her get pounded. Man, love is crazy, right?"

As for me, well, I don't know. Riley actually called a few weeks after canceling the wedding. We talked for about five minutes and she offered to take me back if I admitted to being wrong. She didn't specify what I was wrong about, but it didn't matter. I wasn't looking to get on that merry-go-round again. Zachary and I are good, though I don't see him much anymore now that he's invested in his first genuine grown-up relationship. We still talk and hang out once in a while, but not like before. I'm happy for him, though.

I officially graduated from college and I'm a week into my new career as a kindergarten teacher at Merryhill Elementary School. It's okay so far, though I'm thinking maybe kindergarteners are a bit two young and unruly for me. Frankly, I'm already thinking about my winter break, when I'll get two weeks off from these little hellions. I'm actually thinking about taking another cruise, this time by myself. Maybe another trip along the Mexican Riviera will be just what I need to recharge the ol' battery. And what harm would it do to visit a certain shop in Cabo San Lucas where I might run into a certain shop girl with caramel skin and brown eyes?

Belinda's Edge

One more time.

That's all I need.

One more.

I'll be rid of it after that. I won't crave the screams anymore. The terror. The blood. She'll be my last. I feel good about that. It feels right. It's been a long road. A long journey. A whole lot of memories to last a lifetime. One more time sharpening Belinda. One more time buying rope at the hardware store. One more time slipping on the hood. I'll miss the hood. The smell of it. The weight. That ever-welcoming black hole. Making me invisible.

Invincible.

Inevitable.

I'll remember this one forever. Almost as special as the first. There've been so many in between. So many covered mouths. So many strands of pulled hair. So many torn blouses and yanked jeans. So many crimson smiles opened by Belinda's edge. Butterflies are gathering like it's the first time all over again. I wish I could make it last. I wish the lights could be turned back on just as easily as I turn them off. I wish I could go back to her.

The first.

She loved perfume. Always a different fragrance, each more enticing than the next. She was healthy in body and spirit. So many days and weeks I spent watching her. I was too anxious, too excited. The urge was too strong. I couldn't hold it. Couldn't make it last. How I wish I'd found her later when I was better. More experienced, more able. I'd make it perfect. So many girls later, she still stands out. So many days I watched her examining produce, looking for bruises and brown spots. Discarding the inferior apples and kale, settling for nothing less than what she deserved.

I miss her window. Sometimes I go back just to look through it, remembering how the sight of her slicing fruits and vegetables made me feel down there. How many smoothies did I watch her make? How many salads tossed? So many nights I watched with Belinda. So many nights I felt the pulse against my jeans. I was so naïve. I thought the pleasure was in the end. How wrong I was. The pleasure is in all the moments before. The pleasure is in the longing. The following. The planning. I wish I could go back. I'd enjoy it so much more now. What I wouldn't give to turn her light back on, to do it one more time. To do it right.

The last one will be right.

It will be perfect.

All the others have led to this.

To you.

Nothing good lasts forever. I always knew there would be an end. I'm grateful to have it end on my own terms. I'll remember the close calls. The sirens. The sound of guns drawn. Hurried footsteps on wooden floors. I float through the air. A specter. A phantom. Materializing at your bedside. How easily I enter your home. So many locks, so many hinges. How easily I shatter your illusions.

I'm already in your entryway. Taking it all in. Belinda is in my hand, always a part of me. An extension. A manifestation of what was always meant to be. The rope is heavy. I'll miss the knots and the cinch. I'm already imagining how it will feel against your flesh, how it will pull against your skin. How often I've thought about your skin. Dreamt of it. Longed for it. How many times did I watch you tan beside the pool? How many times did I watch you moisturize after a shower? How many times did I watch you coil in ecstasy at your lover's touch? Too many count. Soon it will be my turn. Soon you will feel Belinda's touch.

You will scream.

You will plead.

You will bleed.

I walk through your hallway and see pictures on the wall. Photographs of you in different phases of your life. Childhood, adolescence, birthdays, graduations, dinners, barbecues. There are your mom and dad. There is your sister. There is your infant nephew in your arms. You were so elated to meet him. Such a nice day for you. There you are with your best friends in the Bahamas. You don't hear from them as much as you used to. Everybody's busy. They'll miss you. You won't know it, but they will. They will be horrified when they learn what happened. They will wonder if it can happen to them. They will double-check their locks every night. They will sleep with the lights on. They will close their eyes to reruns of *The Big Bang Theory*. They will wake up, breath-less, looking around. They don't know about the hood. The rope. Belinda. They will think about me often, wondering what it's like to find me at their bedside.

I hear you stir in your bedroom. So pleasant, so unaware. Adrift in your dreams, never once considering—not even for a moment—that I might be sitting on your couch. Being so close to you is unbearable. Everything in my body is screaming to go now up to your bedroom and begin. My groin aches in anticipation. When I was younger, I would've rushed. I would've relented to my urges. While I wouldn't regret it in the moment, I would come to wish I had been more patient. That I had appreciated it more.

The screams.

The blood.

The terror.

Driving to the hardware store. Walking down the familiar aisles. Knowing exactly where to find rope. Smelling the lumber and the steel. Feeling the benign chatter. Waiting in line at the register. Looking at all the people. All the boring, normal people. Living out their boring, normal lives. I wish they could know my joy. I wish they could feel what I feel. What I have felt so many times. Even the sickness that follows. Even the hot sting of Belinda's edge opening my skin. Bleeding in the bathtub. Pink water spinning down the drain. The tears. The shame. It is all part of it. It all matters.

And it all comes down to you.

My last.

One more time.

I walk up your stairs, wood creaking beneath my boots. I walk down the hall towards your bedroom. There is a mirror on the wall. I'm in it. I take a moment to look. The hood draping my head, my eyes barely visible. My breath gathers inside the black hole. Hot. Minty. I trace the point of Belinda along the mirror, across the reflection of my throat. I am walking again down the hall. I open your bedroom door. You are beneath a sheet, lying on your stomach. One knee bent. The other is straight, your toes peeking out from the sheet. Your delicate fingers, freshly manicured, rest beneath your cheek.

I am standing at your bedside. Belinda. The rope. The hood. Waiting. I will not wake you. I will stand and wait for as long as it takes. You will feel me here. My presence. Your most primal instincts will alert you. You will open your eyes.

Open your eyes.

Open your eyes.

Open your eyes.

Your lids are fluttering. You take in a breath. It's dark. Your eyes don't know yet. They adjust to the darkness. There is the scream. My god, it's even better than I imagined. I have thought of nothing else but this moment for so many weeks and you have already surpassed my grandest expectations. I jump onto the bed, straddling you.

Savor it.

Relish it.

Take it.

I let you scream longer than usual, allowing your terror to fill the room. I close my eyes, soaking it up. That is enough. I blanket your screams with my gloved hand, letting you taste all the screams that came before. You try to fight, swinging your arms, kicking your legs. I introduce you to Belinda, giving you a nice close look. You settle down. I bring the rope. You scream again, so I bring down my fist. The feeling of my knuckles against your mouth makes me swell inside my pants. I bring my fist down again, splitting your lip. You're sobbing now, no longer screaming. Time to tighten the rope, time to bring the knots. You only ask questions now, the same one over and over.

Why?

Why?

Why?

The pressure is unbearable. I want so badly to explode. But, this is the last time, I remind myself. The last time. I run Belinda's edge from your tits to your belly button, opening a seam of red. You try to scream against the pain, but the sound comes out awkward through your broken jaw. Belinda removes your pinky, then your ring finger. Your eyes grow big, each of them clouded with fear and confusion. You have no idea why any of this is happening, why you have been chosen. It is all too much. I cannot wait any longer. I grab your hair and yank your head back, exposing your pretty neck. I run Belinda's edge across your throat, opening one last crimson smile. You choke on your blood as I explode, wetting my jeans. I watch your eyes, waiting and waiting, taking it all in until that one final moment.

Lights out.

There's a knock on your front door. The neighbor asks if everything is okay. You don't answer. They knock again. I don't know what they do next, because I am already outside, walking down the sidewalk, headed home. It's hard to believe it's over. A long journey has reached its end.

I think about the seam of red from your tits to your belly button. Could it have been more straight? I think about the two fingers I cut off. Should I have mirrored the other hand? I think about the timing of my explosion. Wouldn't it have been more perfect to explode just as your lights went out?

The regret is already seeping in. The shame will soon follow. Belinda will punish me, of course. But it doesn't feel right. Not right at all.

One more time.

That's all I need.

One more.

The Big Night

I leave Mona's dorm in the morning at UNLV, stopping for a mani-pedi in preparation of our "Big Night." (You'll have to pardon the quotation marks, but it's hard for me to make any reference to the "Big Night" without imagining quotes around it and it's equally hard for me to take it as seriously as Mona. But, from this point forward, out of respect to my friend, I'll do my best to avoid the quotation marks when referencing the "Big Night." That was the last one, I swear. Maybe. "Big Night.") The Big Night is Mona's idea and, while she said it was for me, I know it's mostly her wanting to make use of my apartment because she doesn't want to risk inviting a stripper to her dorm room.

I'm standing outside my apartment door, digging through my purse in search of my keys, when my neighbor Nicole appears. Leaning against her doorway, arms crossed, phone pinned between her ear and shoulder, she says, "Fucking cable company." She's holding an issue of *Dolph the Unicorn Killer*, which I assume was meant to pass the time while the cable company kept her on hold. I know she's trying to engage me in conversation, but I really don't feel like having a hallway chat. I mean, Nicole is sweet and I've had very nice chats with her before, but sometimes she talks a little too much and isn't always the best at reading the room when my face is doing everything it can to tell her that I don't want to talk anymore. So I smile and nod, before turning to my door, staring intently at the lock as if it needs my full and undivided attention.

"They've got plenty of time to call you when they need money," she says, "but God forbid you need something from them. The only reason I put up with them anymore is for the cable guy. Have you seen him? My god, I'd love to stick a quarter in that ride."

That's the other thing about Nicole. She's cock crazy. Whatever the girl equivalent of a poon hound is, that's Nicole. Not that there's anything wrong with that, by the way. I'm all for us women empowering ourselves and owning our sexuality and getting some good dick when we can, but Nicole is just on another level. And, as best as I can tell, she has a steady boyfriend. Some guy named Zachary. I've met him a few times in the hallway and, while I wouldn't tell Nicole, I'm pretty sure he's trying to fuck me. Anyway, he's nice, too. They seem happy together, from what I can tell.

"What are you doing later?" she asks.

I unlock my door and pretend I don't hear her last question. In fact, I barely acknowledge her as I close the door behind me, because I know she's looking for any window of opportunity to engage me. She really is sweet and I really do like her, but—fuck. Am I an asshole?

You can be honest.

No, wait, don't say anything.

Not yet, anyway.

I'll figure out a way to make it up to her.

Save your judgment until after that.

My phone begins to ring inside my purse as I get into my apartment, so, in a way, I really couldn't make time for Nicole. When I take it out, I see it's Barry, so I don't answer. I plop down on my couch, phone in hand, and try to talk myself out of listening to the voicemail he's just left. He has nothing to say that I want to hear, yet I know I can't *not* listen to it. I pace around my apartment, pretending like listening to the voicemail isn't a foregone conclusion. I open my bedroom door, sounding the familiar squeak from its hinges (the same familiar squeak Barry had always promised to fix!), and belly flop onto my bed. Still clutching Barry's voicemail in my hand, I decide to go ahead and get it over with.

"Carol, honey," he starts. "I am so, so, so sorry."

He's clearly drunk and it wasn't even noon. See, that's just another reason he and I need to be broken up. I mean he wasn't getting drunk before noon when we were together, but it's clear now that he always had the capacity to do it. So, you know, vindication.

"For real," he says, "I don't know what I was thinking. I pray every day that the answers will come to me, but all I see is your face."

Oh, isn't that sweet? He doesn't even go to church, but now he's praying all of a sudden?

Fuck him.

"Listen, baby, I know my armor is chinked, but with you by my side, I can hammer it out. Your love is my hammer, Carol, and I've still got a lot of nailing to do. Please, baby, let me nail you."

By the way, I know you can't hear his voice as he says it, but I swear to you he has no idea that what he just said sounds filthy. He's so fucking obtuse. I really don't know what I ever saw in him.

"Please, Carol," he says, "I want to see you. I *need* to see you. You...complete...me. Just like the movie. Remember that gay movie you made me watch with the guy from *Mission Impossible* who was in love with the football player? We're like that, you and me. Listen, Carol. Listen. Even if you're not home, I'm gonna come over there and wait for you. I'll wait all day and night, because my love doesn't own a watch and, even if it did, I can't tell time when I'm not with you. And you know it. You *know* it, Carol. *Carol!*"

That's the end of the voicemail.

He got a little sloppy at the end, but, if I'm being honest, I could hear the passion in his voice. That part was very real and—fuck, I hate admitting this—it turns me on. That's probably what I hate most about him: No matter how much I hate Barry, I still get horny for him. It's purely biological or primal or whatever it is when people have smells that you can't smell, but your internal senses pick them up and you're attracted to them because evolution says you should make babies together, so, even if they cheated on you with the cute girl they work with at Kwipz, you can't turn off the part of your brain that makes you open your legs for the wrong fucking man.

As it stands, I've simply never had any luck with men I've seen naked. I can almost trace it back to the time I saw my mother having sex with the pool boy when I was I kid, but they were almost completely under water, so I don't count him. With that exception, I've seen a total of two naked men in my life. Gilroy the gray-haired bohemian and Barry the ex-boyfriend. And, after the Big Night, that number would supposedly become three.

Okay, look, you've come along this far, so I'm not going hide anything from you. I'm calling Barry back. It's embarrassing enough to admit, so please don't say anything. But, just so you know, I'm only calling him back to tell him to leave me alone.

"Hey, babe."

"You better not show your ass-face anywhere near here!"

"Carol," he says, "are you home?"

"Stay away, Barry."

"I need to see you," he says. "You're my hammer."

"You're drunk."

"This is why I need you," he says. "And you need me."

"I don't need you."

"Yes, you do, babe," he says. "The world is too dangerous for an angel like you. I was watching the news and some poor girl got murdered last night."

"Well, unfortunately that happens sometimes."

"Yeah, but it happened here in Vegas," he said. "They found her tied up in her bed with her face beaten and her fingers cut off."

"Jesus, Barry, I don't need to hear about that."

"I'm sorry," he says, getting weepy, "I just worry about you. You shouldn't be wearing that skimpy dress, you know. It's cold season."

"Well, I don't need you worrying about—"

Wait a minute.

"How do you know what I'm wearing?"

"I'm sitting at the triple-Q."

Quigley's Quoffee Quafe is a coffee spot across the street from my apartment. During our better days, we would sit under the green awning, drinking coffee like a cute little couple, while Barry did the most spectacular impersonation of a good boyfriend. He nodded his head in rhythm with my words, smiling and frowning at all the appropriate points and, when I was particularly upset about this or that, he said really sweet things, like, "What a bitch!"

I hurry to my bedroom window and look outside, spotting Barry across the street on his iPhone. He waves at me from beneath the green awning, a pair of binoculars hanging around his neck.

"You motherfucker!"

"I was just concerned," he says. "You wouldn't talk to me and I just thought—"

"Spare me," I say. "Just go the fuck home, Barry."

I hang up. I'm done with him. I am completely and totally done. I have to be. I have to cut him out of my life because, for all the wrong he did to me, I still miss the son of a bitch. I miss his smell. His hands. His shoulders. I miss the way he picked me up for surprise dates and the way he'd make love to me with that big goddamned cock of his. I miss ordering pizza for breakfast and watching *Friends* on Netflix (I even sort of miss how Barry called it "that gay show with the hot girl Brad Pitt used to fuck"). The most frustrating part about our break-up is he was perfect when we were together. We never had a fight we couldn't settle or an issue we couldn't compromise. But the Caesar salad incident outweighs every good memory I have about Barry.

The Caesar salad incident took place at an out-of-the-way Thai restaurant near the Strip. It's across the street from UNLV, so the customers are mainly college students and local working folks. If you're just visiting Vegas for a fun weekend, you'll never find it. That was Barry's favorite feature about it, that you couldn't find it unless you were looking for it. I thought it was romantic, but it turns out he was just trying to improve his odds of not getting caught.

I actually don't like Thai food all that much, so, on the day in question, I picked up a Caesar salad on my way to meet Barry for lunch. When I arrived, he was drinking a beer and had ordered me an ice water with lemon. Our waitress was taking his order when I saw a girl standing outside of the restaurant, staring at me. She eventually stormed into the restaurant, marching towards us and planting her fists down on our table, rattling the fork off my plate. I regarded this woman as a deranged lunatic, maybe a lost soul struggling with drug addiction or mental illness. I was scared, but I also knew in my heart that there was no way Barry would let this woman hurt me.

"What the fuck are you doing with my man?" she asked.

It was a strange question to hear because the math hadn't yet begun to compute in my head. Silly me, I was still working under the impression that this very pretty woman was in the throws of schizophrenia, reacting to a reality that wasn't real. She could've easily asked, "Where's my million dollars?" and I would've felt the same confusion. I didn't have a million dollars any more than I had a man who belonged to her.

"I'm talking to you, bitch!"

She punctuated "bitch" by punching the table.

"Hey," Barry said, "take it easy."

The deranged pretty woman looked at him, which, honestly, was a relief because I didn't like having her attention focused on me.

"Who is she?!"

I actually felt empathy for her in that moment—pity even. This poor girl was struggling right before our eyes to make sense of her reality. I figured it would be a matter of minutes before the police arrived (certainly somebody called the cops, right?) and before long she'd be in a mental institution, arms twined in a straight jacket, bouncing her head off a padded wall. I even considered visiting her, befriending her, helping her find her way back to mental stability. Maybe she'd get herself a job and I could be a steady presence in her life. We'd write a book together—mostly me, but her struggle would be the heart of it—and we'd tour the country speaking at bookstores and universities, eventually garnering national attention and being interviewed by Oprah and making a hilarious guest appearance on *Saturday Night Live.*

"Carol," Barry said.

Obviously, I looked at him, because that's what you do when somebody calls your name. But, when I looked at him, I realized Barry wasn't calling my name. He wasn't even talking to me. He was talking to the deranged pretty girl.

"I don't give a fuck what her name is," she said. "I want to know who the fuck she *is*!"

Everyone in the restaurant, myself included, waited for Barry to respond.

"She's a friend."

"I'm a what?"

"No, fuck that," she said. "You think I'm stupid? You're fucking this bitch. I can smell her pussy on you right now, motherfucker!"

Finally, Barry stood up, facing her appropriately, like a man ought to do when defending his woman's honor.

"She meant nothing to me," Barry said.

As little comfort as that remark brought me, I quickly realized he was talking to her.

"I swear," he said, "it was a fling. Nothing serious, babe, I swear." So, it turned out this woman *wasn't* deranged *or* mentally ill. She was heartbroken. Her man was cheating on her—and I was the other woman. As a gesture of solidarity, I wanted to explain to her that I had no idea Barry was a philanderer and, like her, I was also feeling the sting of betrayal. But, as I opened my mouth to talk, she took my water and threw it in my face, before dumping the Caesar salad on my lap.

"You're lucky I'm a lady," she said, "or I would've fucked your shit up."

The scorned woman turned to leave, stopping at the glass door. She then looked at Barry.

"You coming or what?"

You'd think at this point I would have seen the writing on the wall, but even in that moment I was delusional enough to think he'd stay with me. Without a word or so much as a goodbye, he stood up from the table and left the Thai restaurant with the woman he apparently regarded as his girlfriend, leaving me alone with a Caesar salad in my lap. And I haven't heard from him since, until today.

Last night Mona and I got drunk on tequila shots and heartache. We burned love letters over a scented candle, talked about how much we hated boys, and playfully—but optimistically—attempted to put a curse on Barry. Mona wasn't in a relationship herself, nor had she recently suffered heartache, but she embraced my broken heart like it was her own. At some point in the night, she said we should order a stripper. It's probably worth mentioning that most of Mona's solutions to romantic strife involve ordering strippers. We'd never actually done it before and I'd never seriously considered it, but I guess last night she caught me in the midst of a perfect storm of emotional vulnerability.

We were watching *The Office* on Netflix and I'd forgotten what an emotional rollercoaster Pam and Jim put us through, so, by the time we got to the two-part wedding episode, I was a wreck, a veritable faucet of tears and snot. I likely would've said yes to just about anything Mona suggested at that point, so I should be grateful that a stripper was all she asked for. She filled my head with grand notions of us dressing up all sexy, getting our nails done, and acting like total divas with a naked man at our feet. It was a bit over the top and clearly born from her obsession with reality television, but I have to admit it all sounded good in the moment. Before I could come to my senses, Mona was already pulling up the list of stripper websites she'd bookmarked over the years. I laughed hysterically when she actually dialed one of the numbers and started talking to somebody, sharing the features she was most interested in—tall, muscular, and foreign with a sexy accent—before giving them my address. And just like that, she'd made us an appointment with our very own stripper. He'd be coming to my apartment tonight as the centerpiece of the Big Night.

When I woke up this morning in Mona's dorm, I was sort of surprised that the whole stripper thing still sounded kind of fun. The first pang of worry didn't hit until I asked Mona what time she wanted to get our nails done.

"You go on without me," she said. "I've got to study for my chemistry midterm."

"But, the idea was to spend the day together, right?"

"Totally," she said. "The stripper isn't coming until the afternoon, so it's no big deal if I miss the morning bit."

"Wait, he's coming in the *afternoon*," I asked, "as in a couple of hours from now?"

"Yeah, remember? We talked about it."

"I don't remember that at all," I said. "I didn't think he'd be coming until the evening."

Mona rested her chin in her hand, looking up and away as she searched her memory.

"You know," she said, "I must have *thought* it, but forgot to say it out loud."

"Thought what?"

"I figured if we scheduled the stripper for the afternoon, we'd have the rest of the day to go barhopping."

"I guess that makes sense," I said, "but I wish you would've told me. What time this afternoon?"

"I don't remember."

"Mona!"

"What? We were drinking, so it's all a bit blurry. But, I definitely ordered him."

"Do you at least know his name?"

"Pierre."

"Okay, at least we know that," I said. "What time will you be at my place?"

"This afternoon."

"I know, but what time?"

"I don't know," she said, "I have to study."

If you didn't know anything else about Mona or our friendship, her vague answer and shaky commitment might've seemed relatively harmless—I mean, it was *her* idea after all, so why would she back out?—but juxtaposed with Mona's first big idea involving me and a naked man, it makes a lot more sense why I was getting nervous.

A few years back, when Mona and I were freshmen at UNLV, she convinced me to sign up for an art class with her. "It's going to have real live nude models," she'd told me. Being that it was our first year in college and, up to that point, my life had been void of naked men, I decided to take the class with her. I figured that part of being a college student was taking chances and doing crazy things, such as drawing pictures of naked people. Mona showed up for the first few classes with me, but the day we had our first nude model in class—an older man named Gilroy whose gray hairs weren't nearly long enough to conceal his uncircumcised manhood—she was nowhere to be found. So, there I was sitting in an art studio with five relative strangers sketching a charcoal portrait of Gilroy, a man who seemed pathologically comfortable with being naked in front of us.

I called Mona as soon as class was over.

"Where were you?"

"When?"

"Today!" I said. "You weren't in art class."

"Don't you remember?" she asked. "I dropped the class."

"No, you didn't tell me that."

"Really?"

"Yeah, really."

"You know," she said, "I must have *thought* it, but forgot to say it out loud."

I didn't talk to her for weeks and I swore I'd never forgive her, but, of course I eventually did, mostly because she was the only friend I'd made that year. And, interestingly enough, the art thing kind of stuck. It turns out I enjoy sketching and painting, though I'm not great at either. I'm not sure what I'll do with it, but I'm currently an art major. So, in that sense, I had Mona to thank for it. But, none of that stopped me from worrying that she was going to back out on me again.

"You'll be there right?" I asked.

"Yes, of course. This afternoon?"

"Yes."

"Twelve?"

"I don't know what time exactly," she said. "I'll text you."

"Promise?"

"Jesus, yes," she said. "I promise."

Other than Mona—and, until recently, Barry—the only person I regularly called was my mother. So, given that I'm feeling lonely and heartbroken, and I can't quite shake the anxiety of knowing a stripper named Pierre will soon be naked in my apartment, I call my mother for a quick chat.

"Hello," she says, "I was wondering when you'd call your mother on her birthday."

Fuck, I forgot today is her birthday.

"You forgot, right?"

"No!" I say. "It's barely noon, you knew I'd call eventually."

I don't want her to figure out I'm lying, so I change the subject.

"Barry's stalking me."

"What?!"

"Yeah," I say, "he's sitting across the street at fucking Quigley's and he called me this morning and I swear to God if he had the nerve to come up to my apartment I would just freak out."

"That piece of shit," she says. "You know I never liked him."

"I know."

"And I told you he was a piece of shit and you didn't need to be with him."

"I know."

"Did he hurt you?"

"No," I say, "but he's creeping me out."

"Did you call the police?"

"No."

"It's just as well," she says. "There's nothing they could do anyway. I'm glad you called me, though. I'll be right over."

"No!"

Because you can't actually hear me, you'll have to take my word for it when I tell you the "No" I'd just shouted out was way louder and more aggressive than I'd intended.

"What's the matter with you?"

"I'm sorry," I say. "I just don't need you to come over. Not today."

"Listen," she says, "a mother knows things, sweetheart. Your words don't fool me, my love. You're scared and you're heart is broken, so you need your mother. I'll be there as soon as I can. Love you."

She hangs up before I can protest any further.

I definitely can't go through with the Pierre thing now, so I call Mona. She doesn't answer, so I call her again. When she still doesn't answer, I send her a text, telling her to call me back. Almost immediately, she texts back that she's busy studying. I call her again and this time she finally answers.

"Don't hate me," she says, "but I can't hang out today."

"What?!"

"I've got this fucking chemistry midterm and it's got me stressed out," she says, "so I need to spend the day studying."

"But, this whole thing was your idea."

"I know," she says, "but you can still have the Big Night without me."

"That wasn't the point," I say. "Whatever, just cancel Pierre."

"You'll have to call them."

"Why me?"

"We ordered him with your credit card."

"Fine, whatever," I say, "text me the information."

"Are you mad?"

"Would you care if I was?"

"Of course."

"In that case, I fucking hate you."

I hang up and wait for Mona to send me the information, but she doesn't. I don't bother texting her again, either. Instead, I go into my bank account and find the name for the company that charged my credit card. I go online, track down their phone number, and call them up. A woman with a nasally voice answers.

"Strip-o-Rama," she says, "how may I help you?"

"Hi, I ordered a stripper yesterday."

She asks for my name, then types for a few moments on her keyboard.

"Well, fancy that," she says. "It seems *I* was supposed to call *you*."

"You were?"

"Yes," she says, "you ordered Pierre, right?"

"That's right."

"Well, as I'm sure we already told you, Pierre speaks limited English."

"He doesn't speak English?"

"No, he *speaks* English," she says, "but in a limited capacity. We usually send him out to his appointments with a chaperone who can communicate in French *and* English. Anywho, Pierre's chaperone called in sick. Cold season, you know. So, Pierre will be arriving without a chaperone."

"That's fine," I say, "I was calling to cancel anyway."

"Well, we can definitely do that for you, but there is one concern," she says. "Pierre is already on his way. Once our performers leave, we don't offer refunds. The transaction at this point is final."

"I don't care," I say. "Go ahead and cancel."

"That's no problem," she says. "When Pierre arrives, tell him that you talked to me and that you want to cancel."

"Why can't *you* tell him?"

"He's in transit," she says. "It'll be easier for you to tell him."

"I think it makes more sense for *you* to tell him."

"Nonetheless," she says, "is there anything else I can help you with?"

I hang up without another word and go back to my bedroom to look out across the street. I see Barry flirting with one of the prettier waitresses at Quigley's. The asshole can't even *stalk* me monogamously. I have half a mind to call him and tell him I can see what he's doing, but thankfully my ascent into bad decision-making is interrupted by the sound of the doorbell ringing. I walk to the front door and look through the peephole, expecting to see a handsome Frenchmen. Instead, I see my mother holding a box of wine. I take a moment to consider any option that would reasonably allow me to keep her out, but I can think of none, so I open the door.

"Sweetheart," she says, "come here."

She gives me a hug and a kiss, before making her way into the kitchen to pour two glasses of wine. I sit down on the couch and she joins me, handing me a glass.

"We just have the worst luck with men," she says. "I was on a date last night with a young man from your university. He was going down on me, which was lovely, but he kept sneezing. I finally sent him home with some NyQuil and a rain check. It's cold season, you know."

"That's what I hear."

You'll have to excuse my mother's lack of boundaries, but the only thing she loves more than having sex is talking about it. I've never in my life gone out of my way to initiate a conversation about sex with my mother, but that's never stopped her from finding any reason to tell me about her many sexual escapades. I figured out early on that asking her to stop didn't work and ignoring her was completely pointless, so I simply learned to live with it.

"Drink your wine, sweetheart," she says. "I'm going to take you out. We'll get our hair done, get some lunch, and maybe do a little shopping."

This was perfect. If I were out with my mother, Pierre would show up to an empty apartment. He'd have to leave eventually and my mother would never be the wiser. I can't believe I hadn't thought of this sooner.

"That all sounds wonderful."

"Well good," she says. "We'll just finish our wine, then head out."

The doorbell rings.

"You expecting someone?"

I scoured my brain for a decent lie.

"It's the cable guy."

"Carol, darling," she says, "you don't have cable."

"I know," I say. "That's why I called for him."

"When were you going to tell me? Unless you have some other means of paying for it."

"Well, I wasn't exactly planning to order it."

"Then why did you call for the cable guy?"

"He's not just any cable guy."

"No?"

"He's pretty popular with the ladies around here."

"Well, well," she says, "this is a pleasant turn of events."

The doorbell rings again.

"Come now," she says, "let's not keep this gentlemen caller waiting."

She gets up to answer the door.

"Wait!"

"Don't worry," she says, "I won't embarrass you. I'd just like to meet this handsome young man and then I'll be on my way."

I jump from the couch, moving past her and planting my hands against the door.

"I'd sort of rather he didn't see you."

"Well, why not?" she asks. "Aren't I presentable?"

"Of course you are," I say. "You're just *too* presentable."

She adjusts her cleavage.

"You might be right," she says. "But, I'm afraid we can't avoid it."

The doorbell rings again, so I take my mother by the wrist and lead her into my bedroom.

"You can wait in here until he's gone."

"How long will that be?"

"Not long," I say. "Juts a few minutes. Once he's gone, you can tell me more about the boy from last night."

I leave her sitting on the edge of my bed, closing the door behind me. The doorbell rings again as I hurry to answer it. Just before I open the door, I consider the possibility that it could be Barry on the other side. But, when I open the door, it is immediately apparent that the man ringing my doorbell is most definitely *not* Barry. This man is tall with tight muscles and olive skin. He's wearing a police outfit that looks about as convincing as a pre-fab Halloween costume. The pants and shirt are two different shades of blue, while his badge is a cheap plastic toy. He's got a baseball cap on his head that reads LVFRD on the front (an acronym for "Las Vegas Fire & Rescue Department"). In one hand, he holds a large boom box—an obsolete piece of equipment if there ever was one—and in the other, he holds a piece of notepaper with my address and apartment number on it.

"My name is Pierre."

He speaks with a buoyant French accent, which causes me to think dirty thoughts about the dexterity of his tongue.

"I'm very sorry," I say, speaking quickly, "there's been something of a misunderstanding, so as much as I appreciate you coming over, I can't let you in."

He smiles.

"My name is Pierre."

Clearly, this isn't going well, so I do what anybody else would do when faced with a language barrier—I speak in slow motion, emphasizing each syllable.

"Pi-erre," I say. "My...mo-ther... is...he-re."

"Mother?"

"Yes," I say. "Mother. You understand?"

"Mother," he says. "Yes."

"Oh, good," I say. "So, I need you to leave."

He smiles.

"My name is Pierre."

The situation is becoming increasingly hopeless, so I figure I'll just shut the door in his face and wait for him to get the hint. But, before I can, I see Barry peeking his head around the corner at the end of the hallway. He pulls his head back just as soon as he realizes I've caught him spying on me. I know he saw Pierre and I realize that from Barry's perspective he probably looks like a genuine police officer.

"That's right *officer*," I say, ensuring my voice projects down the hall, "my *ex*-boyfriend is *definitely* stalking me."

"My name is Pierre."

"You want to know his *name*?" I say. "His name is *Barry*. That's B-A-R—as in *rat*—R-Y."

I project my voice so effectively that it gets Nicole's attention across the hall, so she cracks her door open and peeks out.

"Is everything alright?"

"What's that?" I say, waving Nicole over, "you need an eyewitness. Yes, I have an eyewitness."

Nicole, bless her heart, scrambles right across the hall without a second thought, looking Pierre up and down as she enters my apartment.

"Why is there a police officer here?" she asks.

"I'll explain in a second."

I hear my bedroom door opening, so I grab Pierre by the arm and pull him inside, before running back to my bedroom. I slip inside, shutting the door behind me.

"Mother, I asked you not to come out."

"I know, but I just heard all that fussing you were doing," she says. "Is everything alright?"

"Yes, I've got everything under control."

"Well, good," she says. "Maybe I can meet your cable gentleman."

"No, no," I say, "that won't be necessary. We're just talking about rescheduling his visit, so please try to keep yourself occupied until I can get him out of here."

"Honestly," she says, "I don't see what harm would come out of me just saying hello."

"He's not going to be here long," I say. "It'll just be easier this way."

"Easier how?"

"I don't know," I say. "Just easier."

The sound of music comes from the living room.

"Is your cable gentleman having a party?"

"God, I hope not."

I leave her in my bedroom and find Nicole sitting on the couch, wide-eyed, watching Pierre as he gyrates in front of her.

I hurry to Pierre's boom box, shutting off the music.

Both he and Nicole seem disappointed.

"Pierre," I say, pointing to the front door, "go home."

He stays put like a lost puppy.

"Oh, don't feel bad," I say. "It's not you, it's me. This whole day has been one big mess. My ex-boyfriend is stalking me, my best friend is a flake, and I'm holding my mother hostage in the bedroom."

"Mother?" he says.

"Yeah, so I just need you to go home."

"He doesn't speak English," Nicole says.

"I know."

"Who is he?"

"He's a stripper," I say. "His name is Pierre."

"My name is Pierre."

"Yeah, I just told her," I say. "My friend Mona thought we should order a stripper to help me get over Barry."

"You and Barry broke up?"

"Yeah, about a week ago," I say. "Barry's hiding at the end of the hall, so that whole display you just saw was me trying to scare him."

"Wow," she says, "you're my new hero."

"Really?"

"You ordered a stripper to come to your apartment in the middle of the day," she says. "I can't believe I've never thought of that myself."

"Don't be too impressed," I say, "it's not exactly turning out well."

"Before he leaves, maybe we can let him finish his routine," Nicole says. "I mean he's already here."

"I'd rather not," I say. "I don't want my mother to see him."

"Mother!" Pierre says.

"Yes," I say, "mother."

"I believe he's talking to me."

I turn around and see my mother strutting out of the bedroom, heading straight for Pierre.

"Hello," she says, extending her hand.

Pierre takes it, kissing her fingers.

"My name is Pierre."

"Carol, dear," Mother says, "why is your cable guy dressed as a police officer?"

I have no idea how to answer that question.

"If I didn't know any better," she says, "I might think this strapping young man is an exotic dancer."

I stay quiet, hoping somehow this will all just go away.

"I think I understand," she says

"You do?"

"Yes, I believe I do," she says. "You didn't forget my birthday at all, did you? You arranged this whole elaborate charade so you could surprise me with Pierre."

I look at Pierre, then back at my mother.

"Surprise."

"Can I stay?" Nicole asks.

"Of course you can stay, dear," my mother says. "Carol, get us some more wine, sweetheart. As for you, Pierre, I think it's about time you get to work."

She sits on the couch and reaches into her purse, pulling out some dollar bills, which prompt Pierre to put his music back on. He takes off his cap, tossing it like a Frisbee to my mother. He then spins around, facing his back towards her, removing his shirt before tearing off his pants in one swift motion. He's naked now, but for his cowboy boots and a tiny red thong. He drops onto the floor, spreading his legs into a perfect split. Balancing himself with his hands, he begins bouncing his tiny red thong up and down on my carpet. He stands to his feet and works himself between my mother's legs, pumping his red bulge in her face.

It's at this point that I step into the hallway, shutting the door behind me. Nicole follows me out.

"Carol," she asks, "can I invite my friend Riley over?"

"Sure," I say, "why not?"

Nicole goes back inside, while I lean back against the wall, sliding down onto the floor. About fifteen minutes pass with my mother and Nicole squealing and laughing when Riley turns up.

"Is this where the party is?"

I wave my hand to the door, inviting her inside.

Another ten minutes pass before Nicole sticks her head out the door.

"Hey, so Pierre's fucking your mom in your bedroom," she says, "and technically my turn is next, but I just wanted to make sure that was cool with you."

"Wait, what?"

"You know what, you're right," she says. "It's your party, you should fuck him next."

I look down the hall and see Barry peeking around the corner again.

"Fuck it," I say, standing up.

Barry runs down the hallway.

"Carol, wait," he says. "What's going on with the cop?"

"He's not a cop," I say. "He's a stripper. And possibly a prostitute, I don't know. I'm going to have sex with him now, so you're welcome to stand by the door if you want to hear what it sounds like."

Barry waits a moment, as he if he's considering the offer, before turning and walking away. It isn't the most dramatic of exits, but it feels good nonetheless. I enter my apartment to the sounds of my mother and Pierre in the bedroom.

"He sounds like a lot of fun," Nicole says.

"Don't you have a boyfriend?" I ask.

"Yeah, but it's okay," she says. "He's on a cruise with Riley's fiancé."

The bedroom door opens and my mother comes out with her hair in tatters as she catches her breath. Through the doorway, I can just make out Pierre's naked legs hanging from the bed, all chiseled and tanned. Nicole and Riley cheer me on as walk inside, climbing on top of Pierre.

Now, before I wrap this up—without any more details than I've already shared—you should know that I'm totally aware of how strange this all is. I'm pretty sure I may live to regret some, if not all, of the day's events and chances are I'll spend the whole rest of my life on a therapist's couch trying to make sense of it all. But, right now, in this very moment, I can't bring myself to care about anything else except fucking Pierre.

"Giddy up."

The Baldies

"**I**, for one, am *not* going to sit around waiting for the Baldies to take advantage of my body!"

"That's not even what they do, Mother."

"And how would *you* know what they do, Son?" Mother asked. "Are you running around with them? Is that one more thing I need to worry about? If that's the case, then it really is well past time we leave this horrible city."

"I'm not running around with the Baldies."

"If *you're* not, then that degenerate boy Rainbow likely is," Mother said. "Isn't he?!"

"How would I know?" Earl asked. "You won't let me hang out with Rainbow anymore."

"Don't talk back to Mother."

"Father, please."

"Sorry, Mother."

It's true that Mother forbade Earl from seeing his best friend Rainbow, but that didn't change the fact that Rainbow was, at that very moment, hiding in Earl's closet, smoking weed from his favorite glass pipe. As the tiny orange embers at the end of the pipe became one with the darkness, Rainbow thought about how he couldn't imagine anyone—let alone the Baldies—wanting to take advantage of Earl's Mother's body. He exhaled a plume of smoke, stifling a laugh that threatened to become a coughing fit.

Earl, for the most part, was an obedient son. The only time he went against Mother and Father's wishes was when he hung out with Rainbow and when he smoked marijuana—though, technically, they never directly forbade him from smoking.

"We're done talking about this," Mother said. "Absolutely one hundred percent done! This town is swarming with miscreants and scoundrels and this family isn't going to be raped or murdered by them."

"But, nothing's ever happened to us before."

"Don't talk back to Mother."

"Father, please."

"Sorry, Mother."

"Nothing has happened because we've been lucky," Mother said. "But, it's only a matter of time before our luck runs out and the Baldies break into our home and take advantage of my body."

"All they do is shave your head."

"How do *you* know that's all they do?"

"That's what they said on the news."

"Well," Mother said, "maybe you should stop listening to fake news."

Earl had lived in Las Vegas since he was in grade school, when his parents moved the family from Utah because Father got a new job. But, after years and years of terrible stories on the news of people being robbed and murdered—and, most recently, being violated by the Baldies—Mother decided it was time to move out of Las Vegas. They bought a house in San Bernardino, California, which was where they'd be moving in a few days. San Bernardino was a large suburban city whose general makeup wasn't all that different from North Las Vegas, which is to say poor, dilapidated, and sketchy. And, like Las Vegas, you can even gamble there, so long as it's at the San Manuel Indian Bingo and Casino. Earl wasn't happy about the move, as he didn't want to part from his best friend. His parents couldn't have cared less, however, and as if to prove the point they decided to spend their last weekend in Las Vegas at Caesar's Palace.

"You're to have no friends over while we're gone," Mother said. "Your food money is under the clock by the front door. There's enough to last you the entire weekend. If you starve to death, it'll be your own fault, so don't starve to death."

"We'll be very disappointed if you starve to death, Son."

"If you need us, the phone number to Caesar's Palace is on the Internet," Mother said. "I suggest you don't need us."

Unlike Earl, Rainbow had lived in Las Vegas his whole life. He knew Earl's parents were right about Las Vegas being full of miscreants and scoundrels—even though he didn't know what those exact words meant—so he could hardly blame them for wanting to get out, but it didn't mean he had to be happy about it. Rainbow pulled out his lighter, intending to light up his pipe for another toke. It was a metal lighter, painted red with a faded picture of a 1920's pinup girl on it. He'd gotten it some years ago in a midway game at the Grambling Brothers Traveling Circus and Sideshow, which passed through town once a year.

As he flicked the lighter on, Rainbow watched the small flame dance, illuminating the darkness with its wavy rhythms. He was the center of his own universe, a god who gave life to tiny flames. He imagined small planets and moons orbiting the flame, pulled by the force of its gravity. He was a giant invisible power looking over everything and, at any given moment, he could make it all go away. He imagined a tiny civilization of human-like creatures evolving over millions of years from sticks and stones to time-traveling machines and the flame got bigger as his universe filled with smoke. He assumed the smoke was all in his head, a manifestation of the mind-altering effects of his marijuana, until he realized he'd unwittingly caught one of Earl's T-shirts on fire.

Because Rainbow was already high, the fire didn't immediately alarm him. He stared at it a few moments, marveling at the threads of smoke twirling up into the darkness. Once the fire grew, Rainbow's survival instincts kicked in. He dropped the lighter and swatted the T-shirt like a cat trying to tame a fiery ball of yarn.

"What's that?"

"What's what?"

"That ruckus."

"What ruckus?"

"Father, didn't you hear a ruckus?"

"Yes, Mother."

"Father heard a ruckus," Mother said. "Why is there a ruckus?"

"I don't know."

"Are you hiding critters under your bed again?" Mother asked. "If you catch rabies, that'll be your burden."

"Do you have rabies, Son?"

"I don't have rabies."

"Then why is there a ruckus?"

"I don't know."

"We're going to get to the bottom of this, just as soon as we get back," Mother said. "You'll see. And this room had better be packed when we get home. You hear me, Son?"

"Tell Mother you hear her."

"I hear you."

"Anything that's not packed stays here," Mother said. "Now, give us a kiss."

Rainbow pulled the smoking T-shirt down, ensuring the fire was out. He then squeezed his eyes shut and stroked the rabbit's foot hanging from his neck. He'd worn it every day since the night he met "The World's Prettiest Fortuneteller" Xyla Peppermint at Grambling Brothers. Rainbow was smitten with Xyla from the moment he first saw her. He'd wanted to get his fortune told, but he didn't have enough money to pay for a proper reading. For what little money he did have, Xyla gave him the rabbit's foot right from around her neck. "The rabbit from whom this foot came was fed a diet of four-leaf clovers and killed by a horseshoe from a seven-year-old stud named Irish," Xyla told him. "It leaves a path wherever it goes. So, when you're lost, you may always be found." That was a year ago, the last time Grambling Brothers was in town.

Rainbow stroked the rabbit's foot between his thumb and fore-finger, the hair worn thin from his familiar fingerprints. He stroked and stroked, hoping Earl's parents would finally leave so he could relax and enjoy his high. He concentrated so hard on hoping that he didn't hear the bedroom door open and shut, nor did he hear Earl's parents shuffle out of the room. In fact, he didn't hear anything until three stiff knocks rippled through his tiny universe. Opening his eyes, he said nothing.

"Dude, what are you waiting for?" Earl asked.

"Oh, hey," Rainbow said. "I can't open the door."

"Why not?"

"There's no door knob in here."

"You don't need a door knob," Earl said. "Just slide it."

Rainbow slid his hand across the door like he was washing the hood of a car.

"It didn't work."

Earl slid the door open for him.

Rainbow smiled.

"There it goes," he said. "It's working now."

"Come on out."

Rainbow held the pipe out to Earl.

"Take a hit, dude," he said. "It'll help you forget about your crazy parents."

Earl would need to take a hit from a bowl the size of the Grand Canyon to forget about his parents, but that didn't stop him from sucking on Rainbow's pipe.

Rainbow and Earl met for the first time at the Grambling Brothers Traveling Circus and Sideshow. Even before Rainbow met his best friend, Grambling Brothers had been a fixture in his life from the time he was a poor kid growing up in North Las Vegas. While his mom took him every year because it was affordable entertainment, as far as Rainbow could tell it was the most extravagant source of fun in the world. The fact that it stayed for a short period of time—usually no more than a weekend—made it all the more magical.

When he first met Earl, Rainbow was in the midway trying and failing to knock over milk bottles with a baseball. His mom was somewhere, doing something, but Rainbow didn't know what or where, nor was he too concerned with finding out. Earl turned up at the same midway game, Mother and Father hovering over him as he handed his cash over to the man behind the counter. Rainbow watched as Earl also tried and failed to knock over the same milk bottles that had defied him only moments before. The boys looked at each other, bewildered at the strength of these milk bottles, marveling as they stood triumphantly against the velocity of their adolescent strength.

And that was it.

That's how they became friends.

Simple as that.

Rainbow's mom met Mother and Father that night, exchanging numbers when they saw how well the boys got along. Neither Rainbow nor Earl had friends, so all three parents felt grateful to see their boys bonding. Mother called Rainbow's mom the next day to set up a play date for Earl and Rainbow. The following Saturday, Rainbow's mom drove him up to Earl's house in Summerlin. She was intimidated by the neighborhood, as it's one of the wealthier areas of Las Vegas and she could never afford to live there herself. She'd spent her whole life living below Rainbow Boulevard (and, yes, that's where Rainbow got his name) in North Las Vegas, much closer to Downtown.

This, of course, meant Rainbow had also lived his whole life in North Las Vegas, so his mom was worried about how he'd fair in this upscale community. But, as soon as he and Earl were together again, they were just boys having fun. Mother and Father invited Rainbow's mom to sit for tea, while Earl took him up to his room to play video games. Rainbow was keenly aware of the expensive video games and consoles Earl owned and how his mom couldn't afford to buy those same games and consoles for him, but even then he didn't feel uncomfortable or out of place. Mostly, he was just happy to have a friend who owned cool toys that he could play with. Having played video games for a while, they went outside to Earl's backyard to jump on his trampoline, which was something Rainbow had always wanted to do but never had the opportunity. Mother and Father ordered pizza for the boys, which they devoured before going upstairs for more video games. It was arguably for all involved—boys and parents alike—the best day of their lives.

While Rainbow's mom was happy to see her boy make a friend, she ultimately couldn't get over her own discomfort with being in such a fancy house or wealthy neighborhood. She simply felt out of place, so the next time they made a play date for the boys, Rainbow took the bus into Summerlin. When Mother and Father found out he took the bus, they offered to pick him up for their play date the following weekend—and after seeing where Rainbow and his mom lived, they decided he was okay taking the bus the next time. Unfortunately, they also became less comfortable with Earl spending time with Rainbow, worried that whatever poverty or disadvantages he'd had in life might somehow be contagious.

Nonetheless, even throughout the disillusionment of their respective parents, Rainbow and Earl's friendship endured. A few years passed and, just like that, Rainbow and Earl were teenagers. They went to different schools but never made any other friends. They didn't need to. They had each other. Rainbow discovered marijuana along the way, as well as the benefits of avoiding barbers. He let his hair grow long and shaggy, totally unkempt. Throughout high school, Rainbow's hair became an inseparable part of his identity. It got to where Earl could hardly remember a time when Rainbow *didn't* have his long curls. Earl even asked him once if he'd ever considered cutting it.

"No way, dude," Rainbow said. "I'm like Samson."

"Who?"

"Samson," he said. "From the Bible."

"Since when do you read the Bible?"

"I don't, but I know Samson's in it," he said, "and his hair's dope as fuck. It makes him strong and shit, so he can kill lions and whatnot. But, when that bitch Delilah cut it, Samson's strength was gone."

"So, you think you're strong like Samson?"

"Nah," he said. "It looks cool as fuck, though."

Earl couldn't argue with that. He loved Rainbow's look, particularly the spirit behind it, in large part because there was no way Mother and Father would ever let him get away with anything other than his neatly manicured hair, short and parted to the side.

What he *could* get away with was joining Rainbow in his discovery of marijuana. Not that there was much discovery involved. Rainbow tried it and loved it, so he told Earl. Earl tried it and loved it, so they kept doing it. Rainbow, of course, was in charge of actually procuring their supply. He happily experimented, trying different strains, until he had a short list of favorites, including Sour Diesel, Fire OG, Super Lemon Haze, Purple Trainwreck, and OG Kush— but he and Earl both agreed their favorite was Blue Dream. Blue Dream was a hybrid of two opposites, blueberry indica with sativa haze, one being sedating and physically relaxing, while the other was uplifting and cerebrally stimulating. And while Blue Dream had medical benefits, Rainbow and Earl weren't exactly using it for pain or nausea, though they might've unwittingly enjoyed the effects it had on stress and depression.

After suffering through several unreliable dealers, Rainbow found Pizza Man. In true stoner fashion, Rainbow had no concrete memory of how he met Pizza Man. If he did remember, though, he'd mostly be disappointed by the mundane nature of their meeting. Basically, Rainbow knew a guy who knew a guy who knew a guy. In his mind, he liked to imagine it was more mythical than that, like maybe Pizza Man came to him in a dream, his long blond hair hanging perfectly beneath his baseball cap.

At any rate, Rainbow and Earl had come to know Pizza Man as a steady presence in their lives, to the point where they knew his schedule, which mattered because he only sold marijuana while delivering pizzas. Even with medical marijuana being legalized in Nevada, it was still easier for Rainbow to use Pizza Man. Ironically, Pizza Man had a medical marijuana card, which he used to stock his inventory. As far as his doctor—or "doctor"—knew, Pizza Man suffered from anxiety, which, also ironically, wasn't far from the truth.

"Did you call Pizza Man?"

"Yup."

"Sweet," Earl said. "We got anything else to burn for now?"

"Just the shake, dude."

"It'll do, I guess."

"Pizza Man will be here soon," Rainbow said. "Plus, guess what."

"What?"

"No, guess."

"I don't know."

"Dude, Grambling Brothers is in town!"

"The fucking circus is here?"

"Yup, it's like they knew this was our last weekend together."

"We should go."

"Obviously, dude," Rainbow said. "So, let's toss the shake, wait for Pizza Man, then get high at the circus."

"You're my fucking hero."

"I know."

Pizza Man deciphered which of his customers wanted pizza and which wanted marijuana using an easily decipherable system that any law enforcement could've figured out if they ever bothered to look into his operation. When he was a kid, Pizza Man watched every movie that came out of his cable box and his favorite was a 1989 comedy called *Loverboy*, starring Patrick Dempsey. The plot of the movie involves Dempsey as a college student who needs to make extra money, so he starts delivering pizzas. He meets an attractive older woman who orders pizza with extra anchovies. She seduces him, then gives him an extra $200 and, just like that, he becomes a gigolo. When neglected women called the pizza shop and ordered a pizza with extra anchovies, it was the secret signal for Dempsey to make the special delivery.

Loverboy was the sole reason Pizza Man took a job as a pizza delivery guy when he was a teenager. He hoped he'd meet his own seductive older woman who would want extra anchovies, but that fantasy never came to pass. He did eventually start selling marijuana and, if only to pay homage to his favorite movie, he set up his own secret signal. Anyone who called up for a pizza with extra anchovies meant they wanted Pizza Man to make the delivery so they could score. Rainbow and Earl were his most loyal and reliable customers.

The boys sat on the couch, entertaining themselves while they waited for Pizza Man. Earl rested his feet on the coffee table, something he'd never do if Mother was home—but, of course, that was precisely the reason he was doing it. He didn't see what was so special about her coffee table. It had a glass top, which Mother was forever worrying over, cleaning and wiping, constantly removing crumbs that only she could see. She wouldn't even let Earl rest a cold beverage on her coffee table, let alone his feet. So as not to be *too* rebellious, however, he took his shoes off before putting his feet up.

While Earl enjoyed the rebellious joy of resting his feet on Mother's coffee table, Rainbow was reading a copy of *Grunt*, which was a long forgotten porno magazine from the seventies. Father had a stack of them, which the boys had discovered while they were in junior high. It would prove to be a fortuitous discovery at the time, given that the Internet hadn't yet become a household staple. While the magazine once served as the source of many masturbatory dalliances, Rainbow now mostly read *Grunt* for the articles, as the abundance of Internet porn had desensitized him to the relatively tame pictures of women spreading themselves open. At the moment, he was completely sucked into a gonzo journalism piece called "Captain Fuckmeister." The journalist in question, a man who called himself Oral Lee, documented the journey of a man named Patrick William Mahoney as he tried to fuck everyone in Mexico.

"Dude," Rainbow said, elbowing Earl, "listen to this. 'Seven days removed from the beginning of his ludicrous endeavor, Patrick William Mahoney is lying naked on the floor of a dirty motel room somewhere in the middle of Tijuana, Mexico, curled into himself, hugging his knees and sobbing quietly.' Dude, this is crazy!"

Earl was too focused on the TV to pay attention to Rainbow.

"Seriously," Rainbow said, trying again to get his friend's attention, "this dude tried to fuck everyone in Mexico. Every motherfuckin' one! *And* it's a true story, dude."

Most any other night, Earl would've been captivated by Rainbow discovering a hidden treasure of gonzo journalism, but at the moment he was watching the evening news, which was his favorite program. Earl had come to enjoy the evening news when he was a kid, after figuring out how much violence and gore was reported. It was almost as good as watching horror movies, which Mother and Father absolutely forbade. The evening news, on the other hand, they watched religiously. Of course, being best friends with Rainbow meant he still got to see cool horror movies like *Nightmare on Elm Street* and *Hellraiser*. They'd watch their horror movies late at night, quietly, sitting inches in front of the TV, while Mother and Father slept. This was back when Rainbow was still allowed to have sleepovers and hadn't yet been banned from Earl's house.

The news story that had Earl transfixed was the same one that had captivated most everybody in the South West, from California to New Mexico, for nearly a year: The Baldies. There wasn't much new news to offer on the Baldies, given nobody knew who they were. There were some firsthand witness accounts from victims of the Baldies, which led to police sketches of three bald men with no unique identifying features, so they were about as useful as sketches of department store mannequins.

For the most part, all the witnesses had pretty similar stories. A group of three bald men followed them home, forced themselves inside, tied them down, and shaved their heads. Some accounts included violence, but not all of them—the variable seemed to be how cooperative the victims were with the Baldies. The witnesses who willingly allowed themselves to be tied up and shaved seemed not to suffer any sort of beatings, while those victims who were less cooperative were usually worse off for it.

Outside of losing your hair, neither Earl nor Rainbow could find too much harm in having your heads shaved against your will. That is, of course, until the news anchor shared a breaking development in the story: "A man with his head recently shaved was found dead inside the tunnels beneath Las Vegas Boulevard and the 15 freeway. Details are still being released, but authorities confirm they're treating the death as a homicide. The underground tunnels, which the Regional Flood Control District estimates are close to 600 miles long, are home to thousands of homeless men and women. Authorities say the victim, who has yet to be identified, doesn't appear to have been part of the homeless population. While authorities haven't made any official comments, all signs point to the man being a victim of the Baldies."

At some point, perhaps unbeknownst even to Earl, he'd developed an affection for the Baldies. He saw them as merry pranksters shaking things up, a trio of tricksters who weren't really doing any lasting damage. Hair would grow back and bruises would heal.

But, murder?

The thought left Earl feeling almost betrayed.

The doorbell rang, causing him to jump.

"Easy, dude," Rainbow said, laughing. "It's just Pizza Man."

Earl got up from the couch, still thinking about the Baldies as he walked to the front door. He found Pizza Man on the porch, scanning the neighborhood as a stray siren sounded in the air. Earl invited Pizza Man in, leading him into the living room where Rainbow was still reading about Captain Fuckmeister. The three of them started eating pizza, but not before picking the anchovies off.

"Dude," Rainbow said, "you don't actually have to put anchovies on the pizza when we order."

"I've gotta be safe," Pizza Man said. "If someone wants the extra anchovies and not the ganja, then I'm fucked."

"What if we came up with our own pizza," Earl said, "like extra anchovies, extra pineapple, extra peanut butter. Then you know for sure it's us and you can just make a regular pepperoni pizza."

"Too risky," Pizza Man said. "Lots of people have strange tastes, so I don't ask questions. They order a pie, I make that pie."

Pizza Man pulled a couple of dime bags from his pocket, tossing them on the coffee table.

"This is fresh inventory," he said. "You'll be very satisfied."

"Awesome."

"You mind if I smoke with you guys?"

"Sure," Rainbow said. "We're smoking at the circus, though."

"Is that some new slang I don't know about?"

"No," Earl said, "the Grambling Brothers Traveling Circus and Sideshow is in town. We're gonna go smoke there."

"Cool."

"You wanna go?"

"Is pussy my favorite snack?"

Rainbow and Earl looked at Pizza Man, waiting.

"That means yes."

The boys celebrated with a high five, before heading out the door.

Blue Dream, Pizza Man, and Grambling Brothers. This had all the makings of becoming the greatest night of their lives. That's exactly what both Rainbow and Earl were thinking, simultaneously, like they were twins. Pizza Man drove, allowing Rainbow and Earl to feel like they were part of a rock star entourage. They'd never hung out socially with Pizza Man before, as it never occurred to either of them to ask. They'd always put Pizza Man up on a pedestal, given that he was older and cooler and sold marijuana. So, outside of occasionally smoking with them during deliveries, this was their first time being out with Pizza Man—and it was awesome.

The Grambling Brothers Traveling Circus and Sideshow was set up in in the dirt lot behind Boca Park, a shopping center anchored by Target and a few small retail stores. Certainly, at least part of the idea was to get people who were out shopping or eating to notice Grambling Brothers in the background with its red-striped tent and hanging string of lights, tugging at their curiosity just enough to wander up to the box office and buy a ticket. The boys drove onto the dirt lot, which also doubled as a makeshift parking lot. The modest stretch of dirt was filled nearly to capacity with cars, but Pizza Man was nonetheless able to find an open spot. It was dark out, on account of there being no lighting beyond what came from the circus itself, but it wasn't quite pitch black. Perhaps it was the poor lighting, or maybe it was the general excitement of the night, but, whatever it was, none of them—not Pizza Man, not Rainbow, not Earl—noticed the rusty orange pickup truck beside them or the three bald men inside.

As Rainbow, Earl, and Pizza Man walked along the dirt to the box office, they could hear the loud voice of a barker somewhere inside the circus, his voice rough and rhythmic, trying to sell an attraction to anyone who would pay him attention. The big tent was in plain view beyond the box office and there was a line of about ten people extending from the window. As they reached the front of the line, a man with his arm in a sling greeted them from inside the small box office.

"Welcome," he said. "How can I help you?"

"Three tickets please," Rainbow said.

The man in the box office rang up three tickets, followed by Earl and Pizza Man each putting money on the counter.

Earl looked at Rainbow.

"What're you waiting for?"

"Can you cover me?"

"You don't have money?"

"I want to save it for inside," Rainbow said. "I'll buy you some cotton candy."

Earl paid for Rainbow's ticket and the three of them headed for the entrance, where they were greeted by a clown.

"Welcome to the Grambling Brothers Traveling Circus and Sideshow," the clown said, taking their tickets and tearing them in half. "The show in the big tent will be starting in a bit, but until then enjoy any one of our many amazing sideshows."

"There're a lot of people here," Rainbow said. "Is this normal?"

"We've grown quite popular ever since the YouTube video a few weeks ago."

"What video?" Earl asked.

"The video of the man on fire," the clown said. "Have you seen it?"

"No," Earl said. "Why was he on fire?"

"Because that's what he does," the clown said. "You'll see him in the main show under the big tent."

"Is the fortuneteller still here?" Rainbow asked.

"You must be talking about Xyla Peppermint," the clown said, "the World's Prettiest Fortuneteller."

"Yes."

"Well, you're in luck," the clown said. "She just so happens to be with us tonight for a limited engagement."

Rainbow could hardly believe his luck. The clown was fibbing, of course, as any good carny might—Xyla always traveled with Grambling Brothers and there was nothing limited about her engagement.

Even if Rainbow knew he was being lied to, he'd still be happy knowing that he was going to see Xyla Peppermint again.

"Head inside," the clown said, "have a look around. I'm sure you'll find her before long."

"Thank you!"

The three of them walked past the clown and entered the circus grounds.

"Enjoy the show, boys," the clown said. "That's what it's here for."

They walked past the tents and concession stands, all three of them unwittingly moving towards the voice of the barker, like so many rats being lured by the Pied Piper.

"You three gentlemen!" the barker said, pointing at the boys. "You look like curious sorts. Step right up and come see the most curious creature this side of Tutu Island."

Motioning his hand behind him, the barker guided their collective attention to the entrance of his tent.

"What's in there?" Earl asked.

"Through this portal is a world where wolf boys live and giants shrink," the barker said. "A world where your brain won't believe a thing of what your eyes tell it are true."

He paused and looked around, before touching his index finger to his ear.

"Do you hear that?"

Just as he said it, the tent moved like somebody was trying to push their way through.

"My, my," he said. "The little guy sounds absolutely famished for company."

"Who's that?" Rainbow asked.

"Good question," the barker said. "That, my good man, is Pedro the Orphan Wolf Boy."

Tiny growls sounded from behind the tent, followed by a hairy little arm pushing through the slit of the closed flaps, fingers grasping at the air.

"Back!" the barker yelled. "Get back, I say!"

The hairy arm retreated into the tent.

"I assure you, gentlemen," he said, "your lives will only be in a *limited* amount of danger should you choose to be an audience to the world's only orphan wolf boy. Be warned, however, the boy's hungry and it's almost feeding time."

"How much?" Earl asked.

"Entering is four dollars," the barker said, "and exiting is almost certainly guaranteed."

"Maybe later," Pizza Man said.

"Not feeling brave, are we?" the barker said. "Come, come! See the Orphan Wolf Boy with your own eyes, let your imagination feast."

Pizza Man walked away, so Rainbow and Earl followed him. The barker barked a few words behind them, but they didn't look back. Pizza Man led them behind one of the tents and asked if they were ready to get high, so Rainbow took out his pipe and the bag of Blue Dream. He stuffed the pipe, before taking out his pinup girl lighter. He sucked hard on the pipe, feeling the hot smoke snake down his throat and into his lungs, holding it down for as long as he could while passing the pipe to Pizza Man. Pizza Man took a similar hit, before passing the pipe to Earl. Earl also took a similar hit, before passing the pipe back to Rainbow. They went on like this for a few more revolutions, before stepping out from behind the tent and back into the dreamlike world of the circus.

"Hello, boys."

Rainbow, Earl, and Pizza Man looked around until their eyes all landed on the same woman.

"Looking for me?"

Hands on her hips, she stood in front of a small tent with a burlap banner hanging over her head, which read, "Xyla Peppermint: The World's Prettiest Fortuneteller."

"It's you!" Rainbow said.

"It is," Xyla said.

"I still have my rabbit's foot."

"You better."

"Do you know the future?" Earl asked.

"Sometimes."

"Are you good?" Pizza Man asked.

"Better than a cookie."

"Fortunes take place in the future, right?" Earl asked.

"Sure."

"So, you're sort of like a *future*-teller."

"I guess if you look at it that way," Xyla said, "but predicting the future is usually about lottery tickets and earthquakes. Think of your fortune more as courses of luck, good or bad, following your progress through life."

"And you predict that?" Pizza Man said.

"I don't *predict* fortunes," she said. "I *tell* them."

Xyla nodded her head towards her tent, before passing through the curtains. The boys followed behind her, pushing through the heavy fabric. The inside of Xyla's tent was dim, illuminated by candles and white Christmas lights. The delicious scent of incense floated in the air. There was a small table covered with an exotic blanket and, sitting atop it, was a genuine crystal ball.

There were only two chairs inside the tent, one on either side of the table.

"So," Xyla said, "who'd like to sit with me."

"Can only one of us do it?" Rainbow asked.

"You all can have your fortunes told," she said, "but only one of you will."

"Is that a prediction?" Pizza Man asked.

"No," she said, "just the truth."

"How do you know?" Earl asked.

"The same way I know you're the one who will sit with me."

"Is it true?" Rainbow asked. "Do you want to sit with her?"

"I kind of do," Earl said.

"That's fucking spooky, dude."

Pizza Man shook his head, seemingly in disgust.

"You think this is silly?" Xyla asked.

Pizza man laughed, but said nothing.

Xyla smiled.

"You should enjoy your good spirit," she said. "It won't last through the night."

"What's that supposed to mean?"

"I don't know," she said. "I don't predict the future. Remember?"

"How do you know something bad will happen?"

"I didn't say it would."

"Fuck this," Pizza Man said, exiting the tent.

Xyla gave her attention to Earl.

"Have a seat."

"Should I leave?" Rainbow asked.

"Do you want to?"

"No."

"Then stay."

Xyla waved her hand over the crystal ball, staring deeply at it, before raising her eyes.

"What's your name?"

"Earl."

"Shall I tell you your fortune, Earl?"

He nodded, yes.

Xyla pulled out a deck of cards, setting them on the table.

"We'll do a tarot reading."

Earl nodded, though he didn't know what a tarot reading was. Xyla slid the deck of cards in front of him.

"Shuffle them please."

Earl picked up the deck and did a half-decent job shuffling, before sliding the cards back to Xyla.

"In just a moment you'll draw three cards," she said. "But, before you do, you need to ask a question of the cards."

"What do I ask?"

"Something regarding your fortune," she said. "Whatever it is you'd like to know."

"I have to leave Las Vegas."

"Okay," she said, "so what's your question?"

"What can I do to *stay* in Las Vegas?"

Xyla smiled.

"Let's begin," she said. "Go ahead and draw three cards."

"From the top?"

"From wherever you like."

Earl pulled the first card, leaving it face down.

"That's not necessary," Xyla said, "you can look at it."

Earl turned the card over, revealing a woman in a long gown and a shawl over her shoulders. She sat upon an exotic thrown, her foot resting atop a half moon. A horned crown rested on her head and a large crucifix hung against her breasts.

"The High Priestess," Xyla said.

"Is that good?"

"It can be," she said. "Draw your next card."

Earl pulled his next card from the deck, laying it beside the High Priestess. Pictured on the card were a man and a woman standing naked across from one another. Behind the woman was an apple tree with a long snake wrapped around the trunk. Behind the man was a tree that was nearly barren but for twelve leaves that looked like flames. Between the man and woman, out in the distance, was a mountain with a sharp peak. Hanging over them in the air, floating on a cloud, was an angel with her eyes closed and arms open. Behind the angel, filling the sky, was the sun.

"The Lovers," Xyla said. "Pick one more."

Earl drew his third and final card, laying it beside the Lovers. Pictured on it was a man hanging upside down, his right ankle tied to a horizontal tree branch. His left leg was bent, the ankle hiding behind the knee, like the number four. His arms were behind his back and his blonde hair reached for the ground. Behind his head glowed a large halo.

"The Hanged Man," she said. "Interesting. Let's begin."

Earl nodded.

"There are many different spreads," she said. "A spread is the number of cards you draw and the manner in which they're arranged. The significance of each card is based on the position it lands in. For your reading this evening, I selected a very simple spread. I asked you to select three cards, which you did. You even laid all three cards down beside each other without me having to ask, which is good because they are now set in the order of your choosing, even though you didn't know you were choosing. Before you drew the cards, each position in this spread already had a determined meaning. The first card represents the past, the second card represents the present, and the third card represents the future. Based on the cards you've chosen and the position they've been placed, I'll use them to help answer your question. You asked, 'What can I do to stay in Las Vegas?' To begin, we'll look first to the past. And for that you drew the High Priestess."

Xyla touched her finger to the card.

"When you find yourself in situations where you're not sure how to act, but you're still calm, then in those times you are subconsciously emulating the High Priestess. The High Priestess card is one about instinct, trusting your inner compass that guides you even when you don't know why or how. The world is full of mystery, full of places, people, and experiences that we often don't understand. The High Priestess embraces all of it, all of the mystery, letting it wash over her until bit-by-bit all of it becomes clear."

Silence.

"Because you drew the High Priestess first in this spread, she represents your past. Her placement could refer to your recent past or perhaps your childhood. She tells me you were a passive child, reared by parents with domineering personalities. You had very little say in what happened to you growing up, but, just as the High Priestess, you stayed calm. You developed your intuition and inner compass, you learned to survive on hunches and gut feelings. Again, your question was 'What can I do to stay in Las Vegas?' Your very question exists on the precipice of past and future. It implies that your past involves your living in Las Vegas, but your future has you living elsewhere."

Silence.

"San Bernardino," Earl said.

"This is where you're moving?"

"Yes."

"But, you don't want to go, do you?"

"No."

"Who's making you go?"

"My parents."

"This explains why you drew the High Priestess," Xyla said. "In your past, which is every moment leading up to now, you have relied on patience and understanding, developing your inner compass which helped you survive, yes?"

"They raised me like I was a pet," Earl said, "telling me what to do, what to eat, who I could and couldn't be friends with."

"Your parents aren't here with you now, are they?"

"No."

"But," Xyla said, looking at Rainbow, "your friend is."

"Yes."

"Intuition," she said. "Understanding. Does the High Priestess make sense to you?"

Earl nodded, yes.

"Good," she said. "Let's move on."

Xyla tapped her finger on the middle card.

"The Lovers," she said. "You can see the angel above protects the Lovers. The snake and the fruit tree allude to the story of Adam and Eve, a metaphor for the temptations of the world. A representation of doing those things that we know we should not, but we do them anyway because we can't stop ourselves. Often it's passion that fuels temptation, which is what the tree of fire behind the man represents."

Silence.

"In this spread," Xyla said, "the Lovers represent your present. Again, you asked, 'What can I do to stay in Las Vegas?' This card indicates you have someone in your life, someone you trust, someone who gives you strength. Your bond is strong and can overcome any obstacle, such as distance or time. The Lovers are soul mates, but, despite the implicit indication of the card, that doesn't have to mean romance—though it *can* mean romance, even if you don't yet see it. But, that's the present. Let's now look at the future."

Xyla tapped her finger on the third card.

"The final card you drew is the Hanged Man," she said. "This card is particularly interesting, given your question. This is the card of ultimate surrender, giving up control and presenting yourself as a martyr. The Hanged Man reminds us that, when it comes to the larger forces of the universe, we have no control, so the only way to gain control is by letting go. 'What can I do to stay in Las Vegas?' you asked. The answer is this: Nothing."

"Nothing?"

"Nothing," she said, taking Earl's hands in her own. "Accept and surrender. By giving up control and letting go, you'll find that all the angst and anxiety will also go away and you'll open yourself up to new possibilities. You'll have a new life, one that you can't yet imagine, but one that you may find more satisfying than the present or the past."

Earl smiled. Rainbow did too. Neither wanted to think about life without the other, but Xyla's words comforted them both.

She squeezed Earl's hand.

"Life isn't always easy," she said. "You will experience bad things—perhaps sooner than you expect—but you'll be okay."

Letting go of his hand, Xyla looked into his eyes and repeated herself.

"You'll be okay."

Earl and Rainbow walked out of Xyla's tent, each buzzing with the transcendent experience they'd just had. Even though it was Earl who had his fortune told, Rainbow felt every bit as invested in the outcome. They were so overwhelmed by the unnamable feelings Xyla left them with that they'd forgotten to pay for her service. Earl turned immediately around and went back to Xyla's tent, but she was gone.

"Should we wait for her?" Earl asked.

"I don't know," Rainbow said. "Maybe she didn't want you to pay."

"Why wouldn't she want me to pay?"

"She didn't ask for money."

"I don't think that's how businesses work."

Pizza Man turned up eating a corndog.

"You guys done playing with the bitch?"

"She's not a bitch," Earl said. "She's amazing."

"Yeah, well, whatever," Pizza Man said. "The main show is going to start soon, so we need to get our seats."

Earl hated to leave the tent before he saw Xyla to pay her, but he didn't want to miss the main show, so he and Rainbow followed Earl to the big tent. Rainbow bought some popcorn for himself on the way in and, as he promised earlier, he bought cotton candy for Earl. They found seats amongst the otherwise packed tent just in the nick of time as the light dimmed and a familiar tune sounded from wonky speakers.

A spotlight shot straight down from the center of the big tent, lighting a perfect circle on the dirt. Inside the circle of light was the Ringmaster, dressed in a red coat, heavy black boots, and a top hat. He brought a megaphone to his mouth and started the show.

"Ladies and gentlemen, boys and girls, children of all ages, for the duration of your stay beneath this magical tent you will be presented with the most spine-tingling, toe-curling, heart–pounding, death-defying collection of spectacles that your eyes will ever see. Just yonder behind those curtains awaits miracles of mischief, hoards of humor, and visions of wonder. The men and women who will soon capture your imagination are globetrotters, trailblazers, mold breakers, and conscience shakers. I am your Ringmaster, Claudius Xavier, and I proudly present to you the Grambling Brothers Traveling Circus!"

The audience cheered and clapped and, for the duration of the show, every act got their due appreciation. Handsome Harry the World's Prettiest Strongman, Swift Sammy Tawker the High-Wire Walker, Charlie Chuckles and the Clown Alley Hooligans, the Soaring Silvas, and Fernando the Fearless Fire Tamer each amazed and enthralled the audience, but there was a palpable buzz in the air which grew through the night, until the final act was set to begin.

Rainbow and Earl had each assumed that Fernando the Fearless Fire Tamer was the final act, given how the clown—who turned out to be Charlie Chuckles, leader of the Clown Alley Hooligans—had told them about the fire-man. Given the build up, they were feeling a bit underwhelmed by the fire act, until the Ringmaster returned to the center and it became clear the show was not yet over.

"Your final performer of the night doesn't simply dance with fire," the Ringmaster said. "He terrifies it!"

The whole audience rose to their feet, cheering as loudly as they had the entire night.

"I can promise you, once he's done, the memory of his feats will sizzle in your memories for the whole of your lives. Ladies and gentlemen, I present to you the Man Whom Fire Fears, Grover Wilcox!"

Fernando the Fearless Fire Tamer was back at center ring, joined by Grover Wilcox, a relatively normal looking man in jeans and a T-shirt. Fernando picked up a large rod, lighting the tip on fire like a giant matchstick while Grover simply stood in the center ring, doing nothing. Fernando circled around him a few times, waving the fiery rod, before stopping so that he was face to face with Grover. Holding the rod in front of him, he took a deep breath and blew a fireball directly into Grover's face, eliciting a combination of cheers and horrified screams from the audience.

As the fireball dissipated, Grover looked around, waving and smiling at the audience. Fernando continued blowing fireballs, hitting every part of Grover's body, eventually catching his clothes on fire. The audience continued to be amazed and scared, trusting that Grover was not burning alive, despite all the evidence to the contrary. As for Rainbow and Earl, even if they weren't under the influence of Blue Dream, they still would've been amazed—but the high they were enjoying was mostly calming, so they never felt the terror that much of the audience was feeling as Grover was engulfed in flames. By the end of the show, Grover's clothes had burned off completely, except for a pair of shiny silver boxer shorts.

Filing out of the big tent, Rainbow, Earl, and Pizza Man were each beside themselves with how amazing that final performance was. Grambling Brothers was mostly shut down for the night as everybody headed back into the parking lot. Earl looked one more time at Xyla's tent, but it was still empty like she'd never been there at all.

"Do you want to just leave the money for her?" Rainbow asked.

"What if she doesn't know it's from me?" Earl said.

Rainbow rubbed his rabbit's foot between his thumb and forefinger.

"I have an idea," he said. "What if we leave the money with my rabbit's foot on top? Then she'll know it's from us."

Earl loved the idea, so he took out the money for Xyla and Rainbow removed the rabbit's foot from around his neck, handing it to his friend. Earl rolled up the money and tied the necklace around it. "Where do I leave it?" he asked. "On the dirt?"

"No," Rainbow said. "Somebody might take it. Put it on her table."

"But, she's not in there."

"Remember how Xyla told you about letting go of control and stuff?"

"Yeah."

"What if maybe she was talking about this?" he asked. "What if maybe you're supposed to let go of being a pussy and do this thing you're scared of?"

Earl stood there, contemplating Rainbow's epiphany when Pizza Man snatched the money from his hand. Before Earl could protest, he walked into the tent and placed the money on the table beside Xyla's crystal ball.

"There," Pizza Man said, coming out of the tent. "Can we leave now?"

The boys joined the stream of people filing into the dirt parking lot, which was just a little bit darker now that the circus was closed for the night. There were so many people walking around and looking for their cars, you could hardly blame Rainbow, Earl, and Pizza Man for still not noticing the three bald men in the truck parked beside them. And, of course, because everybody in the parking lot was driving home from the circus, the boys had no real reason to notice that they were followed out of the parking lot by the rusty orange pickup truck.

It was a short drive from Boca Park to Earl's house, so there weren't a whole lot of turns or intersections to drive through, which might have helped account for why none of the boys realized the rusty orange pickup truck was matching them turn for turn and stop for stop, right up until the moment Pizza Man pulled up in front of Earl's house. Rainbow and Earl got out of the car, but Pizza Man stayed in the driver's seat intending to leave. Rainbow noticed the bald men first, turning his head as the rusty orange pickup truck parked behind Pizza Man.

"Who's that?" Rainbow asked.

Earl looked, watching as the doors opened and the three bald men got out.

"I don't know."

The three bald men moved quickly towards Pizza Man's car, prompting Rainbow and Earl to start running for the front door. Earl fumbled for his house keys, still running until he reached the porch, out of breath. Rainbow stood behind him, panicking as two of the bald men marched towards them. The third bald man was dragging Pizza Man out of his car. Just as soon as Earl got the key in the door, the two physically imposing bald men stood behind him and Rainbow, grabbing them around their necks. The bald man holding Earl—squeezing his neck tight enough that he couldn't scream—turned the key and opened the door. They dragged Rainbow and Earl into the house, while the third man followed behind them, dragging Pizza Man inside.

They dragged them into the living room, throwing them to the floor. Rainbow and Earl stayed put, but Pizza Man jumped up and ran for the front door. He only traveled a few feet before one of the bald men tackled him. They fell onto Mother's coffee table, shattering it beneath Pizza Man. Shards of glass dug into his face and arms, slicing his palms as he tried to break his fall. The bald man began punching Pizza Man relentlessly, first about the head and face, before focusing his blows to the stomach and rib cage. Pizza Man curled into submission, weeping as he begged for mercy. The bald man kept beating on him until he was unconscious. When he stood to his feet, bloody fists hanging at his sides, the bald man stared at Rainbow and Earl. Even though he didn't say a word, the boys new full well what the message was.

One of the bald men grabbed two chairs from the kitchen, setting them in the living room, while the other bald man exited the front door. The bald man with the bloody fists looked at Rainbow and Earl.

"Sit."

They got up from the floor and sat in the chairs. The third bald man returned with a duffle bag, dropping it to the floor. He unzipped it and removed a couple rolls of duct tape, which they used to wrap Rainbow and Earl's waists, arms, and ankles to their respective chairs. Pizza Man remained on the floor, still unconscious, blood leaking from his mouth and nose. One of the bald men fastened Pizza Man's wrists behind his back with duct tape, before wrapping his ankles together.

From the duffle bag, one of the bald men pulled out three candles, each of them made crudely of homemade wax inside of dented tomato cans. He set two of the candles on the floor, near Rainbow and Earl's feet. The third candle he set beside Pizza Man's bleeding face. The bald man dug through the duffle bag again, searching for something else, before quickly giving up.

"We don't have matches."

One of the bald men looked at Rainbow.

"That one has a lighter."

"Get it."

He went to Rainbow, reaching both hands in his pockets, his strong fingers digging into his thighs until he found the red lighter with the pinup girl on it.

"C'mon, man," Rainbow said.

"Dude," Earl whispered, "be quiet."

The bald man with the lighter looked at Rainbow.

"Listen to your friend," he said. "We only need to take one of you, but that doesn't mean we can't take more."

"Take us where?" Rainbow asked.

One of the bald men stepped in front of Rainbow, gripping his face by the jaw.

"My brother asked for silence," he said. "You'd be smart to obey."

Rainbow nodded his agreement as best as he could with the bald man still squeezing his jaw. When he let go, he went back to the duffle bag and pulled out a straight razor and a pair of scissors.

The bald man with Rainbow's pinup lighter lit each of the homemade candles, before slipping the lighter in his pocket. Rainbow watched his lighter disappear and, despite the strange and terrifying circumstances he was currently experiencing, he couldn't help but be a little sad at the thought he'd seen his pinup girl for the last time.

One of the bald men stood behind Rainbow, grabbing a handful of his wild curls and pulling his head back hard over the chair. He cut the handful of hair off, before grabbing another handful and repeating the process. He did this over and over again, leaving small clumps of hair on the floor around Rainbow's feet. The next bald man stepped up behind Rainbow with a bottle of shaving cream in hand, slathering a thick layer of foam all over his head and eyebrows. Then the third bald man stepped behind Rainbow with the straight razor, gripping the back of his neck.

"Don't move."

He began shaving Rainbow's head, delicately, almost lovingly, like a painter working to ensure every detail was exactly perfect. While he shaved Rainbow's head, the first bald man stepped behind Earl and began trimming his hair with the scissors, getting it as close to the scalp as he could without tearing into his flesh. Then the second bald man stepped behind Earl and slathered shaving cream over his scalp and eyebrows. The third bald man was still working on Rainbow, so all Earl could do was sit and wait. He looked at Pizza Man who remained unconscious on the floor, blood still oozing from his nose and mouth, leaving a crimson disc beneath his cheek. He'd been unconscious long enough that Earl was now wondering if he was even still alive. He concentrated his eyes on Pizza Man's ribs, trying to see if they were rising and falling. It was hard to tell, but as best as he could see Pizza Man was completely still. No movement at all.

When he felt the third bald man behind him, Earl tensed up, no longer focusing on Pizza Man. He felt the strong fingers on his neck, gripping him, followed by the edge of the straight razor, cool against his skin, slowly running across the top of his scalp. Other than the scraping of the razor against his skin, the only other sound in the room was Rainbow weeping with his chin against his chest. Earl wanted to look at his friend, but, with the bald man's fingers

gripped on his neck, he didn't dare move. Hoping that his coopera-
tion would lead to the terror being over sooner rather than later, he
stayed perfectly still as the bald man shaved him smooth.

The bald men packed up the duffle bag, putting away the scissors, shaving cream, straight razor, and candles. One of the bald men
picked up the duffle bag, while the other two picked up Pizza Man.
Without a word to signify they were done, the bald men walked out
of the house with Pizza Man, leaving Rainbow and Earl fastened to
their chairs. They would remain exactly there for a full day and night,
occasionally nodding off to sleep, hardly a word spoken between
them, until Earl's parents returned home from their weekend at Caesar's Palace.

Mother was frantic, of course, and she could hardly stop talking while
Father called the police. She was both horrified and relieved, pacing
around the living room, stepping through hair and talking mostly
to herself about miscreants and scoundrels. Father sat on the couch
between Earl and Rainbow, his arms around both of them, squeezing
them in tight while they waited for the police to arrive. He offered to
call Rainbow's mother, but he said it was okay. Two police offers eventually showed up, a young cop and an old cop. Both seemed unusually
unfazed by the scene in the living room. They looked around, taking
note of the shattered glass, the broken table, the duct tape, hair, and
blood. The old cop asked to speak with Earl, while the young cop
asked to speak with Rainbow.

"You're saying there was three of you," the old cop asked, "and the
intruders abducted your friend?"

"Yes."

"That's his blood on the floor?"

"Yes."

"Is that his car outside, parked on the street?"

"Probably, yes."

The old cop looked at his partner.

"The plates gone?"

"Yup."

The old cop looked at Rainbow and Earl.

"These guys steal license plates," he said. "They likely use them on whatever car they're driving. It's hard to say for sure, though. What's your friend's name, the one they abducted?"

"I don't know," Earl said. "We call him Pizza Man."

"You don't know his legal name?"

"No," Earl said. "He delivers pizzas, though. I'm sure the pizza shop would know his name."

The officers offered to call an ambulance, but Earl and Rainbow said they were okay—physically, anyway. They asked everyone to stay put for a little while, so as not to affect any of the evidence. Rainbow and Earl sat together on the couch, watching the next few hours unfold like a television drama. The crime scene investigator showed up, collecting evidence—mostly pieces of broken glass, samples of Pizza Man's blood, and any fingerprints they could lift. A commotion sounded outside in the front yard.

"They're here," the old cop said, shaking his head.

"Who's here?" Father asked.

"The media."

"How would they know?" Father asked.

"Somebody tipped them off."

"Who would do that?"

The old cop shrugged.

"Could be anybody," he said. "Hard to say. You guys don't have to talk to them, of course."

After the crime scene investigator collected what she needed, she spoke with the cops and left. Rainbow and Earl heard the reporters shouting questions at her as she walked to her car. The cops offered to give Rainbow a ride home, which he accepted. The old cop asked

Mother for a blanket, using it to cover Rainbow's head so the media couldn't get any pictures of him. He was still too shaken up to say much of anything to Earl, but he caught his eye on the way out and forced a smile.

Rainbow listened to the pack of reporters light up again, shouting over one another, snapping pictures and begging for answers. A few hours later, Earl saw his house on the news. They didn't mention the address, but they shared the cross streets. The reporter talked about the latest incident of the Baldies striking in Las Vegas and, citing an anonymous source, said there were three victims, one of whom was missing and presumed dead.

The following morning, Earl's family drove to their new home in San Bernardino, California. Earl hadn't slept all night. They didn't bother packing any of their belongings, as Mother just wanted to leave. Father didn't protest and Earl just shuffled behind them into the car, still shell-shocked by his terrifying experience. On their way out of town, they drove by Boca Park where the Grambling Brothers' Traveling Circus and Sideshow had been. The big tent was gone and there was nothing in its place but an empty dirt lot. Earl imagined Xyla Peppermint and the rest of the circus traveling down the road, just like he was.

He thought also of the three bald men doing the same, wondering where they were and if Pizza Man was all right. He leaned his temple against the car window, watching as the Las Vegas desert rushed along, and thought about Rainbow. He wondered if he was awake and what he'd be doing if he were. He wondered if, like him, he wore a baseball cap to conceal his bald head. He thought about how when he got settled in California he'd finally get his driver's license and perhaps he could even save up for a used car. He could drive out to Las Vegas every so often to see Rainbow and they could pick up where they left off. As he thought about the future and what his fortunes held, Earl's eyelids grew more and more heavy until the rushing desert outside dimmed to black, leaving the gentle rumblings of the road to color his dreams.

Captain Fuckmeister

Seven days removed from the beginning of his ludicrous endeavor, Patrick William Mahoney is lying naked on the floor of a dirty motel room somewhere in the middle of Tijuana, Mexico, curled into himself, hugging his knees, and sobbing quietly.

"It hurts so much," he tells me.

I kneel down beside him, tape recorder in hand, and ask him to speak up.

"It hurts! So! Much!"

I believe what I'm looking at is a heartbroken man, choking on the chalky remains of his eviscerated dream, a modern-day Don Quixote whose idealist quest could only ever end in disappointment. Not wanting to put words into his mouth—alas, Mahoney has already put far too much in his mouth this week—I ask him to elaborate on what it is that hurts him so.

"My cock!" he says. "Oh God, it hurts so fucking much!"

But, before I sat with Mahoney on that dirty Mexican floor and before he endeavored to achieve a world record for which there was neither precedent nor a sanctioning body interested in the outcome, there was that first chance encounter at Fucktastic, a sex club tucked away in the desolate desert getaway of San Bernardino, California.

My wife, Jillian—who prefers to remain anonymous—and I frequent
Fucktastic whenever she has "a scratch that means to be itched." It was
exactly the sort of exuberant sexual establishment one might expect to
find in the exotic ruins of Las Vegas. I believe, however, it is *exactly* the
underwhelming nature of this misunderstood city (underappreciated
for many a reason, not the least of which it gave home to the world's
very first McDonald's restaurant) that makes it the ideal location for an
erotic refuge such as Fucktastic. On this particular night at Fucktastic,
Jillian is feeling frisky, which I figure bodes well for me, so I send her
off to retrieve a couple of drinks from the bar. A little sexual lubricant,
if you will.

Nearly an hour passes before I decide it's time I look for my wife
when I see a naked man sitting against the wall nearest the dance
floor, a bag of ice resting on the sensitive part of his lap. He has a
strange smile on his face, like a child with a delicious secret.

I ask him his name and he says, "I'm Captain Fuckmeister, himself." When I ask for his Christian name, he tells me it's Patrick William Mahoney. "But, you can call me Mahoney."

I ask my new friend, Mahoney, why he's icing his genitals.

"Brother," he says, "I just fucked every broad in this joint."

Mahoney pats the icepack to emphasize his point.

It's at this moment that I spot Jillian and call her over. She arrives
with a noticeable hitch in her step and considerably less clothing. I'm
excited for her to meet my new friend, but it seems they've already
acquainted themselves.

"Hey, Captain."

"Howdy, Sugar Twat."

I would be lying if I said I wasn't at least a little jealous. I'd known
Mahoney for at least as long as she had and he hadn't yet offered me
a nickname.

"Darling," I say. "Our drinks?"

"Oh," she says, gazing down at the good captain's icepack, "I guess I got distracted."

"Nonetheless," I say, "the air is warm with sex and I've become quite thirsty."

I hate getting gruff with Jillian, but I really was parched.

"I'll go back to the bar," she says, rushing off.

Excited to have Mahoney all to myself again, I inquire about his ability to copulate with so many women in one night. He tells me that it started when the first petals of puberty blossomed in him and he would "punish [his] meat like the cure for cancer were in [his] chowder."

Mahoney learned early on that he had an ability to orgasm 10 to 15 times a day before his nether region grew too sore for even the gentle lap of his dog's tongue. Through his teen years, he honed this ability, building his endurance to the point where he could climax up to 30 times a day before his "Johnson looked like [he] had just fucked a porcupine with [his] eyes closed." I tell Mahoney that I'm a journalist and his eyes light up almost as quickly as his erection. He tells me that he has a story for me that I won't want to pass up, so we exchange contact information, awakening the butterflies in my belly.

Two phone calls and a fortnight later, I'm sitting shotgun with Mahoney as we sail down Interstate 15, heading towards his date with destiny.

Mahoney, you see, plans to "fuck" everyone in Mexico.

"Everyone?"

"*Every*one."

"But, why?"

"We've all got a number on our back, brother, and one day the man upstairs is gonna call it. I don't know about you, but I, for one, don't want to look ol' white beard in his big fucking face just to tell him I didn't give it everything I had."

Good enough for me.

During our two-and-half hour trip traveling south on that infinite highway towards San Diego, Mahoney tells me that his ultimate goal is to get into the *Guinness Book of World Records* for his tour of Mexican sex. Though I'm hesitant to be a curmudgeon, I remind Mahoney that Mexico is a large country with millions of people. But, he matches my observation with a bit of that sharp wisdom that has come to define him.

"Rome wasn't fucked in a day, brother."

No, it wasn't.

As we approach the Mexican border, we drive beneath signs that read, "Last USA Exit," prompting Mahoney to open his window and yell out, "I may be exiting the USA, but I'm gonna be entering Mexico...all...night...long!" We have a good laugh over this, during which time Mahoney pulls out his member and begins "giving CPR to [his] albino lobster tail."

Leaving the car in an adjacent parking lot, we cross the border on foot, pushing through a large, rotating one-way entrance of horizontal bars. We walk along a concrete bridge, which passes over a long ravine, and from the other end of the bridge, Tijuana spreads out before us like a sea of corrupt pharmacies and gringo tourists.

Mahoney's first stop is Chicago Club, a well-known brothel in Tijuana, which looks like a greasy spoon disguised as a nightclub. Loud music hangs in the air, pulsing rhythmically with its exotic beats. We take a seat in a corner booth and are soon greeted by a chubby waitress with orange teeth.

In an admirable attempt at English, she asks if we want a drink.

"No drinko," Mahoney tells her. "I want to el fucko, por favoro."

I soon find myself alone in the booth, narrating notes into my tape recorder, while Mahoney ascends up the stairs with our waitress, where he will soon tally the first lay of his ambitious journey.

Upon her return, the waitress approaches a scantily clad woman riding solo at the bar, nursing a green cocktail with lots of ice. Leaving her emerald beverage to sweat under the fluorescent lights, Woman #2 ascends up the stairs. Upon her return, she tags in Woman #3, a tall drink of water with bleached hair and crooked toes. She is soon replaced by Woman #4, a cross-eyed gal with a hairy lip and three earlobes. The procession goes on like this for hours and hours, before Mahoney calls it quits, ending his night with 31 conquests. At his request, I carry Mahoney to a nearby motel, where we check in and I promptly supply him with a much-needed icepack.

As the days pass, Mahoney's numbers grow.

33 women on Day Two and 37 on Day Three. A brief altercation with a couple of Mexican police officers resulting in our being handcuffed and robbed sets us back, allowing for a mere 12 conquests on Day Four. Determined to make up for it, Mahoney barrels through 46 women on Day Five. After sleeping in and taking a leisurely walking tour, Mahoney finishes Day Six with a respectable 38 women.

On the seventh day, when Mahoney tells me it's about time for us to move on to the next town, I broach a concern I've had since before we arrived in Mexico.

"It's really just a semantic concern."

"What is it?"

"Correct me if I'm wrong, Captain, but you did say you were going to 'fuck' everyone in Mexico, yes?"

"Hell yeah!"

"*Everyone?*"

"Every fuckin' one of 'em."

Just the mention of it causes his member to swell.

"Well, Captain, the thing is...*everyone* implies men, as well as women."

Mahoney is quiet for a moment and I fear I've offended him. Just as I'm silently scolding myself, wishing I could take it all back, Mahoney speaks.

"Christ," he says, "you're *right!*"

And without another word, Mahoney throws aside his icepack, puts on a pair of blue jeans and walks barefoot out the motel, returning twenty minutes later with the prettiest transvestite my eyes have ever seen.

"Éste costará más dinero," she says, pointing at me.

Mahoney looks at her, confused, so she rubs the pads of her thumb and two fingers together—the universal sign for money.

"Ooohhh," Mahoney says, turning to me. "You're gonna have to wait outside, brother."

"Can I leave my tape recorder?"

"Not unless you want me to fuck her with it."

I consider this for a moment, before deciding I'd best not take any chances.

I take my place in the hallway and sit down against the peeling wallpaper, figuring I'd be out for no more than five minutes, as Mahoney was reliably quick. But the first five minutes come and go and the door remains closed. At the twelve-minute mark, I hear the first screams. At minute twenty-three there are more screams—manly, guttural sounds that remind me of my wedding night. At the conclusion of the first hour, I hear the violent shuffling of furniture, followed by yet more screams and something that sounds like the pulverizing of a large tomato. At the one-and-a-half hour mark, I hear scratching at the door and what appears to be the soft whimpering sound of Mahoney. The scratching quickly stops and is followed by what I am convinced is the dragging of a body across the floor. By hour three, there are no more screams, just a wet pounding sound, like a piston pumping a rain puddle. At the conclusion of hour four, the transvestite emerges from the room. I stand up to greet her, smiling. But she only acknowledges me long enough to push me out of the way.

I rush into the room, tape recorder in hand, and find Mahoney lying naked on the floor, curled into himself, hugging his knees and sobbing quietly. I stand over him for what seems like forever but was really only a few moments.

"It hurts so much," he tells me.

I kneel down beside him, holding my tape recorder to his quivering lips, and ask him to speak up.

"It hurts! So! Much!"

"Please," I say, tears welling up in my eyes, "tell me what hurts?"

"My cock!" he says. "Oh God, it hurts so fucking much!"

"Shall I gather our things, so that we may head onward with our journey?"

But the tears are already falling because I know the answer before he says it.

"It's over, brother," he says, shaking his head. "It's all over."

Upon our return to the States, I never saw Mahoney again.

The last words I got from him came scribbled on an anonymous postcard: "I'm retiring my yogurt shooter, brother. Tell 'em I'm sorry. Hope ol' white beard understands."

There was no signature, but it was Mahoney all the way.

If there is a lesson to be learned in any of this—and I'm not sure that there is—it is that a man's phallus is not as resilient as the human spirit. And though we may not be able to "fuck" our way into immortality, it should not strip away the beauty of our efforts. Reach for the moon and catch a star, they say. I may never be able to "pound a tuna cave" like my friend, William Patrick Mahoney, but, starting with my wife, I'm finally ready to try.

The Flying Game

The towers were down, fires raged, smoke rose to the heavens, and Uncle Mortimer got a new apartment. On the morning of September 11, while thousands of New Yorkers panicked through the streets and millions more around the country sat before their televisions trying to wrap their heads around the unthinkable event that had just a few hours prior become frighteningly thinkable, I was in California sleeping on an inflatable mattress in Uncle Mortimer's new living room. Except for me, the mattress, and a handful of cardboard boxes, the living room was otherwise empty.

I loved Uncle Mortimer in equal proportion to how much I hated my father. He was my mom's brother and it seemed lately about the only time I saw her smile was when Uncle Mortimer came to visit us in Summerlin. Up until recently, he lived in North Las Vegas with his longtime girlfriend, but they'd had a tough breakup and Uncle Mortimer wanted to start fresh, so he decided to move to Rancho Cucamonga, California, which was a well-to-do suburban city in San Bernardino County. He came over to the house to tell my mom and me face to face.

"Really, Mortimer?" she asked. "California? It's so expensive out there."

"Yeah, but it'll just be me," he said. "Plus, you and Rusty can come visit whenever you like."

The omission of my father was no accident. Uncle Mortimer didn't like him any more than I did. My father certainly didn't mind putting a beating on me—sometimes for perceived disobedience and sometimes for reasons he was too drunk to articulate. I'd felt the painful swat of a Ping-Pong paddle on more than one occasion, which was his favorite weapon for doling out punishment. Even more than what he did to me, I hated how he treated my mom. I never saw him lay a hand on her, but that didn't make him any less of a bastard. Long before I knew what an extra-marital affair was, I understood intuitively that my father was doing things away from home that made my mom cry. Sometimes there were late night phone calls that she'd answer and, within a few moments, I'd hear my father get on the phone saying, "I told you not to call me here." Other times he stayed out all night, returning home without an explanation as if nothing were out of the ordinary.

I never understood how she ended up with him, because my mom was a far better woman than he deserved. I know that the only reason I'm here is because she met my father, but I would gladly disappear from this earth if it meant she could live a full and happy life without ever knowing he existed. She was a wonderful housewife, always cooking and cleaning, and she was a lovely hostess, particularly when my father had one of his business associates over for dinner. But, when it was just the three of us at home with none of his colleagues around, he treated my mom like one of his fancy sports cars in our oversized garage that he never drove.

"I was thinking," Uncle Mortimer said, "maybe Rusty could drive out to California with me."

"What for?"

"He can help me move in."

"Mortimer," she said, "he's just a child. What would you have him do?"

"He could keep me company," Uncle Mortimer said. "I'll be all alone in California, you know? It'd be nice to have some family around."

"He just started the new school year last week," she said. "I don't think he should miss class."

"Oh, c'mon," he said. "Rusty, what grade are you in?"

"Fifth."

"See, he's in the fifth grade," Uncle Mortimer said. "They're probably going to be finger-painting until Christmas."

"Mortimer, he's not in pre-school."

"Yeah, but you know they're not going learn anything important this early in the school year," he said. "You can even talk to his teacher and get his homework for the week. I'll make sure he does it."

"A week? Oh, I don't know, Mortimer."

"He'd love it," Uncle Mortimer said. "Wouldn't you, buddy? You want to go to California with Uncle for a week?"

"Yeah!"

"See?"

"Of course he wants to go."

"But, seriously," Uncle Mortimer said, "it would be nice to have him with me for a few days."

Mom sighed.

"Okay," she said, "but I'll have to talk to his father first."

That eviscerated all hope I had of going with Uncle Mortimer to California—but, later that night, my father surprised all of us by saying I could go. He wasn't so much consensual as he was apathetic, which is to say he didn't seem to care one way or the other about me not being home for a week. Apparently, he was in the middle of a major business deal, this time with Pete Peterson. Mr. Peterson had been over for dinner once or twice and he seemed like a nice enough guy, but, even as kid, I had generally low opinions of anyone associated with my father. Ultimately, I didn't care why my father conceded, I was just happy to be going to California with Uncle Mortimer. When my mom wasn't around, he told me I wouldn't actually have to do my homework—at least not all of it. He wanted to take me to Disneyland and Universal Studios and he said we'd go to the beach and to see the Hollywood sign. It was going to be the best week of my whole life.

Uncle Mortimer was set to move a few days later and on Monday morning, September 10, he and I drove to California with a U-Haul trailer hooked to the back of his car. I'd never been out of Nevada before, so a road trip to California felt very much like we were on our way to meet the Wizard of Oz. The drive took three and a half hours and I loved every minute of it. We listened to the radio, sang songs together, and exchanged dirty jokes. Halfway there, we stopped in Barstow for lunch at a McDonald's built inside of a freight train. Normally, I got the Happy Meal, but Uncle Mortimer said I should get a big meal like him, so I did.

When we got to his new apartment, I helped him carry his boxes inside. As soon as everything was in, he set up the TV and ordered us a pizza. We ate on the floor while watching *Buffy the Vampire Slayer*. At the end of the night, we went to sleep on an air mattress surrounded by cardboard boxes.

It was about eight o'clock the following Tuesday morning when Uncle Mortimer's phone rang, waking us both up. I quickly deduced it was my mom on the other end.

"Oh my God!" Uncle Mortimer said, responding to whatever my mom had just told him. "I'll turn it on now."

Uncle Mortimer hung up the phone, before clicking on the TV. A large building was on fire and a headline on the bottom of the screen read "America Attacked." It sounded absurd. The headline could've just as easily read "Martians Find Cure for AIDS" and it would've been every bit as difficult to wrap my head around. Even as a kid, I understood it was *other* countries whose buildings burned, not ours. Yet, there it was—one very large building on fire because somebody had attacked it.

Attacked *us*.

But, *not* us.

Not exactly.

We were in California and this burning building was in New York. I'd never been to New York, but I knew it was far away—far enough away that I'd never before considered myself part of it. Uncle Mortimer and I sat in silence, watching the slow motion video of the airplane that attacked America. It was a seemingly tiny airplane until I realized it wasn't the airplane that was tiny, but the building that was huge. And there wasn't just one attacked building, but two.

"The fucking Twin Towers," Uncle Mortimer said. "Jesus Christ."

I had no idea what the Twin Towers were. I'd never heard of them before that morning. The Statue of Liberty I knew. The White House, of course. Mount Rushmore, the Empire State Building, and Disneyland. But, somehow these two large buildings, which towered over the New York skyline, had fallen through the cracks of my America.

"Your mom said there's another plane in the air and they don't know where it's at," Uncle Mortimer said. "It might be headed for Los Angeles."

"Are we close to Los Angeles?"

"It's about an hour away," he said, "but if someone's looking to attack it then we're much closer than I'd like to be."

Images of fire and rubble and foreign men in army uniforms began populating my imagination. I imagined being placed in a concentration camp or, worse, tortured and killed before our own American army could rescue me. Ideas like these would have sounded preposterous before that morning, but that headline, "America Attacked," meant anything was possible. Right that very moment I wanted to go home to be with my mom in Summerlin. It turned out that Uncle Mortimer was thinking the same thing.

"If the world's gonna end," he said, "we need to be with family."

Uncle Mortimer never had kids of his own and it seemed that he never would, but I know he would've been an amazing dad. My mom loaned me out every now and again to spend the weekend with Uncle Mortimer and his now ex-girlfriend. I spent countless weekends at their house when they still lived together in Las Vegas. She was always in the middle of cooking something delicious and Uncle Mortimer let me drink non-alcoholic beer at the dinner table. I always knew somewhere between dinner and bedtime I could count on hearing my favorite sentence in the whole world.

"You ready to play the flying game?"

Uncle Mortimer would lay on the floor, his chest facing the ceiling, hands in the air. I'd take hold of each hand in my own and he'd place his barefoot on my belly, the crusty skin of his heel catching on my T-shirt. "On the count of three," he'd say, before counting down. At the end of his count he'd lift me up, his arms steady as concrete. I kept my head straight and my toes pointed, pretending to be Superman. When his arms began to quiver, Uncle Mortimer would lay me on his chest and I'd roll over next to him, resting my head on his arm like a pillow. We'd laugh until our bellies hurt and, after he'd caught his breath, we would do it all over again.

Uncle Mortimer and I got dressed with the news coverage playing in the background and a few minutes later we were in his car, headed back to Summerlin. Before we connected onto the 15 Freeway, we drove through some residential neighborhoods and I saw two men painting a house. It wasn't their house, I gathered, but a house they were likely being paid to paint. I wondered if they'd seen the news that morning, if they knew that America had been attacked. I wondered if, like me, they'd never heard of the Twin Towers. I wondered why, if the world was indeed going to end, they weren't driving away to be with *their* families.

The drive home to Summerlin was much less festive than the drive to California. There was no singing or joking. We really didn't even talk all that much. Uncle Mortimer had the radio on, so, for the whole three-hour drive, we listened to news coverage of the attack. As we got to Las Vegas and drove alongside the Strip, I felt a great sense of relief, because we were almost home. But, that relief went away when I looked at the Stratosphere, which was the pointy tower that stands over 1,000 feet high at the end of the Strip. If tall buildings in America were under attack, then I worried that the Stratosphere—and, more specifically, my city— was now in danger.

"Do you think they'll attack Las Vegas?" I asked.

Uncle Mortimer laughed.

"No, kiddo," he said, "I think we'll be safe here."

"But the Stratosphere is so tall."

"I don't think it's tall buildings they're mad at."

"Are you sure?"

"Yeah."

"How do you know?"

Uncle Mortimer let a brief pause float between us.

"I guess I don't, kiddo," he said. "I wish I had a better answer for you."

We were soon driving into Summerlin and onto the private road that led back to my house. Uncle Mortimer pulled into the long driveway, parking in front of the garage nearest the front door. I didn't have a key, so I rang the doorbell. My mom opened the door and immediately picked me up into her arms, kissing my cheek. Then she hugged Uncle Mortimer, before bringing us into the house. My father, who normally would have been at work, was on the couch watching the news. Uncle Mortimer and I sat down beside him.

We watched New York residents running around, panicked, their faces white with ash. Policemen and firefighters displayed otherworldly feats of courage and heroism, transcending before our eyes from government employees to mythical heroes. Airports were shut down and no planes were allowed in the sky. My father changed the channel periodically, looking for other coverage, but it was the same three or four news anchors monopolizing every channel, telling us the same thing over and over again.

America attacked.

My mom started sweeping the floor in front of the TV.

"You got a phone call from you-know-who," she told Uncle Mortimer.

"What did she want?"

"What do you think?"

He shrugged.

"It's been a scary day for everyone, Mortimer," my mom said. "You should call her."

He didn't respond, so my mom shook her head and continued sweeping.

A few hours later, Uncle Mortimer called his ex-girlfriend. He sat alone in the living room talking to her, while I sat at the top of the staircase and listened. They talked and laughed and, for all I could tell, they hadn't broken up at all. Uncle Mortimer pulled a pack of cigarettes from his pocket, sticking one in his mouth. As he got up to walk outside, he saw me sitting at the top of the stairs.

"Rusty," he said, "do Uncle a solid and grab me a light."

I went into the kitchen and retrieved a matchbook, quickly taking it to him. Nodding his thanks, he walked outside and closed the door. I could hear him talking on the other side, but I couldn't make out the words. After he was off the phone, Uncle Mortimer decided it was okay to go back to California. He asked my mom if I could go back with him and she said it was up to me. I wanted to stay home with my mom, but I didn't want Uncle Mortimer to be alone. So, we said our goodbyes and got back on the road, making the three-hour drive back to Rancho Cucamonga.

Back at his empty apartment, Uncle Mortimer ordered us pizza again. We ate it on the floor and watched TV, but, instead of *Buffy the Vampire Slayer*, it was the ongoing news coverage. The death toll was estimated to be in the thousands, which was very overwhelming to wrap my brain around. I wanted to think about something else, so I asked Uncle Mortimer about his phone call.

"What would you like to know?"

"Was she scared?"

"A little."

"Do you miss her?"

"Every day."

"Why did you break up if you miss her?"

"I wonder that all the time, kiddo."

"Does she miss you, too?"

"Probably."

"Then why aren't you together?"

Silence.

"I don't think we miss who we are today," Uncle Mortimer said. "I think what we really miss is who we used to be."

"I don't think I understand."

"That's okay," he said, "I wouldn't expect you to. Not yet, anyway."

When the pizza was gone, we got under the covers on the air mattress. I couldn't close my eyes without seeing the Twin Towers crumbling down, down, down to the paved New York streets. I curled into Uncle Mortimer, resting my head on his arm like a pillow. As I drifted off to sleep, I thought of my mom and the Stratosphere and New York and all the thousands and thousands of people who were hurt or killed. I wanted things to be simple and fun again, not scary and uncertain. I wanted Uncle Mortimer to lie on the floor and hold his hands in the air. I wanted to feel him pressing me up towards the ceiling, my arms extended like Superman. I guess really I just wanted things to be the way they were before we learned the world had changed and would never be the same again.

The Plan

Sex was in the air, pungent and thick, suffocating the half-truths and unspoken words that hovered over the young lovers like a swelled bubble waiting to burst. The afternoon sun, unimpeded by the drawn curtain, lit their hair and warmed their skin. Curled together in his bed, wearing only his underwear, he thought about tomorrow. She pressed her back against his chest and pulled his arms tightly around her, securing his fingers over her belly. She smiled, despite knowing what was to come. He lay soundly, oblivious.

His room was empty, save for the bed and a cool afternoon breeze. Were it not for the two of them and a single blanket, the bed would be empty as well. On the floor, beside the bed, were three cardboard boxes marked in big black letters: COLLEGE STUFF. Inside the boxes, which had yet to be sealed, were most of his clothes and baseball magazines, his favorite glove, some trading cards, and several issues of *Dolph the Unicorn Killer*.

"When does your flight leave?"

"Did you forget again?"

"Sort of, I guess."

"It's a wonder you remember I'm getting on a plane at all."

From the time he was a kid, his dad played ball with him, filling his head with dreams of playing in the major leagues. By the time he was a sophomore in high school, he was regarded as one of the best baseball players in Nevada. He was the star athlete at their school and she loved that about him. Being on his arm out in public always made her feel special. Just a few hours prior, they'd spent the evening at the Grambling Brothers' Traveling Circus and Sideshow watching the man from YouTube light himself on fire. Despite the spectacle, it seemed to her that every pair of eyes was on them, which only reaffirmed how desperately she didn't want him to leave.

"I'm not dumb, you know," she said. "I just forget things sometimes."

"My flight is at five o'clock."

"In the morning?"

"Yeah."

"Why so early?"

"Coach wants me to be settled in my dorm as soon as possible," he said. "I need to get in as much work as I can before classes start. I've told you all of this a million times."

"I know," she said. "It's just that you're starting a whole new life. You're so lucky."

"Luck is the residue of design," he said. "My dad taught me that. You've got to have a plan."

She caressed his ankle with her toes, but he moved his leg away.

"I don't want you to go."

"I have to."

"I wish you could stay."

"Things won't change much."

"Yes, they will."

"I'll be back for Thanksgiving," he said, "and Christmas."

"That's not enough."

He shrugged.

She turned on her other side to face him, but he turned at the same time. Pulling herself into him, she sighed against his neck.

"You've got everything figured out."

"It's not too late for you to figure out a plan of your own," he said. "You've got a year of high school left."

"That only gives me nine months."

"As long as you know what you want," he said, "things will work themselves out."

She squeezed him in her arms, before letting her hand move down the ripples of his stomach, slipping beneath the elastic waistband of his underwear. Taking him into her hand, she gently squeezed and caressed, waiting for him to grow hard against her touch. He removed her hand, letting it fall limp on the mattress.

"What if something happens to me while you're gone?"

"Like what?"

"I dunno," she said, "but what if? Would you come back?"

"Depends."

"On what?"

"How serious it was."

"How serious would it have to be?"

"I don't know," he said. "Just serious, I guess."

"But you'd come back if it was serious enough?"

"Sure."

She reached behind her back, unfastening her bra, letting her naked breasts fall against his shoulders. She wrapped him again in her arms, but he sat up, breaking away from her embrace. She removed her panties, laying them beside her bra. He stood from the bed, walking over to his crumpled blue jeans.

"What if something happened to me *before* you left?"

"Nothing's gonna happen."

"You don't know that," she said. "Something could."

He looked at her.

"What're you talking about?"

"I don't know," she said. "Nothing, I guess."

He walked back to the bed, planting his fists in the mattress.

"Don't give me that."

"Forget it."

"You thinking about hurting yourself?"

Silence.

"That would be really dumb, you know?"

"I'm not dumb."

Silence.

"I didn't say you were."

"Don't be mad at me."

"I'm not mad."

"I did something."

"What do you mean?"

"I might've done something bad."

"What'd you do?"

Silence.

"Hey," he said, "what did you do?"

"I forgot one."

"What are you talking about?"

"I forgot a pill."

"What pill?"

Silence.

"What pill did you forget?"

Silence.

He gripped the blanket into his fists and, in a hiccup of fury, yanked it towards the ceiling, knocking her off balance. He pulled his fist back like he meant to strike, causing her to cross her arms around her belly. Startled by her fear, he dropped his fist and got back onto the bed.

He looked directly into her eyes.

"Are you...?"

She nodded, yes.

He dropped his face into his hands and began to cry.

"You were going to leave me," she said. "What was I supposed to do?"

Silence.

"Nobody has to know," she said. "We can run away together. We can get married and make it right. It'll be our little secret, just the three of us."

He cried some more, crumbling into the fetal position.

She took his head into her lap, like a mother soothing a child, humming a familiar lullaby.

The Revenge of
City Marlow

Timber Marlow, in the moments before he tried to kill her, had no idea City Marlow was lurking in the darkness. He watched her beneath the black sky, moon overhead, leaves rustling against a faint breeze. City had no weapon, nothing beyond his fists. He was a teenage boy who wasn't very strong for his age, but he figured he'd be strong enough to kill a girl. Of course, Timber wasn't exactly a normal girl. She was much stronger than every other girl in the Divinity, as well as many of the boys. City knew this only too well, as Timber had made a fool of him in front of his peers, knocking him to the dirt and sticking an ax in the ground so close to his head he could hear the hum of steel as it vibrated the earth.

City resented Timber even before that incident, but now he downright hated her. The resentment came from Timber's status in the Divinity. She was protected by Daddy Marlow and everybody in the Divinity was well aware of it. It had been that way ever since Daddy Marlow placed her in the Sustenance Dwelling where she cut up bodies, preparing them for Sustenance Portions alongside her mentor, Luna Marlow. City would've loved that job, but he was never given a chance, not like Timber. It didn't matter, though, not anymore. All that mattered was this would be his last night in the Divinity. He was going to run away to the Outside, but not before exacting his revenge on Timber Marlow.

City Marlow had never heard the word cannibal before. Yet, that's what he was, along with every other member of the Divinity. The Divinity was what most people would call a cult. Loosely defined, a cult is a fringe group of people with a core set of beliefs—sometimes unique, sometimes bizarre—and they're always led by a singular charismatic presence, who, more times than not, is a man. The Divinity fits this definition to a T. Its members lived and died on a remote combine deep in the San Bernardino Mountains, so nobody—save for a few people in the Outside—knew they existed at all. Aside from being cannibals, members of the Divinity were made to regularly shave all the hair off of their bodies, because hair was believed to be the physical manifestation of evil. The one man who didn't shave any of his hair also happened to be their singular charismatic leader. His name was Daddy Marlow.

Daddy Marlow was a big man, both in brawn as well as character. The hair on his head grew so long that it nearly dragged on the ground when he walked, bouncing off the heels of his boots. Because he was in charge of everything in the Divinity, it was well understood that placing Timber in the Sustenance Dwelling was *his* decision. Outside of knowing that the Sustenance Dwelling provided cooked human flesh, as well as vegetables provided from the Divinity's very own crops, neither City nor any other member of the Divinity knew what happened behind its doors. So, for Timber, a youngling who had fewer years than himself—and a *girl* no less—to be chosen by Daddy Marlow to work in the Sustenance Dwelling left City Marlow feeling more than a little envious.

The Sustenance Dwelling served a very important function,

providing everyone in the Divinity with two daily meals, one in the morning and one in the evening. And because for City's entire life it had only been run by Luna, it took on a sense of mystery, which, mingled with its inherent sense of importance, gave the Sustenance Dwelling an aura of mystique. All Timber ever did, so far as City could tell, was run around with her best friend, Jupiter Marlow, laughing and playing, engaging in nothing more urgent than adolescent concerns. He just couldn't understand why Daddy Marlow thought *she* was so important. City didn't know, for example, that Timber saved Daddy Marlow's life. He wouldn't have known that, because there were only two other people in the world who were there and they're both dead now: Idea and Pepsi Marlow.

Idea and Pepsi were lovers, a dynamic that was frowned upon in the Divinity. To be clear, sex wasn't frowned upon. In fact, men and women were encouraged to engage in as much sex as they could handle. It was the notion of a sustained romantic relationship that was frowned upon. Because Daddy Marlow's presence was far reaching within the Divinity, it was only a matter of time before he became aware of Idea and Pepsi's secret affair. In response, he made Pepsi join him in the Main Dwelling and kept her there for several days, fucking her whenever he liked, leaving her alone in his bedroom when he was done.

Idea Marlow knew exactly where Pepsi was, because Daddy Marlow made a point of telling him personally. He didn't tell Idea *why* she was there, but he trusted that he knew precisely the reason. Perhaps it was Daddy Marlow's hubris that led him to believe Idea wouldn't seek vengeance, but vengeance was exactly what he sought. And in the middle of the night, Idea waited in the darkness, wielding a knife outside of the Main Dwelling, waiting for Daddy Marlow to show himself. On that night, after he finished fucking Pepsi, Daddy Marlow walked outside nearly naked but for a sheet wrapped around his waist. Idea charged at him with his knife and, had Timber not been there to save him, Daddy Marlow surely would've met his end.

Timber was only there by coincidence, having snuck out of her dwelling in the middle of the night. She'd been playing a game with Jupiter in which they hung from the longest branch of the Learning Tree for as long as possible and the winner was whoever hung the longest. More than a game of *physical* strength, it was a game of *mental* strength, because the branch extended in front of Daddy Marlow's bedroom window, which meant she and Jupiter risked being seen by Daddy Marlow. The punishment that would've come from being caught by Daddy Marlow in the middle of the night when they should have been deep into the Hours of Recuperation would have been disastrous.

Neither Timber nor Jupiter wanted to concede to being any less brave than the other, so they hung from that branch until their shoulders burned—and even then, they continued to hang. It wasn't until a stirring came from Daddy Marlow's bedroom that Jupiter dropped from the branch and ran away back to his dwelling. Despite the stirring, Timber continued to hang from the Learning Tree, ignoring the pang of fear that blossomed in her belly. When finally she dropped from the tree, Timber's intention was to go back to her dwelling, but, before she could, she saw Idea Marlow come out from the darkness with the knife meant for killing Daddy Marlow. Timber ran towards Idea as fast as she could, burying her shoulder in his belly, which knocked the knife from his hand. As soon as Daddy Marlow became aware of what was happening, he grabbed Idea and knocked him unconscious. While Daddy Marlow gathered himself, Timber looked in through his bedroom window and saw Pepsi Marlow standing naked on the other side.

The next day Daddy Marlow privately rewarded Timber by placing her in the Sustenance Dwelling to learn under Luna Marlow. Idea Marlow was placed in a Prison Dwelling, where he stayed for a few days until it was time for his sacrifice. On that day, he was dragged to the Sustenance Cradle in the middle of Marlow Square with a burlap hood over his head and strapped down by the brawny triplets known as Daddy Marlow's Boys. An audience of Marlows, which included Timber and Luna, watched as Daddy Marlow chopped off Idea's head. Pepsi Marlow wasn't there to see her lover killed and, a week after his death, she took her own life with a piece of broken glass.

City Marlow, of course, knew none of this. All he knew was this girl, Timber Marlow, had been bestowed a role of prominence in the Divinity for what he imagined was no good reason—and it irked him. Then again, lots of things irked City Marlow, not the least of which was two Sustenance Portions a day wasn't nearly enough to quell his large appetite. He eventually solved this dilemma by stealing Sustenance Chips from Flower Marlow.

Every morning, Sustenance Chips were delivered to each dwelling in the Divinity—two chips for every man, woman, and youngling. The Sustenance Chips themselves were actually poker chips, black and red mainly. One of Timber's chores, upon being placed at Luna's side, was to deliver Sustenance Chips to every dwelling in the Divinity. Before City began stealing Flower Marlow's Sustenance Chips, he would simply wander about, begging for leftovers. Whenever he was lucky enough to get some extra food, it was almost always from one of the girl younglings, as they generally had smaller appetites.

Eventually, City found that begging for portions wasn't a reliable enough solution for satisfying his appetite. The only solution was to get more Sustenance Chips and he knew the only way to do that would be to get them from other Divinity members. He approached a few of the girls, but none of them were willing to part with their Sustenance Chips. Flower Marlow was the last girl he asked and, perhaps his hunger put him in a particularly ornery mood that day, but in response to her rejection City pushed her to the dirt and picked up the Sustenance Chips that fell from her hand. It was so easy that he did it again the following day and the day after that until eventually Flower started volunteering one of her two Sustenance Chips to City Marlow every day.

Flower was easy to bully, as she was much younger and smaller than City Marlow. The fact that she was a girl didn't have much effect on him, however if she were a bit older, more mature and sexually aware, he might've treated her differently. He likely wouldn't have bullied her at all or stolen her Sustenance Chips, but instead he might've tried to figure out how to have sex with her. City had reached that point in his life where his body was changing and hair grew more prominently—and was consequently shaved—in places where it had not grown before. He also got hard in his pants with hardly any provocation. For as little as he understood about sex, he knew that he wanted it desperately.

Sex in the Divinity wasn't something regarded as sacred. It was enjoyable, obviously, and most every member partook in sexual activities often and with multiple partners. While sex wasn't hard to come by—whether you were looking for it or not—there were the occasional anomalies, such as City Marlow, who'd never had sex. He knew what sex was, as he'd seen other boys engaging in it through the windows of their dwellings, but he'd yet to have an opportunity to do it himself. Part of the problem was no girl in the Divinity had yet offered herself up to him. While it wasn't a rule, City understood that the boys who enjoyed the most sex with the most women were the older ones who worked along with the men in the Divinity in Service Activities, such as building dwellings and tending crops, digging wells and guarding borders—basically anything that involved sweat and testosterone. City, despite being twice as old as most of the younglings in Daily Lessons, had yet to graduate into Service Activity, thereby keeping from him the sort of status that might've actually gotten him laid.

Daily Lessons were conducted several times a day beneath the Learning Tree and various women within the Divinity taught them. The lessons ranged from the history of the Divinity and its rituals to the dangers of the Outside. The Outside was the world beyond the Divinity and its invisible borders. City Marlow couldn't even imagine what the Outside looked like or how the evil people within it acted. There were rumors that people in the Outside let their hair grow and engaged in exclusive relationships between men and women.

City thought about the Outside often, his imagination unable to put together any sort of concrete image of how it must look or sound. He was happy in the Divinity, but, if he really thought about it, he wasn't happy all that often. He was lonely most of the time and whatever friends he made had all graduated into Service Activities. The two younglings closest to his age in Daily Lessons were Timber and Jupiter, but they'd both graduated into Service Activity, leaving City as the only big youngling under the Learning Tree.

Sometimes late at night, he would go out into the woods and put his feet in Marlow Stream and imagine running away into the Outside. He wondered if anybody would miss him, if anybody would even notice he was gone. Algebra Marlow would definitely miss him. She was his Dwelling Mother and the thought of ever being separated from her broke his heart. She was the main reason he'd never before considered running away into the Outside—well that and the fact that he lacked any real athletic ability, the sort that would be necessary to run away without being captured by Daddy Marlow's Boys.

City had soft muscles. He couldn't lift as much lumber as the boys his own age and he had a severe lack of cardiovascular endurance. He understood that this was the reason why he'd not yet graduated into Service Activity. The only thought that gave him hope was that they couldn't keep him in Daily Lessons forever—at least, he hoped that was true. But, until Daddy Marlow saw fit to give him a Service Activity with the men and older boys, he was stuck with the younglings. It wasn't until City's seventeenth year that he was finally approached by Daddy Marlow's Boys.

Daddy Marlow's triplet sons—One, Two, and Three Marlow—served as their father's enforcers. Where Daddy Marlow provided the word, his boys provided the muscle. They were also in charge of ensuring the Divinity's various moving parts ran smoothly and according to Daddy Marlow's wishes. City Marlow was in the middle of the Purity Ritual when his Dwelling Mother, Algebra, saw Daddy Marlow's Boys approaching. The Purity Ritual was the process of having all the hair shaved from your body. City Marlow sat on a stool, hunched over and naked, while Algebra wet his skin with soapy water and shaved him from head to toe.

This had been one of her chief roles as his Dwelling Mother and when she saw Daddy Marlow's Boys approaching, she suspected—just as City had—that they were coming to enlist his services. While Algebra wasn't City's biological mother, she was the only mother he'd ever known. Algebra, like so many of the women in the Divinity, had made children biologically, but, just like the other women, they were taken from her immediately after birth. Mothers in the Divinity neither raised their biological progeny nor even knew who they were. The moment a child was born, they were placed in the Nursery Dwelling, before eventually being put into the custody of another woman who would become their Dwelling Mother. This was how City came to be with Algebra and she knew it was only a matter of time before Daddy Marlow's Boys made their inevitable visit.

Algebra, who was only a teenager herself when City came into her care, had been a constant presence in his life. Always seeing him off to Daily Lessons when the Marlow Bell rang, always welcoming him back to their dwelling with a smile and a hug. Up until a few months prior, two other younglings had lived in the dwelling with City and Algebra—a boy named Shoe Marlow and a girl named Barkley Marlow. Barkley, having recently made her first child, was deemed ready to become a Dwelling Mother and placed in a new dwelling with three infant younglings. Shoe, just a month before that, had been killed in a Sustenance Sacrifice. His departure was sad for City, Algebra, and Barkley, but, as it was with any Sustenance Sacrifice, they all put on a happy face. So, for a short while, City and Algebra had the dwelling all to themselves, which was rare in the Divinity, as most dwellings housed at least three or four people at a time.

When Daddy Marlow's Boys stood before City and Algebra, it was Three Marlow who spoke.

"City Marlow," he said, "your services have been requested by Daddy Marlow. In the morning, report to the Main Dwelling and we will assign you to your Service Activity."

City nearly jumped from his stool, which would've been dangerous given the proximity of the razor Algebra held over his head. As Daddy Marlow's Boys walked away, Algebra hugged City around the neck, kissing his soapy head.

"Congratulations," she said. "This is wonderful."

"Thank you."

"I told you," she said, "you just needed patience. The Creator would find a place for you and when he did he would tell Daddy Marlow. And now it's happened."

When City reported to the Main Dwelling the following morning, Daddy Marlow's Boys placed him on wood chopping duty. It wasn't flashy, nothing like building dwellings, but he was happy for the opportunity. Wood chopping was important, as he'd help provide firewood to keep Daddy Marlow warm in the Main Dwelling or to heat the shovel during Sustenance Sacrifices. The wood was also used for building chairs and tables, among other necessities.

For the next several weeks, City threw himself into his new role. While he wasn't quite as strong as his new peers, City loved the work and took to it with gusto. It gave him a purpose, filling his days with a meaning that had previously eluded him. And, as if his good fortune couldn't have gotten any better, he caught the eye of Battery Marlow, a pleasant young girl in her sixteenth year.

City Marlow worked with three other men of varying ages: Crispy Marlow (nineteen years), Cinnamon Marlow (fifteen years), and Delicate Marlow (twenty-two years). Their duties included both chopping down trees in the surrounding forest, as well cutting it into squared-off pieces of lumber that could be delivered anywhere in the Divinity for any purpose that required it. City bonded first with Cinnamon Marlow, as they were closest in age. Cinnamon was easily the strongest of the four woodchoppers, which accounted for why he'd been placed with them at such a young age.

The three of them shared delivering duties, taking wood to the various dwellings that needed it. City always looked forward to delivering wood to Blue Marlow. Blue was the Dwelling Mother to a sweet little girl with a tiny voice named Miracle Marlow. As City knew only too well, it was rare for a dwelling to have only two people living in it, but that was the arrangement Blue and Miracle currently had. Blue wasn't a particularly old woman, but she was certainly older by Divinity standards. Her age gave her perspective and a certain level of bravery to speak freely about things that City never heard other Divinity members talk about.

"I'm sure I won't be at the Divinity much longer."

Blue offered this thought during one of City's deliveries.

"What do you mean?"

"I've lived here longer than most," she said. "I don't think they have much use for me anymore beyond a Sustenance Sacrifice."

Miracle was in the room, playing with some twigs and rocks in the corner.

Blue looked at her, smiling.

"She's the one I worry about," Blue said. "If I'm not here, who'll take care of her?"

"I think you'll be here for a long time," City said.

Blue chuckled.

"We'll see."

She looked again at Miracle.

"Come here, sweetie bird," she said. "I'd like a hug."

Miracle jumped to her feet and hurried over, throwing her arms around Blue's neck.

City and Cinnamon spent a good deal of time together when the day's wood chopping was done, forming a male friendship that City had never previously enjoyed. One evening, City and Cinnamon sat along the bank of Marlow Stream, skipping pebbles along the water, when Cinnamon first told him about Battery Marlow.

"She lets us fill her up."

"Let's who?" City asked.

"Me, Crispy, and Delicate."

"Really?"

"Yup," Cinnamon said. "She's got sixteen years and has already made two younglings. Daddy Marlow said he wants more wood-choppers, so she's trying to make him one. She asked about you."

"She did?"

"Yup," Cinnamon said. "She wanted to know who the new wood-chopper was. I told her Daddy Marlow picked you out himself. We're all going to Battery's dwelling tomorrow after the second Sustenance Portion to fill her up. She wants you to join us."

"She does?"

"Yup," he said. "She said so herself."

City stared off at the water.

"I ain't never filled a girl up before."

"It's easy," Cinnamon said. "Just stick it in her until your juice comes out."

That night, as he lay in bed, City could hardly get to sleep. The anticipation of finally fucking had him wide-awake, staring at the ceiling, fantasizing about what it would be like. His fantasies, along with his relentless erection, were all too much, so, in order to relieve himself, City masturbated beneath his blanket. The sound of his fist pumping against the blanket stirred Algebra awake, as she was sleeping beside him. She turned over, unfazed by City's bedtime activity, as it wasn't the first time she'd been awoken in this manner. When he finished, City rolled over himself, closing his eyes in the hopes that he might get at least a little sleep before it was time to chop wood.

When City arrived at Battery's dwelling, along with Cinnamon, Delicate, and Crispy, Flower Marlow answered the door. Flower had grown up with Battery, though she was several years younger. When their Dwelling Mother, Switch Marlow, was sacrificed two years prior, Battery took over as Flower's new Dwelling Mother. Along with Flower, Battery was the Dwelling Mother of an infant youngling named Ticket Marlow who was now two years old. Flower was holding Ticket Marlow on her hip when she opened the door for the boys. Flower rolled her eyes at the sight of them, knowing full well what they'd come to do. Before she turned to let them in, she noticed City Marlow. She held her eyes on him longer than the others and he worried she might ruin this opportunity by snitching on him for taking her Sustenance Chips. To his great relief, she said nothing.

Battery sat at the foot of her bed, eating Sustenance Portions. "C'mon on in."

City entered the dwelling with the rest of the boys.

"Flower," Battery said, "take Ticket outside for a walk. The boys are gonna fill me up."

"How long will that take?"

"I don't know," she said. "Just go on."

The last few times Battery had invited the boys over to fill her up, Flower stayed in the dwelling with Ticket, playing games with him in the corner. Ticket, however, kept wandering over to the bed, wanting Battery's attention while the boys took their turns mounting her. Every time Flower took him from the bed, Ticket began crying. Now when she had her male visitors over, Battery simply had Flower take Ticket out of the dwelling until she was done. With Ticket still in her arms, young Flower made her exit, leaving City and the boys alone with Battery.

Setting her empty plate aside, Battery hastily pulled her long dress up over her head. Cinnamon, Delicate, and Crispy all began kicking off their shoes, pulling off their trousers, and removing their T-shirts. City watched, feeling like something of an outsider. Delicate was the first to climb on the bed with Battery, kissing her on the mouth as she guided him inside with her hand. As the rest of the boys waited, watching Delicate pumping on top of her, Cinnamon noticed City was still dressed.

"Hey," he whispered, elbowing his ribs. "Take your clothes off."

City hesitated a few moments longer, intimidated by the surreal nature of this new experience. Battery howled as Delicate worked up a sweat, his backside pumping up and down. City had watched girls get filled up before, but he'd never actually been close enough to hear the sounds a girl makes when she's being fucked. Delicate pumped harder, more frantically, just moments before telling Battery he was nearly finished. Hooking her feet around the small of his back, she held onto to Delicate's bucking body as he thoroughly filled her up.

Delicate was barely out of Battery, not even completely off the bed, when Crispy hopped on for his turn. And still, City hadn't removed his clothes. Cinnamon gave City another nudge as Crispy finished filling Battery up, before getting on top of her himself. Both Delicate and Crispy noticed City was still dressed, but neither said anything about it. It wasn't until a few minutes later when Cinnamon was done and Battery waited for City to take his turn that she realized he was still dressed.

"You don't want to fill me up?"

"I do," he said, "very much."

"Then remove your clothes."

City looked away, staring at the floor.

"He's just nervous," Cinnamon said. "He's never filled up a girl before."

Crispy and Delicate snickered at this but were quickly quieted by Battery.

"You boys need to leave now."

They all picked up their clothes and headed out. City started to follow behind them, before Battery stopped him.

"I want you to stay."

Within a few moments, City was alone with Battery.

"How many years do you have?" she asked.

"Seventeen."

"Why have you never filled up a girl?"

"No one asked for it, I guess."

"I asked for it," she said. "Don't you want to fill me up?"

He nodded.

"Then why are you still dressed?"

He shrugged.

"Are you scared?"

City dropped his eyes, saying nothing.

"It's fun, you know," she said. "Nothing to be scared of. And, more importantly, it's your duty to the Divinity and Daddy Marlow."

Battery got up from the bed and approached City, taking his shirt and pulling it up over his head. She took his wrists, guiding City's hands onto her breasts, before pushing his pants down to his ankles. Battery started walking backward towards her bed, pulling City along as he stepped out of his pants. Lying back, she smiled at him, opening her legs. City settled on top of her, his body quivering with nerves and adrenaline. A jolt of electricity coursed through his groin as Battery took hold of his erection, guiding him inside of her. Battery held City's face in her hands, smiling up at him and after a few ephemeral pumps he'd successfully filled her up.

That night City lay awake in bed with Algebra, telling her all about his afternoon with Battery. He told her about how he was the last to go and how he was too nervous to remove his clothes. He told her about how Battery made the others leave, before pulling him on top of her. He told her about how Battery let him fill her up twice, all alone, just the two of them in her dwelling. And he told her about the disappointment of having Flower Marlow turn up before he had an opportunity to fill up Battery a third time. Flower, it seemed, had tired of walking around with Ticket. She watched City as he gathered his clothes, holding them against his weary erection. He'd hoped Battery might invite him to stay a little longer, but she simply smiled and said goodbye, before giving her full attention to Ticket. Flower ignored him as he passed her on his way out the door.

"It sounds like you had a good experience with Battery," Algebra said.

"It was wonderful!"

"And she took you alone," she said, "without the other boys. That's a good sign."

"It is?"

"Certainly," she said. "When a girl is filled with youngling juice, the youngling that forms in her belly is a combination of all the men who filled her. For her to take you alone, twice, means she wanted to have more of your juice than the others."

"That *is* a good sign."

"I take it you'll continue to fill her up until she's round?" "I hope so."

For the next handful of weeks, City regularly visited Battery— sometimes in her dwelling, sometimes in the woods, sometimes with his wood-chopping mates, and sometimes all by himself. Between filling her up and chopping wood, City was as happy as he could ever imagine being. And then one evening he got back to his dwelling after a day of chopping and Algebra wasn't there. Instead he saw Camera Marlow, a teenage girl he hardly knew. She was cradling an infant youngling in her arms. Over in the corner were two other younglings, each of them about three or four years old. City was about to apologize, thinking he'd entered the wrong dwelling, before Camera spoke.

"You're City?"

"Yes."

"Three told me I was to live here now," she said. "Daddy Marlow wants me to be Dwelling Mother to these younglings. You're supposed to go to talk to Daddy Marlow's Boys now."

"Where's Algebra?"

Camera shrugged.

"You'd best go on," she said. "Three said to find him soon as I told you so. I don't want any trouble."

City, still sweating from chopping wood, ran through the combine, kicking up dirt across Marlow Square, past the Sustenance Cradle, not stopping until he reached the porch of the Main Dwelling where Daddy Marlow's Boys were waiting. Three Marlow sat on the steps, sipping water from a metallic cup. One and Two Marlow stood at his side. City stood hunched over, his hands on his knees as he fought to catch his breath.

"You got a new dwelling," Three said. "You'll be sleeping with the boys you chop wood with. Know where to find it?"

City nodded, yes.

"Alright then," Three said. "Leave us."

"Where's Algebra?"

"You don't need a Dwelling Mother anymore," Three said. "She served her purpose."

"Where is she?"

"Sacrifice Dwelling," he said. "Waiting."

City stood up straight, balling his hands into fists.

"The Creator decided it was her time," Three said. "Daddy Marlow said so himself."

City's body shook, but he didn't know what to say.

Three stood up and at stared down at him.

"You wanna take it up with Daddy Marlow?"

City dropped his eyes, shaking his head, no. Three sat back down on the steps, sipping from his cup. He turned his back to Daddy Marlow's Boys and walked away, a hundred different emotions coursing through his heart, each of them some version of anger and grief. Outside of feeling what he was feeling, City knew there was nothing else he could do. He walked to his new dwelling, but the others weren't there, so he took a bed and cried himself to sleep.

City Marlow walked about the Divinity, lost in thought, torn up inside about Algebra. Her Sustenance Sacrifice was set for the following day. City had watched Sustenance Sacrifices all his life and more than once he'd watched somebody he knew get sacrificed, but never in his life was he ever faced with losing anybody as intimately connected to him as Algebra Marlow. These feelings confused him, because he knew, like everybody around him, that he was supposed to be happy and grateful, celebrating the gift that Algebra would soon give.

But he wasn't happy and he wasn't grateful. His heart ached and all he knew was that he didn't want Algebra out of his life. Not now, not ever. He felt helpless in the face of it all and, more than that, he felt selfish for wanting what he wanted. He cried often in the days leading up to Algebra's Sustenance Sacrifice, but never in front of anybody. He didn't want anybody to know how he was feeling, especially since so many Divinity members were coming up to him, smiles on their faces, clapping him on the back and offering their congratulations.

He never cried in his dwelling for fear of one of the boys showing up and seeing his tears. So, in those moments where the grief was too heavy and he couldn't keep his emotions to himself, City ran off into the woods, away from the fold. He'd sit in the dirt, leaning against the bark of a gigantic tree, crying and crying, tears gathering in the bend of his arm. During one such episode, when he thought he was alone, City heard the crunching of leaves and twigs. Lifting his eyes, he saw little Flower Marlow standing before him, her hands in the pockets of her dress.

"What are you doing here?"

"I followed you."

"Why?"

She shrugged, smoothing a patch of dirt with her foot.

"I want to be alone."

"Battery says you're probably crying over Algebra?"

"She knows I'm crying?"

"Yes."

"How does she know?"

"I told her."

"Why'd you do that?"

"Because I didn't know why you was crying," she said. "I told Battery and she said you was probably confused. She said that we get attached to our Dwelling Mothers and one day I'll probably feel like crying when it's her time. But she says not to cry because a Sustenance Sacrifice is a celebration."

City said nothing.

"Should I go?"

City nodded, yes.

Flower turned and walked away, stopping when City called for her.

"Give me your Sustenance Chips."

"Both of them?"

"Yeah," he said. "That's your punishment."

"Punishment for what?"

"For telling Battery I was crying."

Flower reached into her dress pockets and pulled out her two Sustenance Chips, handing them to City. He stayed in the woods a while longer before heading back to start his day of wood chopping. After the day's work had been done, the boys said they were headed for Battery's dwelling, as she'd invited them over to fill her up. City reckoned a visit with Battery was just what he needed to brighten his mood.

Flower was in the dwelling playing with Ticket Marlow when City arrived with the boys, each of them still sweating from hours of chopping wood. Without needing to be told, Flower gathered up Ticket and took him out of the dwelling, ignoring City as she passed him on her way out. All the boys—Cinnamon, Delicate, and Crispy—took their clothes off as Battery lay on her bed, naked and waiting. City, too, took off his clothes. Each boy took his turn, before putting his clothes back on and waiting for the others outside. It went like this until it was City's turn. As he approached, Battery stood up from the bed and picked her dress up from the floor.

"What about my turn?" City asked.

"I don't want your youngling juice today."

"Why not?"

"Flower said you was crying."

City was quiet.

"Listen," she said, "You're real nice and I enjoyed laying down with you, but I'm trying to make a strong youngling for Daddy Marlow and I don't think it's a good idea for me to use your youngling juice anymore."

City stood there, naked, unsure what to do next.

"You can leave now," Battery said. "If you see Flower, tell her she can come back in."

City picked his clothes up from the floor and shuffled out. The boys were outside waiting for him, but City ran away before they could see him cry. He carried his clothes with him into the woods, the tears falling heavy and fast, his face red with shame and hurt. He knew he'd never be naked with Battery again. He wondered if he'd ever fill *any* women up again for the rest of his life. He ran until he reached Marlow Stream, galloping into the water and letting the gentle ripples cool his skin. Floating on his back, he stared up at the moon and thought of Algebra. He wondered what she was doing, which Sacrifice Dwelling she was waiting in, whether or not she was thinking of him. He missed her already and she wasn't even gone yet. The thought of the Divinity without her filled him not just with sadness, but anger.

The sacrifice of Algebra Marlow was about the worst thing City had ever experienced. He'd seen many Sustenance Sacrifices in his life. He'd seen familiar faces and relative strangers walked out to Marlow Square and strapped down to the Sustenance Cradle by Daddy Marlow's Boys. He'd seen Daddy Marlow preside over them, ax in hand, speaking to the surrounding crowd of Marlows, giving some version of the same speech he always gave, thanking the man or woman for their sacrifice, and reminding his followers what an honor it was to be sacrificed into Better Days.

He'd seen it so many times that, really, it had sort of lost its meaning. It was just one more ritual hollowed out by time and repetition. But now he stood alone amongst the crowd, watching Daddy Marlow's Boys bring Algebra out to Marlow Square and strapping her down. He even watched as Daddy Marlow came out, ax in hand, addressing the crowd before pulling the burlap hood from Algebra's head. Nearest to the Sustenance Cradle, standing beside Luna Marlow, City saw Timber looking on. His heart filled with anger as he imagined what she and Luna would do to Algebra in the Sustenance Dwelling, chopping her up and giving her out as Sustenance Portions. But, before the moment of her death, City knew he couldn't watch his Dwelling Mother's head chopped off, so he turned and walked away.

He heard the thud of the ax as it hit the Sustenance Cradle, followed by the cheers of the surrounding Marlows. He realized in that moment that every Sustenance Sacrifice he'd been an audience to probably made somebody else in the Divinity feel the way he was feeling at that moment. As the crowd dissipated, City walked back to his dwelling. He lay facedown on the bed, crying until he fell asleep. He woke up the following morning to the sound of the Marlow Bell chiming to announce the distribution of Sustenance Portions.

City was hungry, so he left his dwelling, collecting the two Sustenance Chips on his doorstep, and headed for the Sustenance Dwelling. On his way there, he saw Flower Marlow walking alone. He marched towards her, grabbing her by the arm and demanded she give him her Sustenance Chips. When she opened her hands, there were two—one for her and one for Battery. He took only one.

"I don't want to chase you down anymore," he said. "From now on leave one Sustenance Chip in front of my door. And you better not tell anybody, got it?"

Flower nodded, before running off.

City went to the Sustenance Dwelling and waited in line, collecting just one Sustenance Portion, choosing to save his extra portion for later. He wasn't even that hungry, but he ate his portion, forcing it down before joining the boys to chop wood. Later in the day, when he and the boys finished chopping wood, City waited in line for his second Sustenance Portion. Despite his grief, a full day of chopping wood properly stirred his appetite, so after he finished eating he got back in line with the Sustenance Chip he'd take from Flower and collected his third portion of the day. The following morning he collected the Sustenance Chips on his doorstep for he and the boys. And when he finished distributing them, there was exactly one extra chip.

City made a delivery to Blue and Miracle's dwelling. Blue was alone, as Miracle was away at Daily Lessons. When City arrived with her wood, she invited him in. It wasn't unusual for Blue to engage City in polite conversation, but something about her demeanor felt different, even before she spoke.

"I'm getting out of this place."

"You're moving into a new dwelling?"

She laughed.

"No, I'm getting out of the Divinity," she said. "I'm taking Miracle and going to the Outside."

"Why?"

"It's the only way I can know for sure that she'll be taken care of."

City could hardly wrap his mind around the idea of Blue and Miracle sneaking out into the Outside.

"When?"

"Tomorrow evening," she said, "after everyone is asleep."

"How?"

"I've got a plan," she said. "Nothing too complicated. The only thing that matters is getting out."

Blue touched his shoulder.

"I thought it was a shame they took Algebra away from you," she said. "They didn't need to do that, but they did. And I know you've been awful sad about it."

City dropped his head and began to cry.

Blue wrapped him up in her arms.

"I'm not telling you what to do," she said, "but I wouldn't object to you coming with us to the Outside."

"I don't know if I could do it."

"Just think about it," Blue said. "You don't have to decide until tomorrow night."

City's new arrangement with Flower Marlow was quickly brought to an end the following day. Truly, the beginning of the end came a few days prior when he showed up to the Sustenance Dwelling for his third portion of the day, something he'd been doing regularly, only on that day Timber Marlow leaned her elbows on the window where she handed out the portions and looked down at him with suspicious eyes. City held out the Sustenance Chip and, despite whatever reservations she had, Timber handed him a Sustenance Portion.

On the day where it all ended, City joined the boys to chop wood after eating his morning meal. It was a good day, too, better than most. City found himself smiling easy, laughing even as he worked with his peers. It was the first time since the sacrifice of Algebra Marlow that he hadn't felt completely sad. The thought even crossed his mind that he would soon leave Flower Marlow alone and let her keep both her Sustenance Chips. He was in the middle of chopping a piece of lumber when he saw Timber marching toward him.

Without any consideration for the ax he held, Timber grabbed City by his shirt and threw him to the ground. He hit the dirt hard, dropping the ax. Timber picked it up and told Cinnamon, Delicate, and Crispy that they'd best leave her and City alone. The boys heeded her warning, running off. She wasn't a big girl at all—short in height, slight in build. But, when she put hands on him, City realized just how deceptively strong she was. He tried to get up from the dirt, but Timber stomped her foot on his chest, knocking him back down. Setting her knee on his sternum, she pinned him to the ground. With one hard swing she stuck the ax deep into the dirt, landing it so close to his head he could hear the hum of steel as it vibrated the earth. With her free hand, Timber gripped City's throat, leaving just enough slack for him to gasp for air.

"Now listen up, you," Timber said, "I'm not as stupid as you think I am. Starting tomorrow, my little friend Flower is going to get all of her Sustenance Portions and, for the rest of the week, she's going to get one of yours as well."

City managed a slight nod, as he tried desperately to breathe through Timber's iron grip. When she finally let go, City rolled into the fetal position, gulping in air and dirt. Timber stood over him, kicking him in the gut for good measure, before leaving him where he lay. Tears flowed down his cheeks and into the dirt. He whimpered in pain, barely able to sit up. He watched Timber out in the distance marching back to the Sustenance Dwelling, anger blooming in his belly. When the boys returned, City got up and left, running into woods. He removed his clothes and went into Marlow Stream, trying literally and figuratively to cool off, but his anger only grew the longer he thought about Timber.

He got out of the water, putting his clothes back on and lay between the trees, staring up at the sky. He watched it go from blue to black, all the while thinking of the many ways he wanted to hurt her. He was tired of being made the fool, tired of being rejected, tired of living in the Divinity. City knew in that very moment that he would take Blue Marlow up on her offer to escape into the Outside. Before escaping the Divinity for good, however, he intended to exact brutal revenge on Timber Marlow, making her regret ever putting her hands on him.

The next morning, City collected his Sustenance Chips from the doorstep and went out to find Flower Marlow. She looked nervous when she saw him approach. He took her hand, placing his two Sustenance Chips in her palm. He told her he wouldn't be needing them anymore, then walked away. He joined Cinnamon, Delicate, and Crispy, chopping wood and laughing like everything was normal. When the day was over, the boys went to collect their Sustenance Portions, but City told them he'd catch up with them later.

He walked to Blue and Miracle's dwelling. Blue sat with Miracle on their bed, telling her a story. Miracle's head rested on her lap, her eyes struggling to stay open.

"Are you still going?" City asked.

"Yes."

"I want to go with you."

Blue smiled.

"Good," she said. "After nightfall, Daddy Marlow's Boys are driving into the Outside. We have to wait for them to be gone. When that happens, nobody will be standing guard of the road. That's when we'll go."

City's heart raced just talking about it.

"Okay."

He left and walked out into the woods nearest Timber's dwelling, sitting down in the dirt and waiting for nightfall. He watched as the Divinity wound down for the day, its members wandering about, talking with one another, laughing and socializing, before disappearing into their respective dwellings for the night. He watched as Timber walked to her dwelling, saying goodnight to Luna Marlow as they parted ways. He watched Timber close the door behind her and, through the window, he watched her slip into bed. He ran his fingers across the dirt, picking up pebbles and squeezing them in his palm. Stepping out from the woods and threw a pebble at her window—then another and another, until the door opened and Timber stepped out. City stayed back near the trees, watching Timber look around.

"Who's there?" she whispered.

City stayed quiet.

"Jupiter, is that you?"

City laughed in the darkness.

"What are you doing out there?"

City threw another pebble, pinging it off of Timber's dwelling. Then he threw another, hitting her on the arm.

"If I have to come out there and find you," she said, "you're gonna get it."

City laughed again, louder this time.

Timber grabbed her shoes from inside the dwelling, putting them on and running out into the darkness. She stopped and listened to the night, trying to figure out where the pebbles were coming from. City picked up a heavy rock and began walking towards her, throwing it as hard as he could. It sailed past her head as closely as possible without making contact.

"Jupiter," she said, "that wasn't funny!"

"It wasn't supposed to be."

City pulled all of his anger up from his belly and charged towards her, tackling Timber to the dirt. They struggled against each other, clawing and grappling, both trying to gain control. Timber broke loose from City, standing to her feet just long enough for him to charge back into her, his momentum driving her into the trunk of a large pine tree. He'd stunned her, knocked the wind out of her, and for the time being she wasn't fighting back. City threw a couple of wild punches, but, on account of the darkness—and his general lack of athleticism—he had trouble connecting.

The first punch landed flush on the side of Timber's head, stinging her ear. The second punch, however, missed the mark completely and City inadvertently punched the tree trunk, breaking his hand. He bent over and held his broken hand against his belly, wailing in pain. This gave Timber time to recover. She charged into City, tackling him back onto the dirt. The pain in his hand throbbed as Timber sat on his chest, pinning him down. He nearly forgot about the pain in his hand altogether once she started raining down punches on his face. With the last of his energy, City managed to buck Timber off his chest. But, as quickly as she was off, she hopped back on, punching and clawing, relentlessly pulverizing him.

Unable to fight back with any amount of success, Timber reduced City to holding his arms over his head in self-defense. On the ground, beside City's head, was the rock he had thrown at her. So overwhelmed by her vicious offense, City didn't notice the pause in violence as Timber picked up the rock. Still covering his face, he never saw her raise the rock over her head and, in the moments before she brought it down like a hammer, crushing his skull, he had no idea he wouldn't be joining Blue and Miracle on their journey to the Outside. If he had known death was just a few short moments away, he might've taken a fraction of a moment to think of Flower and how he regretted bullying her. Perhaps he might've taken another fraction to remember how lovely it was to be with Battery Marlow. Then maybe he'd use whatever fractions he had left to thank his lucky stars for Algebra Marlow, the best Dwelling Mother he could've hoped for.

In the meantime, there was the matter of Timber Marlow, the rock, and the final blow that cracked City Marlow's skull open, spilling his life into the dirt until the stars melted into the sky and there was nothing else to see but darkness.

The Night Owl

Uncle Leo didn't put up much of a fight when Aunt Laura left him on our doorstep, even when she swung her pudgy fists at his head. That part I saw from my bedroom through my cracked door. I'd been in bed reading my favorite comic book, *Dolph the Unicorn Killer,* when I heard the yelling, so I got out of bed to see what was happening. My parents were downstairs with Uncle Leo and Aunt Laura in the entryway. The front door was open, but nobody seemed to be coming or going. It was after dark and way past my bedtime, so it seemed strange that they were just now showing up for a visit. Aunt Laura was screaming at Uncle Leo and my mom was trying to calm her down, telling her that I was asleep, but she wasn't listening.

"If you're so miserable," Aunt Laura said, "then don't come home!"

I wondered if any of our neighbors were outside. And, if they were, I wondered if they were feeling scared like I was. This wasn't the sort of scene I'd ever witnessed in my house before. I mean, I'd seen anger and violence like this on TV and sometimes on the playground, but that could be chalked up to fiction and adolescence. But, these were grown-ups. Grown-ups who'd played with me, cooked for me, hugged and kissed me.

"Laura, stop!" my mom said.

Uncle Leo was my mom's little brother and I could see on her face she wanted to protect him. I didn't have siblings of my own, but, if I did, I think I would protect them just like that.

When Aunt Laura finally stopped hitting Uncle Leo, she turned and walked out of the house.

"I mean it, Leopold," she said. "Don't come home."

The front door slammed shut and there were no more voices.

During my most recent spring break just a few months ago, I'd spent a week with Uncle Leo and Aunt Laura. They took me to California and we went to Disneyland and we ate at sit-down restaurants every night. I wondered now if I'd ever see her again. I wondered if Uncle Leo thought the same thing. I watched him standing with his back against the wall, staring at his feet. My mother took him into the living room, sitting him down on the couch. I'd seen this before with Uncle Leo. It meant they were going to have a grown-up conversation. They would use words I didn't recognize, speaking in tones I didn't like.

My dad got up from the couch and made his way up the stairs to check on me. I quickly turned off my light and jumped into bed, pretending to be asleep. He peeked in for just a moment, before closing the door.

It was midnight when I heard the TV turn on downstairs. I left my room, walking barefoot through the hallway as I made my way down to the living room. I found Uncle Leo sitting by himself, flicking his Zippo lighter on and off. He smiled when he saw me.

"There's the night owl," he said. "What's shaking, Felix?"

"Nothing much," I said. "You?"

"You know how it goes," he said. "Looks like Uncle's gonna be crashing with you guys for a while."

"Cool," I said. "How long?"

"Just long enough to figure out what I'm gonna do and where I'm gonna do it at," he said. "You hungry?"

"Yeah."

"Let's get something to eat."

"I'm supposed to be in bed," I said. "I have school in the morning."

"Yeah? What are you doing in school?"

"Miss Claudia is testing us on our timetables," I said. "My friend is scared of the sevens, but that's my best number."

"Let me hear."

"Seven, fourteen, twenty-one, twenty-eight, thirty-five—"

"Well, shit," he said, "you've got me convinced. I think you're gonna ace that test."

I wanted to keep going, at least until seventy-seven, because I liked impressing Uncle Leo.

"Go put some shoes on," he said. "Uncle's hungry."

I put on my shoes but stayed in my pajamas. Inside Uncle Leo's car, there was a red smoking pipe on his seat. He asked me to hand it to him, before putting it in the glove box. He handed me his Zippo to play with during the car ride to Lola's Diner. I flicked it on and off, just like he always did. When we arrived at the diner, we were greeted by Lola. I only knew it was her because that's what her nametag said. She told us to sit anywhere we liked, so Uncle Leo chose a booth in the corner next to a window. There were other people in the diner, but not many. Most of them sat alone.

Lola took our orders without a notepad.

"Just some coffee for me, darling," Uncle Leo said. "Get whatever you want, Felix."

"Can I have a cheeseburger?"

"Sure you can, sweetheart," Lola said. "You want some fries, too?"

I nodded, yes.

"And how about something to drink."

"Coke."

"Coming right up."

Lola came back a few moments later with our drinks.

"Run away with me, darling," Uncle Leo told her. "I'll name an island after you and we can grow coconuts together."

Lola laughed, touching him on the shoulder before walking away.

I was pouring ketchup on my fries when I saw a woman walk in with a kid who looked about my age. He didn't go to my school, so I didn't know who he was. They sat down at a booth near the window, like Uncle Leo and me. I watched Lola talk to them, taking their orders. I wondered what they were going to eat. His mother looked around the restaurant, turning her head and rising in her seat until she saw Uncle Leo.

She said something to the kid then walked outside, back to her car. I watched her get inside and wondered if she was going to leave her son by himself.

Uncle Leo stood up from our booth.

"I'll be right back, kiddo."

"Where're you going?"

"Uncle needs a smoke."

"Can I go?"

"No, it's bad for your lungs," he said. "Enjoy your cheeseburger. I'll be back in a few minutes."

Uncle Leo went outside and I watched him through the window. He walked to the woman's car, getting in on the other side. I wondered if maybe he was asking about her son, checking to see why she'd left him alone in the restaurant. I could just barely see through the back of her car window, their heads moving as they talked. From the kitchen, Lola came out with a strawberry sundae that looked delicious. She sets it on the counter and calls for the kid to eat it there. I looked back out the window to see if Uncle Leo was still talking with the woman, but her back window fogged up, so I couldn't see inside anymore.

I looked back to see the sundae again. Lola stood on the other side counter, talking with the kid. She looked over at me and smiled.

"You want a sundae?"

I nodded, yes.

She waved me over to the counter, so I left my cheeseburger and fries behind. I sat next to the kid, but he didn't look at me. He just ate his sundae.

"You want strawberry or chocolate?"

"Strawberry."

Lola went back into the kitchen and came out a few minutes later, setting a strawberry sundae down in front of me.

The kid looked at my sundae.

"She said they taste better when you eat at the counter," he said. "It's a secret, though."

"Is it true?"

"Yeah," he said, "I think so."

Now that I knew Lola's secret, I was grateful to eat my sundae at the counter.

I was nearly done when Uncle Leo turned up behind me.

"You got yourself some dessert," he said. "Good man. What do I owe you, Lola?"

"My treat," she said. "The boys kept me company."

Uncle Leo took out two twenty-dollar bills and left them on the counter.

"What's this for?" she asked.

"Getaway money," he said. "There's an island out there some-where with your name on it."

Lola giggled as she put the twenties in her apron.

I got down from my stool and walked with Uncle Leo through the diner, passing the woman as we exited. I thought she and Uncle Leo would say hi, but they didn't seem to notice each other.

"Who was that?"

"Who was who?"

"The woman."

"What woman?"

"The woman you were in the car with?"

"Nobody," he said. "She was lost, so Uncle gave her some directions."

Back at home, I sat on the bumper of Uncle Leo's car. I was cold in my pajamas, but I didn't want to go inside yet. I watched Uncle Leo pull a plastic baggy with dark green fur in it from his pocket. Pinching some of the fur out, he put it inside the end of his red pipe.

"You still got my Zippo?" he asked, patting his pockets.

I pulled it from my pocket and handed it over to him. He flicked it to life, holding the flame over the fur and sucking on the pipe until his cheeks collapsed. He closed his eyes, exhaling a big cloud of smoke. He kept them closed for what felt like a very long time. When he opened them again, he looked at me. He seemed almost surprised to see me outside with him.

"Go to bed, Felix," he said. "You gotta do your sevens in the morning."

I gave Uncle Leo a hug and he kissed the top of my head.

"Take your shoes off before going upstairs," he said. "You don't want to wake your parents."

He sucked on his pipe again, holding the Zippo over the green fur. Leaning on his car, he closed his eyes as I went back in the house. I took my shoes off before going upstairs, which worked because I made it all the way up and into my bed without waking my parents. I closed my eyes and spent the rest of the night dreaming about strawberry sundaes.

Footsteps

Driving home from the morgue, my thoughts filled with death, I marveled at how comfortably I wore my newly acquired secret. Maybe it was all the dinners my father missed because he was too busy bending his secretary over to check his watch. Maybe it was the residue of white powder on his nostril the night he gave me a black eye for smoking pot. Maybe it was all the times I watched my mother cry herself to sleep in the middle of the day. Whatever the reason—and, believe me, there're plenty to choose from—I didn't want to follow in my father's footsteps.

Regardless of what strings he'd pulled, I decided not to attend the Peterson and Glasgow College Fair. Peterson and Glasgow were a couple of wealthy corporate types that my father regularly did business with. They hosted the exclusive college fair every year, bringing together a collection of prestigious universities, mostly from the Ivy League. And, as it was every year, the Peterson and Glasgow College Fair was held at the Sands Expo and Convention Center, which was part of the plush Venetian hotel.

The fair itself was invitation only and, from what my dad told me over and over again it was a nearly impossible invitation to receive. "Pete Peterson is a very wealthy associate of mine, with tremendous connections," he'd said. "Five minutes with him can secure your future for the next fifty years, so don't fuck it up." But college, like the fair itself, wasn't something I planned on investing my time in. I had simpler interests, such as hanging out in women's dressing rooms at Fashion Show Mall.

The morning of the Peterson and Glasgow College Fair, I stayed in bed as long as I could. I knew that my father would be sitting at the breakfast table, drinking his black coffee, and reading the section of the newspaper that told him about his money. He'd be waiting for me. Not to give me a ride, mind you. He'd just want to watch me go out the door, making sure I went to the fair.

Lying in bed, I heard my mom call me from downstairs.

"Rusty, come eat your breakfast before it gets cold."

I got out of bed and went to my closet, pulling out the fancy suit my father had bought me to wear at the fair. He'd insisted I be dressed appropriately, so he picked out the suit himself and had it tailored to fit me just right. He wanted to make sure that anybody I met at the fair would think I was a chip off the old block. Every thread of that suit was brand new—even the white dress shirt that had my father's initials, R.H. II, monogrammed over the breast pocket. He had an entire inventory of these shirts, still in the plastic, lining his drawers. I was my father's namesake, the third generation of Rusty Hankovers.

The smell of black coffee, which I'd learned to disdain, met me at the bottom of the stairs as I entered the kitchen. I didn't even bother looking in the mirror because I already knew that I looked like a disheveled version of my father, the tie hanging around my neck like a flimsy meat hook.

As I entered the kitchen, I saw my mom standing over the sink, washing dishes.

"Sit down and eat, honey," she said. "You don't want to be late."

There were two plates of food on the table, each of them equally untouched.

One was mine.

The other my father's.

"Where's dad?"

"I don't know," she said, setting down a glass of orange juice. "He had a late meeting last night. He hasn't come home yet."

I was just happy he wasn't in the kitchen, so, beyond that, I couldn't care less where he was.

"I'm beginning to worry."

"I'm sure he's fine."

She handed me one of her tabloid magazines, opening it to a story buried in the middle: THE BACK ALLEY CANNIBAL EATS AGAIN!

"What if some wild man ate your father?"

"I think we would've found out by now."

"But, this Back Alley Cannibal has eaten a lot of people already," she said, "and the police don't have any leads."

"If there really is a cannibal on the loose," I said, "I'm sure a super-market tabloid wouldn't be the only one with the scoop."

"You'd be surprised how often they get things right," she said, putting the magazine away. "What time are you supposed to be at the fair?"

"Nine," I said. "If I take the bus, I'll be late. Can I drive your car?"

"You know your father wouldn't want that."

"He doesn't have to know."

"I don't know if that's such a good idea, Rusty."

Taking hold of my tie, she worked it into the same complex knot my father had tried to teach me when I was a kid. Whenever I got it wrong, he'd make me stand with my nose against the wall, while holding a Ping-Pong paddle as high up as my arms would stretch. He told me he would beat me with it if I lowered it before he gave me permission.

Sometimes I made it.

Sometimes I didn't.

"Listen," she said, smoothing the tie against my chest, "if you don't get that car back before your father comes home, you and I both are going be in a lot of trouble."

"No problem!"

Grabbing my backpack, I went into the garage. Inside my backpack was a shopping bag for Carnage, which was a trendy shop at the Fashion Show Mall frequented by women with well-to-do husbands. I took my mom's keys off the hook and got into her car. Starting it up, I backed out of the garage, down the long driveway and onto the private road that would guide me along the steep hill through Summerlin towards the Las Vegas Strip. I might've skipped the Peterson and Glasgow College Fair altogether—accepting my father's wrath in whatever form it took—had the Venetian not been conveniently across the street from the Fashion Show Mall.

I parked my mom's car on the fourth level of the large garage at the Venetian and, feeling all sorts of uncomfortable in my suit, made my way down the elevator and through the casino, following the signs and trying not to get lost, until I found the Sands Expo. I had no intention of spending any significant amount of time at the fair. In fact, my only goal was to get my nametag with Rusty Hankover III on it, so, when my father came home later that night from wherever he was, I could prove to him that I'd shown up. At the entrance of the Sands Expo was a nice woman in a business suit sitting behind a desk, checking people in.

"Your name?" she asked.

"Rusty Hankover," I said, "the third."

She quickly perused the list and, upon finding my name, her face lit up.

"Mr. Peterson would like to see you," she said, smiling. "You must've made a good impression on somebody."

I smiled, hoping she got the impression I cared, as she handed me my nametag.

"Go on and I'll let Mr. Peterson know you've arrived," she said. "If you don't mind, stay near the entrance."

"I don't mind at all."

I really didn't care to stay, but, along with the nametag, I figured spending a few minutes with Peterson would go a long way towards keeping my father off my ass. I clipped my nametag over the R.H. II monogram, obscuring it from view.

Inside of the Sands Expo a lot of slick looking guys, no older than me, maneuvered from booth to booth like sharks in suits. They collected business cards, drank complimentary coffee, and talked about golf with any balding man that would give them their attention.

After a few minutes of waiting, a husky man with a thick beard approached me.

"Rusty the *third*, I presume," he said with a big yellow smile. "I haven't seen you since you were a kid. You probably don't remember me. The name's Pete Peterson."

He shook my hand, squeezing it with intent.

"I don't want to take up too much of your time," he said, "as I'm sure you have a lot of networking you want to do. I've been trying to track down your father. We were supposed to get a round of golf in this morning, but he never showed."

"I haven't seen him since yesterday."

"He's a slippery one that dad of yours," Peterson said. "I called him a few times at his office and on his cell phone, but he's not answering. It's nothing urgent. I just wanted to touch base with him since I hadn't heard from him this morning. Anyway, Rusty, you go on ahead and enjoy yourself out there. And, please, make sure you come and see me before you leave."

"You got it," I said. "Thank you, Mr. Peterson."

He smiled and started to walk away.

"Say," he said, turning around, "how's that lovely mother of yours?"

"She's well."

"She's a good woman," he said. "Please tell her Pete Peterson says hello."

"Will do."

When Peterson was finally out of sight, I exited the Sands Expo, made my way back through the casino and up the elevator, back to the fourth level of the parking garage where I got into my mom's car and drove across the street to the Fashion Show Mall. Before I got out of the car, I took the Carnage bag out of my backpack and stuffed my suit jacket inside to give it some weight, before loosening my tie and rolling up my sleeves. Walking into the mall, I held the Carnage bag at my side, creating the illusion that I was in the middle of a shopping trip.

I made stops at all of my favorite women's clothing stores and, in each one, I'd sit in the dressing room area, slouched back with my Carnage bag between my feet. A few years ago, I was shopping at the mall with my mom and every time she tried on clothes I had to sit and wait on whichever nearby chair was in the dressing room area. On one particular day, as women came in and out, trying on clothes, I realized they weren't paying me any attention. I figured out very quickly that a guy alone in the dressing area was virtually invisible because everybody assumed he was just a bored boyfriend or husband waiting for his lady to finish trying on clothes.

I fancied the more upscale stores because those are the spots where rich women shopped. Rich women with rich feet killed me. I loved the pretentiousness of a French manicure, the gaudiness of a toe ring, the way an ankle bracelet rested just on top of the foot, framing it like a masterpiece. I loved watching a woman stand on her tippy-toes, raising her smooth heels and creating that sexy stream of pampered skin, carrying right into the curves of her calves. Carnage was the best store of the bunch, which was why I always made it my last stop. Not only did they attract the most beautiful women, but they also had the most comfortable sofa and the best doors for admiring feet.

I wasn't in Carnage for very long before I spotted a wrecked pair of feet that looked absolutely out of place. The nails were yellowed and overgrown, the skin was ashy, and the heels were dried with deep cracks. A pair of old blue jeans dropped around the ankles, each foot stepping out, before kicking them to the side. A small pair of hands, which didn't belong to the ugly feet, reached down and picked the pants up. Next, a white T-shirt speckled and splashed with reddish-brown stains fell to the floor and, almost as soon as it touched down, the small hands picked it up. Moments later, a nice pair of black pants unfurled, the length of which was being measured against the legs attached to the abominable feet. One foot at a time rose up and disappeared, reappearing with toes pointed as they slid through the pant legs.

A tiny voice sounded from behind the door.

"Are his pants too big?"

"A little, sweetie bird."

"Will they fit?"

"They'll fit fine."

I assumed it was a mother and child behind the door. The mother reached down and rolled up the pant legs, before slipping on a beat-up pair of sneakers. As she tied her shoes with fingers that matched her gnarly feet, a phone rang from behind the dressing room door.

"Can I answer it?" the tiny voice asked.

"No, sweetie bird."

"Why not?"

"Because," she said, "I don't like you talking to strangers."

I next heard what sounded like the fumbling of a cellphone, which lasted a few moments until the ringing stopped. Then the door swung open and I got my first look at the mother and daughter pair. They each had very short hair, nearly bald like their heads had been recently shaved. The daughter was a tiny little thing who couldn't have been more than five or six years old. She wore pink corduroy pants and a Supergirl T-shirt. The mother was wearing an oversized black suit with the sleeves rolled up above her wrists. Under the jacket was a white dress shirt that hung to her knees. She carried a duffle bag in one hand and her daughter's hand in the other.

The mother caught my eye.

"What are you staring at?"

I felt awkward and exposed. She eyed my nametag, which I forgot I was wearing, so, not wanting her to know my name, I took it off and tossed it at the trashcan. My aim was poor, so the nametag landed on the carpet.

The little girl picked it up.

"You shouldn't leader."

Her mother smiled.

"You mean *litter*," she said. "You shouldn't *litter*."

"Like follow the *leader?*"

"No, sweetie bird," her mother said. "Litter and leader *sort of* sound the same, but they're different."

"They're different *and* the same?"

"Something like that."

The mother and daughter left the dressing room and I followed behind them. Before they could exit the store, however, the manager of Carnage stopped them. She was a glamorous woman with long legs and high heels who I'd seen her many times before. In the past, she was one of the few people in Carnage who looked at me strangely, like maybe I didn't belong there. To throw her off my trail, I would—from time to time—purchase accessories at the counter for an imaginary girlfriend.

The manager looked at the mother.

"What were you doing in there?"

"Trying on clothes."

"Where are the clothes you were trying on?"

"I left them in there."

The manager called to the shop girl behind the counter.

"Check the dressing room for loose clothes."

They all stood silently until the shop girl returned empty handed. The manager gave her attention back to the mother, clearly annoyed.

"Where are the clothes?"

"It's not my job to keep track of your clothes," the mother said. "Can I go now?"

"No, you can't."

The little girl looked up at her mother.

"We didn't do anything wrong, did we?"

"No, sweetie bird," she said. "Not a thing."

The manager started eyeing the duffle bag in the mother's hand.

"I'm going to have to look inside your bag."

"There's nothing in here for you to look at."

"If you don't want to cooperate," the manager said, "I'll call security."

"I didn't steal any of your clothes."

"We'll see about that."

The mother spotted me standing not too far away

"I can prove I didn't steal anything," she said. "Just ask *him*."

"Sir," the manager said, "can I have a word with you?"

I pointed at myself, feigning confusion.

"Yes, *you*, sir."

I approached the manager, feeling like a kid at the principal's office.

"Are you here with this woman?"

"Of course he's with me," the mother said. "You don't think he's hanging out here by himself, do you?"

The manager ignored her, waiting for me to answer.

I said nothing.

"I believe your friend is trying to steal merchandise from my store."

When I didn't respond, the manager turned to the shop girl.

"Call security."

I looked at the mother.

"Maybe you should just show her what's in the bag."

"Mind your business."

The little girl tugged her mother's hand.

"I'm hungry," she said. "When can we eat?"

The mother turned to look at her daughter and, in that brief moment, the manager snatched the duffle bag from her. Before the mother could react, the manager unzipped the bag and rifled through it, until something inside caused her to shriek, dropping it to the floor. She frantically wiped her hands against her skirt, while the mother picked the bag back up.

"Next time you need someplace to change," the manager said, "go find a goddamned YMCA!"

In the commotion, the mother's jacket slid off of her shoulder. Before she straightened it back on, I spotted my father's R.H. II monogram on the breast pocket of her shirt. I was too stunned to speak, so I could only watch as she took her daughter's hand and walked out of Carnage. Before I could leave myself, the security guard showed up.

"Is this the troublemaker, ma'am?"

"No, they're gone," the manager said. "But, get him out of here."

The security guard walked me out of Carnage and escorted me all the way out of the Fashion Show Mall—but not before I could get one last look at the mother and daughter walking away in the opposite direction. I headed into the underground parking garage, got in my mother's car, and drove back to Summerlin. As I pulled into the long driveway leading to our garage, I saw a police car parked along the curb. Walking inside my house, I found my mom sitting in the living room, crying with her face buried in her hands. There were two officers inside, a young cop and an old cop. The young cop sat beside my mother, his hand on her shoulder. The old cop approached me as I walked in.

"Are you the son?"

"Yes."

"I have some unfortunate news," he said. "Your father was found dead this morning."

He said it straight away, no frills, the way you might tear off a Band-Aid.

"What happened?"

"We don't know yet," he said. "Forensics is investigating it. There appears to have been foul play. We found him not far from his office building. We need someone to identify the body. Your mom said her brother is on his way from California."

I looked at my mother.

"Uncle Mortimer's coming over?"

She nodded, yes.

"When he gets here," the old cop said, "we'll have him do the identification."

"I can do it."

"It's okay to wait for your uncle," he said. "I know this is a difficult time."

"I want to do it," I said. "When should I go?"

"If you're up to it," the officer said, "I'd have you do it as soon as possible."

"Right now?"

"It doesn't have to be right this moment," he said. "You can take a little time if you need it."

"I'd like to see him now."

The old cop nodded like he thought I was being brave.

"I'll get one of my men to give you a ride."

"I'll drive myself."

He squeezed my shoulder.

"Okay."

I drove my mom's car down to the morgue where a sympathetic woman was waiting for me. She was the forensic pathologist in charge of determining how my father died. She took me into a large, cold room, where the walls were made of steel and lined with large drawers. Leading me to one of the drawers, the pathologist pulled it out from the wall. She unzipped the body bag, careful not to expose more than his face.

"That's him," I said.

Even with the fingernail scratches on his cheek and the bite mark behind his ear, he looked relatively normal. But the body bag, like a playground snitch, told a fuller story. Where his thighs were, the bag sunk low as if he were an amputee. His legs, for the most part, were still there. The bag also concaved into his chest like an invisible bowling ball had been dropped on his sternum. His shoulders and arms appeared intact, which made the crater in his torso look all the more pronounced.

In the moments before the pathologist escorted me out of that cold room filled with death, I thought of the sweet little girl with the nearly bald scalp walking by her mother's side, holding her hand, trusting she would lead her wherever she needed to be.

Peppermint Breath

It's after midnight when I hear Mommy's phone ring in the kitchen. I'm in bed, but not asleep. She'd gotten me an iPad a few months earlier, which was awesome because it wasn't my birthday or anything. Most nights, when I'm not sleepy, I sit in bed with the covers pitched over my head and play with my iPad. I usually watch TV shows on it, but I also enjoy reading. I mostly read comic books, like *Dolph the Unicorn Killer*, but I have some regular books, too, like *Dracula*. I mainly got it because Dracula's a famous vampire, but also because Mommy made me promise to sometimes use my iPad for smart stuff. I was in the middle of watching an episode of *Buffy the Vampire Slayer* on Netflix when I heard Mommy's phone.

I've seen every episode of *Buffy* already, because it was Mommy's favorite show when she was a kid, so from the time I was born she'd been watching it with me. I honestly can't remember a time in my life when I didn't love *Buffy*. The particular episode I was watching when Mommy's phone rang was "Hush." That's the one where these creepy monsters called the Gentlemen steal everyone's voices in Sunnydale. Because nobody can talk, the Gentlemen can hurt people without them being able to scream for help. They also steal people's hearts, cutting them right from their chests. They don't show the cutting part on *Buffy*, though, probably because they didn't want too much blood on TV. I was at the scene where the Gentlemen were chasing

Buffy's best friend, Willow, down the hall of her dorm when I paused it to see listen to Mommy.

Sometimes I'd wake up in the middle of the night after having a nightmare and go to my Mommy's room to lay with her. But, the last time I had a bad nightmare, Mommy wasn't there. I'd walked around our whole apartment, but I couldn't find her. I went outside and stood against the rail, crying as I stared at the parking lot, convinced I'd never see Mommy again. I fell asleep in front of our door and when I woke up I was in bed with Mommy sitting beside me, stroking my hair. She said she was sorry over and over again, but I told her it was okay. Later that day, after she picked me up from school, she took me to the Apple Store and bought me my iPad. She bought herself an iPhone, too, which was what she was talking on in the kitchen. She told me the last time her phone rang in the middle of the night that she would try to keep it on vibrate, but sometimes she forgets.

I get out of bed and go into the kitchen. The light is on and Mommy is leaning against the sink, talking quietly. She opens her arms when she sees me, inviting me in for a hug while continuing to talk. I wrap my arms around her hips, pressing my ear against her belly. I asked her once where she was when I couldn't find her in the middle of the night and she said she was outside smoking. She told me that if I ever found her gone like that again not to worry because she was never far away.

"Okay," she says. "Yes. That'll be fine. Yes. Okay."

She hangs up the phone, putting it on the counter.

"What are you doing up, baby boy?"

"I heard your phone."

"Sorry about that."

"Who were you talking to?"

"A friend."

I didn't know Mommy had a friend because nobody ever comes over to our apartment and we never go to anybody else's apartment. Mommy always tells me I'm her best friend and I always tell her she's mine. It's true, too. I don't really hang out with kids from school because I have so much fun with Mommy. She doesn't have a job, so we hang out pretty much all the time. I mean, she still makes sure I do homework and stuff. She's always making a big deal about school and getting an education and how she wants me to go to college and make lots of money one day.

"Do I know your friend?"

"No."

"Are you leaving?"

"For a little bit."

"Can I go with you?"

She smiles.

"Of course."

"Where're we going?"

"To get a late-night snack across the street."

"Lola's!"

Lola's Diner is across the street from our apartment. Mommy takes me there every Sunday morning to eat scrambled eggs and Belgian waffles. Sometimes after school, she takes me to Lola's for French fries and a strawberry milkshake. I love it there. We go often enough that Lola actually knows who we are. It's a 24-hour diner, which I think is just the coolest thing. I love the idea of this small diner being awake in the middle of the night, people reading menus and ordering food, carrying on conversations like normal while the rest of the world is asleep. If I were a vampire, I'd probably spend most of my time at Lola's, though I suppose I wouldn't be able to order off of the menu.

This is the first time Mommy has ever taken me to Lola's in the middle of the night. We usually walk there, because it's so close. But, tonight Mommy says we'll drive.

"Why?"

"Because the world is a little more dangerous at night," she says, "so you have to be careful."

I wonder if maybe she's talking about vampires. I know vampires are supposed to be make-believe and all, but I can't help but wonder where the idea for vampires came from. I mean, it makes sense to me that somebody probably met a real vampire once and then told a story about it, then other people heard that story and re-told it and that happened over and over again for a very long time until we ended up with stories like *Dracula* and *Buffy the Vampire Slayer*. When I told Mommy my idea, she said, "That's a very interesting theory." I like having a theory, even though I don't know what it means. Mommy agreed that vampire stories had been around pretty much forever, way before Bram Stoker and Joss Whedon.

She told me about Vlad the Impaler, who was an emperor or something, and how he'd kill people and sometimes dip his bread in their blood at dinner. She also told me about Countess Bathory, who was this crazy lady that took baths in the blood of virgins because she thought it would keep her young forever (I asked Mommy what a virgin was, but she said she'd tell me about it another time when I was older). She told me that vampire stories probably came from people like Vlad the Impaler and Countess Bathory, but she didn't know for sure. I asked her if that meant there were no such things as vampires and she said yes. But, when I asked her if she was one-hundred percent certain that there was absolutely no such thing as vampires, she smiled and said, "No, I'm not one-hundred percent certain."

Lola is working at the diner when we arrive. I love seeing her because she feels like a celebrity to me. I know she isn't on TV or anything, but having a restaurant named after you is pretty cool. I would've been just as happy to know Ronald McDonald or Little Caesar.

"Well, isn't this a pleasant surprise," Lola says. "Hello, little man."

"Hi, Lola."

"And what are you doing up so late?"

"We're getting a late-night snack."

"Well, that sounds delightful."

Lola's older than Mommy and she looks like she might be some-body's grandma, which I find fascinating because I never imagine anybody's grandma staying up all night with the vampires. Lola takes us to a booth with a view of the parking lot. There are a couple of men at the counter drinking coffee and eating pie. A few tables away, I see another kid like me. He's eating a cheeseburger and fries, which looks good, but I want dessert. It's weird to see another kid out in the middle of the night, so I wonder if maybe he's a vampire like the little girl in *Let the Right One In*. That's a foreign movie about vampires I watched with Mommy once on Halloween. I decide to keep an eye on him, just in case.

After Mommy and me are seated, Lola takes our orders. She always takes our orders without a notepad, because she has an amaz-ing memory. Whenever I'd ask her how she remembers stuff, she tells me, "I don't know, I just always have." I wonder if there's something I've always been able to do, but don't know about yet. Staying awake has always come easily to me since I've never liked sleeping anyway. I'd like to think that one day I might be a vampire slayer like Buffy.

"What can I get for you?"

"Coffee for me," Mommy said.

"And how about you, little man?"

I looked at the menu, then at Mommy.

"What can I have?"

"Anything you want."

"*Anything?*"

"Anything at all."

"Can I have a sundae?"

"Sure."

"I'll have a strawberry sundae, please."

"You got it," Lola says.

She rests her elbows on the table and motions for me to lean in like she has a secret to tell me.

"Listen," she says, "I've got too much whipped cream in my fridge

and I'm having the darndest time getting rid of it. You'd be doing me
a huge favor if you let me put some extra on your sundae."

"Really?"

"Honest to goodness."

"Okay."

"Thanks, little man."

I look again at the kid and see his daddy looking at Mommy.

"Is that your friend?"

Mommy smiles, kissing me on the top of the head.

"I'll be right back."

She goes to the counter and says something to Lola. Lola looks
over at me and smiles, before going back into the kitchen. Mommy
comes back to me.

"I'm going to go to the car for a little bit."

"Why?"

"I won't be gone long," she says. "Lola's going to bring your sundae, okay?"

"But, isn't it dangerous at night?"

"I'll be okay."

"Are you sure?"

"Yes," she says. "Just wait here for me."

Mommy exits the diner, walking quickly through the cold air.
Her breath comes out like smoke until she reaches the car. I watch
her get inside and close the door. Inside the diner, the vampire kid's
daddy stands up and also goes outside. He doesn't seem afraid at all
to be outside in the middle of the night. I figure maybe it's because
he was a man and men always seem braver than other people. I don't
really know any men, though, except for my teacher. I know I have
a daddy somewhere, but I've never met him. Mommy never really
talks about him, but she'll usually answer questions if I ask. I know it
makes her sad, though, so I don't ask questions anymore.

I watch the vampire kid's daddy walk to our car, getting inside
with Mommy. It's very dark outside, but there's just enough light

from Lola's bright red sign for me to see them talking. I'm scared at first because I think maybe he's a vampire like his kid, which means Mommy would be in a car by herself with a vampire. But, then I figure if he *is* a vampire, he wouldn't have a vampire kid that likes cheeseburgers.

Lola calls me from behind the counter.

"Hey, little man."

She's got my strawberry sundae.

"Come sit over here," she says.

"Mommy told me to wait here."

She leans over the counter and whispers loud enough for me to hear.

"I don't normally tell folks this," she says, "but ice cream actually tastes *better* when you sit at the counter."

"It does?"

"It truly does," she says. "But, if folks knew that, they'd stop sitting at my tables. And *then* what would I do?"

I look back out the window, but I can't see Mommy's head anymore. I can only see the vampire kid's daddy. His head is leaning back on the seat like he's trying to fall asleep, which I guess makes sense because it's so late.

"Come and get it, little man," Lola says. "You don't want your ice cream to melt, do you?"

I take a seat at the counter and start eating my sundae. I'm not one-hundred-percent certain, but I think it might be the best sundae I've ever tasted. I turn to look out the window, hoping to see Mommy, but I don't have a good view from the counter. Plus, the back window of our car is fogged up now. I look back at the vampire kid and start thinking about that foreign movie, *Let the Right One In*, and how the little girl vampire lives with this old man who seems like her daddy, but really he's more like a servant. He helps get her blood and stuff while trying to make sure people don't know she's a vampire. I start to think that maybe that's what the vampire kid and his daddy are like.

What if the vampire kid wants Mommy's blood? I hope he doesn't because I don't think I can protect her against a vampire, even though he's a kid vampire, because even kid vampires are very strong and very dangerous. Thinking that I can't protect Mommy is an awful feeling. It makes me wish I had a Watcher like Giles. Giles is Buffy's Watcher, so he helps train her to be a vampire slayer. One time Mommy pointed out to me that Giles also helped look after Buffy like a daddy because Buffy's daddy wasn't around to take care of her.

"Hey," Lola says, leaning her elbows on the counter, "you think he'd like a sundae, too?"

"I don't know," I say. "I think he might be a vampire."

Lola laughs.

"Maybe vampires like ice cream."

She looks at the vampire kid.

"You want a sundae?"

He says yes with his head, then comes to the counter and sits next to me.

"You want strawberry or chocolate?" Lola asks.

"Strawberry."

I've never been this close to somebody who might be a vampire before, so I'm nervous. Lola doesn't seem nervous at all as she goes to the kitchen. She isn't gone long before coming out and setting a strawberry sundae in front of the vampire kid. If he really is a vampire, I need to say something to him, so, when I'm older, I can tell my future son that I once talked to a vampire.

"She said they taste better when you eat at the counter," I say. "It's a secret, though."

"Is it true?"

"Yeah," I say, "I think so."

The vampire kid and me eat our sundaes, but we don't talk anymore. He still has more ice cream left when his daddy comes back in.

"You got yourself some dessert," his daddy says. "Good man. What do I owe you, Lola?"

"My treat," she says. "The boys kept me company."

His daddy takes out some money and leaves it on the counter.

"What's this for?" Lola asks.

"Getaway money," he says. "There's an island out there somewhere with your name on it."

I wonder if maybe it's a vampire island. I'll have to remember to warn Lola, just in case. After the vampire kid and his daddy leave, Mommy comes back inside. She grabs a piece of peppermint candy from the bowl beside Lola's cash register, popping it in her mouth before joining me at the counter.

Mommy smiles at Lola.

"Thank you."

"No problem."

She kisses me on the cheek and runs her fingers through my hair.

"You all done, baby boy?"

"Yes."

"Then I guess that means it's time for you to get to bed."

Mommy takes some money out of her purse and puts it on the counter. Lola picks it up and gives it back.

"Don't worry about it."

"You sure?"

"Absolutely," Lola says. "Use it to buy your boy something nice."

"I will."

Lola touches the top of my head with her fingers, which are cold from making sundaes.

"I hope I see you again soon, little man."

"Me too."

By the time we get home from Lola's Diner, I can hardly keep my eyes open. Mommy comes around and picks me up from the passenger seat. I sometimes think I'm too old for her to carry me, but I still love it. My ear rests against her cheek and I can feel the peppermint candy clicking against her teeth. Mommy carries me all the way to my bed, removing my shoes and tucking me under the covers.

"Did you enjoy your late-night adventure?"

"Yes."

"Good," she says. "If you're too sleepy to get up in the morning, you can stay home from school."

"Okay."

"But *only* if you're too sleepy," she says. "Got it?"

"Got it."

She leans in and kisses my cheek, before whispering goodnight, her warm peppermint breath lingering as I drift off to sleep.

Sonia Billings and the Tall Red Door

Back when I was twelve years old, still six years away from being a legal adult, Uncle Leo told me, "Every man should see a naked woman on his eighteenth birthday." To the best of my recollection, his words of wisdom were completely unsolicited. That wasn't unusual with Uncle Leo because as I grew up he sort of saw me as a younger version of himself. So, whenever he offered me unsolicited—and borderline inappropriate—advice it was more like he'd gone back in time to warn his younger self about what he'd learned in the future.

For example, when I was about fifteen years old, he told me, "What's your favorite cereal? Cap'n Crunch, right? Can you imagine eating Cap'n Crunch every day for the rest of your life? I mean, sure, they're delicious for a little while, but eventually you're gonna want some Lucky Charms or Cocoa Pebbles. You may even want to experiment with some Fruit Loops one day. That's why you should never get married. Being married is like fucking Cap'n Crunch every day for the rest of your life."

I hadn't even enjoyed my first kiss at the time of Uncle Leo's cereal advice. My first kiss, incidentally, came about a year later with a pretty girl named Yvette. It happened in the midway of Circus Circus during a schoolmate's birthday party. I can't even remember who's birthday it was, but I know Yvette was his cousin—or one of those close family friends who seems like a cousin. Either way, she spent all night talking to me, which was cool, because girls usually didn't pay much attention to me. And I could tell she liked me, which made me nervous because I had no idea what I was supposed to do about it.

When it became clear to me that Yvette and I had reached the point of the night where a kiss was supposed to happen, I invited her outside to "talk," though I think we both knew what was going on. We stood against the wall, near the valet, face to face, and I knew, just like in the movies, this was the moment when it was all supposed to go down. The only problem was I'd had no idea what to do.

So, I did nothing.

Luckily, Yvette was the sort of girl who *did* know what to do, so she made the first move. And the second move. The third move, which involved me sweeping a curl of hair behind her ear, was all mine. I called Uncle Leo that night to tell him it had finally happened, that I'd actually kissed a girl—or, rather, she'd kissed me. Nonetheless, I was still very much involved in the whole ordeal and I made sure Uncle Leo knew that as well. "That's great!" he'd said, genuinely excited. He was working late at Kwipz.

"Did you get your dick wet?"

"We were at Circus Circus."

"It's just as well," he said. "If you fuck a girl at your age, you're likely to marry her. That's just how it goes. Probably would've gotten her pregnant. And believe you me, you don't want a baby. Not now, not ever. They are loud and expensive and will throw up on your good shirt every chance they get. Count your blessings, kid."

Yvette gave me her phone number and we talked a few times, but it turned out she was visiting from Arizona at the time of the birthday party, so the phone calls and texts eventually dried up and we never saw each other again.

"You're better off without her," Uncle Leo told me. "Love 'em and leave 'em, kid. You got your kissy-kiss on and now she's out of your hair. We should all be so lucky. If you knew how much money I was shelling out to your Aunt Laura, you'd know what I was talking about. Frankly, I hope you never have to find out. Believe me, kid, you're doing it right." I knew he was only trying to make me feel better, but it worked like a charm. It always worked with Uncle Leo. He could put a smile on my face just by standing in the same room. "You had your Cap'n Crunch, now go get some Lucky Charms."

Yvette was a pretty girl and all—and, believe me, as first kisses go, I could've done much, much worse—but she wasn't my dream girl. That title belonged to Sonia Billings. I'd been admiring Sonia Billings from afar since junior high school. She was a year ahead of me and had no idea I existed in the world at all. We'd never officially met and, to be honest with you, I have no idea how I even knew her name. We had no mutual friends, primarily because her friends were popular and mine weren't.

All through high school I admired her, savoring every pass in the hallway, the smell of her perfume, the sound of her laugh, the flow of her raven black hair, and the sheen of olive skin. Sonia Billings was probably the sort of girl Uncle Leo had been warning me about, as I would've gladly enjoyed her for breakfast every morning for the rest of my life. "The thing about dream girls is every guy thinks they can be happy forever with them," Uncle Leo told me, "but we're just not built that way. It's not in our DNA, kid. From the time we sprout pubes, our seed is screaming to be planted in as many broads as possible."

I'd been out of high school for about a month when I turned eighteen and Uncle Leo, who'd been counting down the days, insisted on taking me to my first strip club. "Let's face it," he'd said, "your old man's not gonna take you, so it's up to Uncle to make sure it happens." Uncle Leo figured I wouldn't want my parents to know, which was true, so he told me to meet him at Little Darlings after his shift was over at Kwipz. "I'm working the graveyard shift on Tuesday night," he'd said, "with a bit of overtime to boot. I'll be done by noon, so I'll meet you there around 12:30 or so."

I'd driven by Little Darlings hundreds of times over the years, usually in the backseat while my mom or dad was driving us into Downtown Vegas. Every time I saw it off the freeway, I imagined what it was like inside, though I never imagined myself actually going inside. The thought of going to Little Darlings in the middle of the afternoon, with the sun still high up in the sky, filled me with anxiety. If it were up to me, we'd go under the veil of night, hidden from passing cars and familiar eyes. But, Uncle Leo didn't really leave much room for me to say no and, to be honest, I didn't want to turn him down, because, as scary as it was, it was also sort of exciting in that forbidden fruit kind of way.

I arrive at Little Darlings promptly at twelve o'clock, which is actually a half-hour sooner than I wanted to be there, which means I'll have to sit in the parking lot and wait for Uncle Leo to show up. It's a small parking lot and there are only two or three other cars. For the first ten or fifteen minutes of my wait, I attempt to read the latest issue of *Dolph the Unicorn Killer*, but I'm so anxious I can't get past the first page. I watch various men go in and out of Little Darlings, many of them wearing suits and ties. A bouncer stands at the entrance—stone-faced, arms crossed. I see a couple of women come and go as well, presumably dancers crossing paths between shifts. One particularly attractive woman with raven black hair and olive skin pulls into the parking lot around the corner. I watch her walk towards the entrance in overalls and a baseball cap, her hair in a ponytail. The bouncer greets her with a smile as she walks in.

Checking the time, I'm alarmed to find it's now 12:45 pm. Not only have I been sitting in the parking lot for forty-five minutes, but Uncle Leo is fifteen minutes late. A wave of anxiety washes over me and all I want to do is go home and forget I was ever here. I call Uncle Leo to tell him I'm not up to it anymore.

"No, just stay there," he says. "I'm about five minutes away."

He shows up twenty-five minutes later.

The bouncer takes a moment to frisk Uncle Leo and me at the entrance, before letting us in. At the front counter, sitting behind a cash register is a young man reading a textbook, seemingly unaware that Uncle Leo and I are standing in front of him. Beside the counter is a heavy black curtain separating us from the inside of the club.

"How's the read, pal?" Uncle Leo asks.

The clerk puts his book aside and looks up.

"IDs."

Uncle Leo and I each gave him our driver's licenses. The clerk stares at mine for what feels like forever, before giving it back.

"Happy Birthday," he says. "Ten bucks each."

Uncle Leo gives him a twenty-dollar bill, but, before we step through the black curtain, the same attractive girl I'd seen earlier pokes her head through. Only now, I realize she is no ordinary attractive girl.

She's Sonia Billings.

"Can you plug this in, hun?" she asks, handing the clerk her iPhone. "All the outlets are taken back here."

"Sure."

It's the first time I've seen the clerk smile since we'd arrived. Sonia Billings says a quick thank you, before disappearing back behind the curtain. Turning his attention back to Uncle Leo and me, the clerk waves us through. On the other side, a man in a shiny suit greets us. He seems much more important than anyone else there, which I attribute to the walkie-talkie in his back pocket and his metal-detecting wand.

"Sit anywhere you like," he says, as he waves the wand over Uncle Leo and me. "There's a two-drink minimum. One drink per hour or you gotta go."

When he's done, Uncle Leo and I officially enter and start looking for a seat. I'd always imagined Little Darlings would be large and sprawling inside, the sort of place you could sit in for hours without ever being noticed. But, now that I'm inside, it's much smaller than I expected. There are a few men scattered about, but the club is mostly empty. A handful of dancers walk around half-naked, mostly socializing with each other. In the back of the club, away from the stage, I see a tall red door. A large man in a black suit stands beside the door, holding a clipboard.

Onstage I see a blond dancer performing her routine. She sits on the floor, her back arched against the metal pole, and removes her bra—and, in so doing, she becomes the first topless woman I've ever seen in real life.

"Wanna sit at the stage?" Uncle Leo asks. "We can get a closer look at the snatch parade."

"Do we have to?"

He shrugs, before taking us towards the back wall where we find a couple of seats. Once we sit down, I give my attention back to the blond dancer, who is now laying on her back and lifting her legs, toes pointed to the ceiling, as she slides her panties off—and, in so doing, she becomes the first bottomless woman I've ever seen in real life.

I'm both aroused and anxious, wanting to take it all in, but not wanting to appear rude for staring. There are three men sitting around the stage, each of them laying down money for the dancer. Crawling on her hands and knees, she approaches each man, collecting the money between her teeth, before giving them each a kiss on the cheek.

Uncle Leo, without warning, stands up and walks to the stage, taking a seat. He places a five-dollar bill in his teeth, prompting the blond dancer to crawl towards him. Squeezing his face between her breasts, she pinches the bill from his mouth. While I watch Uncle Leo and the blond dancer, a waitress turns up beside me.

"What would you like to drink?"

"What do you have?"

"Soda, mainly," she says. "And water. Bottled."

"Coke?"

"Is that what you want?"

"Yes, please."

She scribbles my order down, then walks away.

When the blond dancer finishes her routine, she puts her clothes back on and exits the stage, but not before saying an extra thank you to all the men who tipped her. When she gets to Uncle Leo, she takes a seat on his lap like he's Santa Claus. After a minute or so of chatting, she stands up and takes Uncle Leo by the hand, leading him to the back of the club. As he passes me, he stops and leans in.

"I'm gonna hit the private room for a few songs," he says. "You having a good time?"

I nod, yes.

Pulling out his wallet, Uncle Leo hands me a couple of twenties.

"There's more where that came from," he says, "so *don't* spend it wisely."

The blond, feigning impatience, tugs on Uncle Leo's hand until he relents, letting her lead him to the tall red door. She says something to the man in the black suit and he, in turn, scribbles something on his clipboard, before opening the tall red door and letting them in. Another dancer is on the stage now, beginning her striptease, and I find myself growing ever more comfortable with my surroundings.

The waitress comes back with my Coke.

"Five dollars."

I hand her one of the twenties Uncle Leo gave me and she hands me back fifteen singles. As I put the money away in my pocket, she stands there, staring at me.

"Nothing?"

"Pardon?"

"No tip?"

I quickly pull out the money and hand her two dollars.

"Really?"

"What?"

"Two dollars?"

I don't know what to say.

"Keep your fucking money," she says, walking away with my money.

I have no idea what just happened, but I'm now too distracted to properly enjoy the dancer on stage. I take a sip from my five-dollar Coke, which is watered down and filled with ice, and come to accept that this whole experience is beginning to sour at a rapid pace. All I want is for Uncle Leo to come back so we can leave.

"Don't worry about her."

I look up and see Sonia Billings.

I can't speak.

I literally can't say a word.

"She's a bitch," she says. "Nobody here likes her. She blows the manager on her breaks, so he keeps her around."

"Thanks."

"What's your name?"

"Felix."

"Nice to meet you, Felix," she says. "I'm Twilight. I've never seen you here before."

"It's my first time."

"What other clubs do you go to?"

"None."

"Really?" she says. "So, this is your first time to *any* strip club?"

I say nothing, feeling shy all of a sudden.

"I think that's sweet," she says. "Is that why you were sitting in the parking lot for an hour?"

"You saw me?"

"Some of the girls were talking," she says. "No big deal."

"I was waiting for my Uncle Leo."

"He's here?"

I nod, yes.

"Where's he at?"

I point at the tall red door.

"Who's he with?"

"The blond girl who was just on stage."

"Interesting," she says. "Your uncle's probably getting more than a dance back there."

"Really?"

She nods, yes.

"But you didn't hear that from me."

She brings her thumb and forefinger to her lips, pretending to zip them shut.

"How about you?" she says. "Would you like a dance?"

Of course, I want a dance with Sonia Billings, but I'm not really sure how to tell her yes.

So, I say nothing.

"It's okay to say no," she says. "I just have to ask."

"Okay."

"Unless you *want* a dance."

She smiles, touching my leg with her hand.

I'm speechless all over again.

"If you decide you're interested," she says, "it's twenty for topless and forty for nude. A dance lasts for one song, but they usually have two-for-one specials every hour or so."

"Okay."

"Okay, you want a dance?"

"No," I say. "I mean, I was just saying okay. Sorry."

She laughs.

"You're cute," she says. "You don't have to be nervous, by the way. I don't bite. Unless you ask me to."

She squeezes my leg, laughing and leaning in, giving me a whiff of her sweet perfume. I laugh with her, trying to act like this is all so very normal, that talking to a beautiful half-naked woman was par for the course. But, really, I'm mostly concerned with not letting Sonia Billings discover my hard-on.

"You having a good time?"

I nod, yes.

"It's a little slow today," she says. "I usually work nights. Week-ends are better, but those shifts are tough to get. Unless the manager likes you."

"He doesn't like you?"

"Well," she says, leaning in, "let's just say I don't let him like me the way he'd like to like me."

She keeps her face close to mine for an extra beat, her breasts pressing against my arm. She brings her lips within an inch of my own, causing my heart to flutter.

"I have to circulate a little," she says, "so the manager thinks I'm busy."

"Okay."

"I'll check on you in a bit," she says, standing up. "Think about that dance, Felix."

I smile and she walks away.

I sit alone for just a few minutes, enjoying the phantom grip of Sonia Billings' fingers on my thigh, when Uncle Leo comes out from behind the tall red door.

"What'cha got there?" he asks, helping himself to my five-dollar Coke.

He drinks it down to the bottom, as the blond comes out a few moments later from behind the tall red door. She says something to the man in the black suit, before winking at Uncle Leo.

"That gal's got talent to spare," Uncle Leo says. "How about you? Any action?"

"I talked to one girl."

"Yeah?" he says. "You get a dance?"

"No."

"Why not?" he asks. "She wasn't offering?"

"She was, but—"

"You weren't interested?"

"I was interested."

"Well, listen, it's your birthday," he says, "and Uncle's paying, so get as much snatch in your face as you like, all right?"

It's a generous offer, but I mostly just want to talk to Sonia Billings some more. I want to smell her perfume again and hear her say my name. I want to feel her hand on my thigh and her breasts against my arm. I want her lips to approach mine, stopping just before they touch, and I'll listen to anything she has to say for the whole rest of my life, till death do us part.

I spot her sitting at the stage, chatting with an older man with a thick beard and gray temples. I watch her lean in close, pressing her breasts against his arm, whispering something in his ear. She stands up and takes him by the hand, leading him back to the tall red door. The man in the black suit scribbles something on his clipboard, before letting them through.

"Where's your girl?" Uncle Leo asks.

"I don't know."

"What's her name?"

"Sonia Billings."

"First *and* last name, huh?" he says. "She must really like you."

I shrug.

"If you don't see her," he says, "she's probably on a break or something. Wanna wait for her?"

"I think I'm ready to go."

"No dance?" he asks. "You sure?"

"Maybe next time."

As we exit through the heavy black curtain, the same clerk is still behind the register, reading the same textbook. Sonia Billings' cell phone is still charging beside him. We pass by the same bouncer at the entrance and he nods to us as we head back to our cars. I give Uncle Leo a hug, thanking him. "Give your mom a kiss for me," he says. "And tell her I'll bring my laundry by this weekend." Driving home, I continue to enjoy the phantom touch of Sonia Billings' hand on my leg, fantasizing about what might've been.

Dolph the
Unicorn Killer

My name's Dolph. Short for Adolph. I dropped the "A" for what I assume are obvious reasons. Mother and Father fancied themselves hilarious. They thought it would give me character to be made fun of. Kids can be cruel. They called me a Nazi and a killer. Turns out they were half right. Not the Nazi part. I am a killer. I kill unicorns. I'm Dolph the Unicorn Killer. When I say unicorns, I'm not talking about rich dudes with big dicks or hot girlfriends who insist on threesomes. I kill *real* unicorns. The mythical ones. Yeah, they're real. Now you know. What you do with that information is between you and your God. If you're squeamish about the details of what it looks like when a horned beast that sneezes rainbow sprinkles and shits ice cream dies beneath my sword, then you'd best stop reading now.

Let's start with where I live, where this story is set. It's set in the time of now. And we may as well be in your backyard. There're streets and schools and traffic lights, just like where you live. We've got assholes in elected government and shitty reality TV. There're multi-millionaire athletes posing as role models and role models posing as schoolteachers. Just like every fucking neighborhood in the whole fucking world, we've got superheroes supplementing our local law enforcement, helping to catch the bad guys. And we also have unicorns, just like where you live.

Oh, what's that?

You've never seen a unicorn?

That's exactly right, Einstein. You're not supposed to see them. If you could, then they wouldn't be special. They also wouldn't be dangerous. And I wouldn't have to be on the streets, night after night, taking them out with liberal violence. I'm one of those superheroes mentioned earlier, but not everyone sees it that way. If you ask the Superhuman Squad, they'd tell you I'm an anti-hero. Fuck them. You know, I've tried to get into their group before, filled out my application like a good boy, got some solid letters of recommendation—I even printed everything on that fancy paper you use for résumés. Every time, they say, "The Superhuman Squad is a family friendly group that doesn't endorse vigilante anti-heroes. Thank you for your interest, but for now, we'll have to pass. Should a position open up that fits your qualifications, we'll be in touch." Well, they've never been in touch, because apparently killing unicorns isn't family friendly.

And what the fuck do they even mean by "family friendly." We're not a fucking feature length cartoon meant to bring parents and kids to the movie theater to spend boatloads of money on tickets and snacks. We're fucking *superheroes!* We smash bad guys. At least I do. But, they're all caught up in their branding and toy deals and T-shirts and their fucking movie which I am so goddamned tired of hearing about. You know, I don't need toys or movies to know the work I do matters, that it keeps people safe so they don't have to worry about unicorns.

But, that's the other thing. You can't see unicorns. Literally, to the human eye—unless you're me—unicorns are fucking invisible. So, not only am I the asshole who kills unicorns, but I'm also the crazy guy who claims they exist even though nobody else can see them. The only other people besides me who can see unicorns are kids, but they can only see them for the first couple years of their life. Right around the age a kid becomes aware of himself and his surroundings, his ability to see unicorns goes away. But, even when the ability to *see* unicorns goes away, kids still *remember* them. Subconsciously, the image of unicorns is always in their brain. It's why kids get so excited when they see unicorns in cartoons and on cereal boxes.

Now, since I'm the hero of this story, it only makes sense that I have a villainous counterpart. There was Rainbow Kisses. Killed him. Hurricane Hugs. Killed him. Princess Pollywog. Killed her. Lollipop Love Bucket. Killed him. And still there were others and if I were to rattle off all of my unicorn kills, we'd hardly have time to talk about the real reason I'm here. The reason I am who I am. My white whale.

Golden Showers.

Every time I get my hands on a unicorn, thrusting my sword elbow deep into their sugary guts, I wish it were Golden Showers laying beneath me, snuffing his last breath. Not only is he the son of a bitch who killed Mother and Father, but he used to sneak into my bedroom in the middle of the night, his big candy hooves pinning me down by my pajama gown, and pee on me.

But, I'm getting ahead of myself.

Like every other superhero, I've got an origin story.

So, here it is.

I grew up rich as fuck. Mansions, toys, personal water slides, butlers, family vacations—you name it, I had several of them. I was so busy playing with myself my parents hardly had to spend time with me at all, which was good for them as it allowed them to focus on the family business. My parents were the founders and owners of the world's most famous candy company: König Kandy. You've likely had our chocolate and licorice and suckers and jawbreakers and Whatnot®. If it's got sugar and it's delicious, we probably made it. And we made a metric shit-ton of money with it. Mother and Father did, anyway. I had nothing to do with it. The company is still around, obviously, and it still makes a shit ton of money. Obviously. A boardroom of suits runs it now. I have nothing to do with it. I couldn't tell you a thing about how it runs. I just know where to get money when I need it. And I need money for all my toys. Not kids toys, either. Not anymore.

Blades.

Knives.

Swords.

Mainly swords. Superheroes don't use guns. At least they shouldn't. Leave that for the cops. If I'm gonna kill a unicorn, all I need is a sword. And my superpowers. Yeah, I've got those, too.

So, check this shit out. My parents and I were leaving the theater on a Tuesday night. Father wore his favorite overcoat and Mother wore her favorite pearl necklace. Father decided we should walk through the alley, which was strange because we were rich and alleys were for hobos and runaways. A man named Joe held us up at gun-point, threatening to kill all of us if Mother didn't give him her pearl necklace. Father snapped immediately into action and protected Mother by placing me in front of the gunman.

The irony of the situation is Father had a million dollars in his overcoat pocket. Literally. It was actually kind of obvious if Joe had bothered to notice. But, all he wanted was the necklace. I guess he'd seen some show about appraising stuff and he was convinced he could get a whole lot of money for Mother's pearl necklace, which is ridiculous because that necklace is virtually worthless. They weren't even real pearls. It was a candy necklace from König Kandy. The pearls were little balls of sugar called Whatnot®. They weren't even flavored.

Mother started taking the necklace off and the three of us could hardly keep from laughing. Then the sky opened up and shit out a bolt of lightning, striking me right between the eyes. The last thing I remember was Father's hands shoving me in the back. I woke up at home surrounded by doctors, nurses, Mother, Father, and Joe. The consensus was nobody could believe I'd survived the lightning bolt, especially Joe. Turns out Joe wasn't so bad after all. While Mother and Father were in a tizzy about me getting struck by lightning, Joe carried me to the hospital. Mother and Father followed behind in a cab, wringing their hands over my wellbeing. When they saw the condition of the hospital, they insisted I be treated at home and overnight they turned a wing of our mansion into a state of the art medical center.

Mother and Father hired Joe on as one of our many butlers and for the first year he worked for us they paid him with Whatnot® candy necklaces. Joe didn't know they were candy, despite the man at the pawn shop telling him so every week. When he finally figured it out, Joe shared a good laugh with the family. But, before all of that, I had to heal and shit. Through the wonders of medical science and my Mother and Father's unlimited bank account, I made a full recovery. I also came away with a unique superhuman ability, which I wouldn't learn about until the first time I met Golden Showers.

I was ten years old, lying in bed fast asleep. The time was well past midnight, so Mother and Father were also asleep, as was Joe and the other butlers. I never heard the wings flapping outside my window or the hooves landing on my balcony. I couldn't have imagined the dexterity of his mouth picking the lock and opening the doors. Some part of me is convinced I felt his presence in the room even before he climbed onto my bed. I assume he used his horn to remove my blanket, leaving me there in my pajama gown. It was a long gown, which spread out wide enough on either side of me that Golden Showers could step his hooves onto it, pinning me down.

I opened my eyes to the sight of that big fucking beast standing over me, pissing all over my pajama gown. His lemonade shot out like a fire hose, drenching me in its citrus scent. More than a few drops splashed onto my lips and—as if to add insult to injury—it was fucking delicious. But, it wasn't so delicious as to wipe away the humiliation of being pissed on in the middle of the night. It was also terrifying because there was a goddamned unicorn in my room. It didn't even occur to me to scream until after he'd emptied his bladder and galloped out of my bedroom, exiting off the balcony and flying away.

Joe arrived in my bedroom first, followed by Mother and Father thirty minutes later. They didn't know what happened or what sort of horror might've caused me to scream like I did, so they went to the kitchen and had one of the butlers fix them each a glass of tea to help calm their nerves. When they finally arrived in my bedroom— laughing over a joke Father told on the way up from the kitchen— they found me cradled in Joe's lap as he soothed me. I told them all about the giant unicorn who'd snuck into my room and pissed on my pajama gown. Mother and Father shared a look of disappointment.

"One must always take accountability for one's own piss, Adolph."

These were Father's words, but Mother agreed. I asked if I could change into a clean pajama gown, but Mother suggested I sleep in the piss pajamas.

"It's the only way you'll learn."

Joe raised the possibility that me sleeping in piss pajamas wasn't going to teach me anything and was ultimately just cruel. So, I slapped him across the cheek and told him to mind his own business. When everybody went back to bed, I remained cloaked in Golden Showers' piss and stared at the ceiling. Mother and Father thought I was a bed wetter and, worse than that, they thought I was a liar. I hated having them disappointed in me and I hated even more that Joe instigated their disappointment by speaking out of turn. But, more than anything else, I hated Golden Showers for igniting the whole pissy predicament. Of course, I didn't know the unicorn's name was Golden Showers. I wouldn't learn that until the following evening when he snuck back into my room and pissed on me again. "I forgot to tell you," he said, leaning in close so his snout touched my nose, "my name's Golden Showers."

I screamed again, Golden Showers fled from the balcony, Joe rushed in to comfort me, and Mother and Father joined thirty minutes later. It was uncannily similar to the previous night, including Mother and Father's disappointment and me slapping Joe across the cheek. Within a few days, the kids at school began taunting me, calling me "the bed wetter" and the "fag who believes in unicorns." I couldn't figure out how they found out, but later that evening Father told me he'd alerted the children at school.

"It'll be good for you," Mother said. "You need character."

Golden Showers pissed on me every night until I was a teenager. I eventually stopped screaming and resigned myself to the inevitability of being pissed on by a unicorn. Then one night Golden Showers didn't show up in my room. I was thirteen years old. I could hardly imagine what it would be like to sleep in dry pajamas. As I lay in bed thinking about it, a terrible crash sounded downstairs. I leaped out of bed and ran to the banister to see our front door had been busted through. A trail of hoof prints indented our marble floor, leading into the kitchen. I heard Mother and Father scream, followed by more violent crashing sounds.

I ran down the stairs and into the kitchen, where I found Mother and Father dead on the kitchen floor, each with large holes clear through their chests. The holes were the exact width of a unicorn horn. Joe ran into the kitchen, but he was too late to be of any use. And, making things worse, he slipped on the puddle of Mother and Father's blood, cracking his head against the tile floor, leaving him concussed and unable to comfort me in my darkest moment. Soon there were police officers and reporters and paramedics and spies from competing candy companies filing in and out of our home. A few days later I was standing with Joe at Mother and Father's duel Kandy Kane Kasket® for the funeral service. It rained that day, running the color off of the Kasket® and filling the air with the sugary scent of peppermint. This caused a good bit of laughter that Mother and Father surely would've enjoyed, as they were always the first to crack a joke at a funeral. From then on, I began the rest of my life without Mother and Father. All I had left in the world was Joe, our countless other butlers and servants, a shit ton of money, a mansion, and the raging cancer of vengeance burning in my heart for the son of a bitch who orphaned me.

Golden Showers.

Then there were the years of training and studying, building up my body and my mind so I could one day find Golden Showers and rip his cherry flavored heart out. Joe helped, too, but that would be just like him to take more credit than he's owed. He made my meals, got me ready for school in the morning, read me stories at night, taught me how to fight, showed me how to exercise, assured me there was nothing wrong with whatever I was doing during my extra long showers, and helped me build a cave beneath the mansion equipped with all the tools I'd need to maintain my full-time career as a super-hero who kills unicorns.

Joe never did believe in unicorns, even up to the day he died. He didn't actually die, mind you. I was just mad at him for something, so I told him he was dead to me. That lasted about two years. I haven't a clue what he did for those two years, but I'll be damned if my meals didn't continue to get made. After Joe was alive to me again, he started coming around to the possibility that unicorns might be real. Not because he'd seen any compelling evidence, but because Mother and Father's murders remained unsolved.

No matter how many unicorns I successfully hunt and kill, I haven't gotten any closer to finding Golden Showers. So many years have passed, I fear I might not even recognize him if I see him—but who am I kidding? I can still see him, smell him, and goddamn taste him like he was standing over me right now and pissing in my face. That golden mane, those pink wings, and that deadly fucking pink horn. I know that when I finally find Golden Showers, I will rip that pink horn off of his head and stab him to death with it just like he did to Mother and Father.

I got another rejection from the Superhuman Squad. Honestly, I don't know why I keep seeking their acceptance. Joe tells me I'm good enough on my own and I don't need to be part of a team. So, I slap him and tell him to mind his own business.

"And when you're done minding your own business," I say, "make me a sandwich."

When he comes back with my sandwich, he continues to explain his logic.

"Honestly," he says, "they would gain more from having you, then you would gain from having them."

I take a bite of the sandwich, before throwing it in Joe's face.

"Too much mustard."

"What I'm trying to say is they would be lucky to have you."

Joe picks the sandwich up from the floor.

"Eat it," I say. "Don't be wasteful. And make me a new sandwich."

There are four members total in the Superhuman Squad. Courageous Man, Fantastic Femme, Lima Lad, and Book-Hockey Man. Courageous Man has super strength, super speed, the power of flight, and x-ray vision. He was orphaned from some distant planet that exploded after he left as a baby. He landed on earth, met some really nice old couple and grew up poor as fuck on a farm. To tell you the truth, he deserves all those powers for the lame ass life he had growing up. Lima Lad is his sidekick. He's about seventeen and dresses up as a lima. I really don't think he has any abilities—super or otherwise. He's a handsome kid, though, and if I'm being honest I think Courageous Man is watching the calendar for his eighteenth birthday. Fantastic Femme rides a badass motorcycle and chokes bad guys with her Whip of Integrity. Apparently, her whip has some mythical powers that convince criminals to stop committing crimes when it's wrapped around their necks and cutting off their air supply.

She's also strong as fuck. I think her dad knew Zeus or something like that. Finally, there's Book-Hockey Man. He's the newest member. He's one of those DIY superhero types that has no superhuman abilities, so he's got to work extra hard to look like he fits in. I think his gimmick has something to do with combining intellect with physical strength, which is where the name comes from, but whenever someone says Book-Hockey Man, all I hear is Bukkake Man. I mean, he has to know, right? Anyway, that's the Superhuman Squad. And when it comes to Dolph the Unicorn Killer, they're all filled up.

Whatever.

Fuck 'em.

Maybe next time I'll include a personal essay.

I can break down for them the anatomy of killing a unicorn. I know death is the part they frown upon, but we're talking about fucking unicorns. Cows are way cooler than unicorns, but that didn't stop the Superhuman Squad from signing an endorsement deal with McDonald's. For Christ's sake, there are Happy Meals with their faces on them all over the country and inside are little action figures tucked beside the remains of murdered cows. But, somehow I'm the asshole for killing unicorns.

My process is pretty simple. I walk around the city and look for unicorns. If I see one, I kill it. I make it sound easy, of course, but it's not. For one, unicorns have wings and I can't fly, so if I can't keep the fight on the ground, then they usually get away. Not always, though. I've got gadgets for shooting them down, but it's always best if I don't have to use them. Unicorns are also really strong. I mean, they're basically horses, but magical. No matter how strong they are, my blade slips into them just as easily as it would you. So, put me in striking distance and I can kill the fucker.

Unicorns don't exist in huge numbers and they generally don't travel in groups. Last time I killed a unicorn was about a week ago. Lemon Drop Sunshine was his name. He'd been on my radar for a few months, especially with the rash of unsolved human murders that have been piling up at an alarming rate. I know Golden Showers is out there and he's got his horn involved in these murders, but he's not doing them all. The unicorn I killed before Lemon Drop Sunshine dropped his name right before I decapitated her and shoved her horn up her ass.

I saw Lemon Drop Sunshine walking around the park in the middle of the day. I was decked out in my unicorn killer gear, ready to roll as always. Lemon Drop was sniffing around a family that was having a picnic. The only member of the family paying Lemon Drop any attention was the toddler on the middle of the blanket. The toddler's parents thought the goofy sounds and expressions he was making was for them, but he was responding to Lemon Drop. I marched toward the picnic, hoping to close in before Lemon Drop knew I was there. But when he lowered his horn, I knew I couldn't wait. I drew my sword and began sprinting.

"Hey!" I yelled.

They all looked at me, including Lemon Drop. The toddler's mom and dad screamed as they picked up the kid and ran in the opposite direction. I didn't mind that they thought I was coming to kill them, so long as they left me alone with Lemon Drop Sunshine. The unicorn snorted and shook out his mane, before pointing his horn in my direction.

"You want some of this, bitch?"

"I don't want *some*," I said. "I want it *all!*"

He charged towards me, horn first. I kept sprinting forward. Just when he was a few feet away, I slid on my back between Lemon Drop's legs, and sliced my sword through his knees.

"You fucking son of bitch!" he screamed.

"Scream all you want, motherfucker," I said. "I'm the only one who can hear you."

Lemon Drop Sunshine opened his wings, hoping to take off, but I was already anticipating this move. I swung my sword through the stem of his left wing, clipping it clean off his back. He rolled around the grass, crying and blubbering. I slipped my sword back in its sheath and took out my knife, the one I use for up-close-and-personal attention. I straddled his neck, holding my blade just beneath his throat.

"You're as good as dead, Lemon Drop."

His eyes grew wide.

"That's right," I said. "I know your name."

"Fuck you," he said, spitting his sugary saliva in my face. "You think I don't know who you are? You think any of us don't know? You're a fucking murdering coward!"

"I'm tired of listening to you talk," I said. "I'm going to kill you no matter what, but you have a chance to make it easier for yourself. Unless you want to die with your horn shoved up your ass, tell me where I can find Golden Showers."

Lemon Drop didn't say anything. I would've ripped his head off right then, but I realized he was looking past me, over my shoulder.

I turned and saw a pink unicorn standing in the grass on her hind legs, wings fully expanded. Turning back to Lemon Drop, I quickly punched my blade into his throat fifteen or twenty times, until crimson corn syrup was bleeding from his nose and mouth. I jumped up, ready for another fight, but the pink unicorn just stood there.

"You want to avenge your friend?" I asked. "Come get some."

"I wouldn't call him a friend," the pink unicorn said. "I barely knew him. What I did know, I didn't like. You're Dolph the Unicorn Killer, right?"

"The one and only," I said. "And you're about to find out why."

I pulled out my sword and started towards her.

"If you really want to find Golden Showers," she said, "you'd better play nice."

I stopped in my tracks.

"Atta boy," she said. "Now put your sword away so we can talk."

I hesitated, but if this unicorn knew anything about Golden Showers, I couldn't take a chance.

"What's your name?"

"Pink Gash," she said. "My friends call me Pinky. So, you can call me Pink Gash."

"All right, Pink Gash, tell me everything you know about Golden Showers."

"Easy, cowboy," she said. "What kind of floozy do you take me for?"

"I don't have time for banter."

"Look, I'm not an idiot," she said. "I tell you where Golden Showers is and you have no more use for me. You'll kill me just like you did ol' Sunshine here."

She was one hundred percent right.

"How long do I have to go without killing you?"

"Is that a real question?"

"You got a real answer?"

"I'd rather you not kill me at all."

"I'd rather you not be a unicorn," I said, "but those are the cards we've been dealt."

Pink Gash lifted her hoof, so I pulled out my sword.

"Easy," she said, reaching into her mane. "I'm just grabbing a smoke."

She pulled a cigarette from her mane, placing it on her bottom lip.

"Got a light?"

I did.

Turns out Pink Gash worked for Golden Showers. He was some sort of entrepreneur in the unicorn community. Before she got involved with him, she was living in a small town a hundred or so miles from where we are now. She went to unicorn school, had crushes on unicorn boys, and generally drove her unicorn parents crazy. One day she was walking home and she got snatched up.

"Kidnapped," she said.

"You guys call it *kid*napped?"

"You think humans have a monopoly on words?"

"I just thought maybe *unicorn*napped."

"You're being ridiculous," she said. "*You're* not a kid. What would you call it if someone snatched you away from your family? *Unicornkiller* napped?"

"Fair enough."

When she was kidnapped, Pink Gash found herself in the back of a large truck with several other unicorns, all of them in various states of confusion and distress. They drove like that for days, before ending up in the backroom of an ice cream shop. That's where she met Golden Showers and his two human collaborators.

"We create the supply."

"What do you mean?"

"We stock the ice cream shop with our excrement," she said. "We poop ice cream, we ejaculate syrup, we shake dandruff toppings from our fur. They take shavings from our hooves and even bottle our tears and urine. Whatever they can get from us, they use. They even poke needles into us and draw our blood. We're dessert slaves."

Dessert slaves. I'd never heard of such a thing, but my gut told me Pink Gash was telling the truth. She said different unicorns produced different flavors, so they had all sorts locked up to produce inventory for the ice cream shop.

"What's it called?"

"I can't tell you that."

"Why?"

"Then you'd be able to find it," she said, "and you won't need me alive anymore. And I've done too much to survive this long to let you go and kill me."

"Speaking of which," I said, "if you're a slave, how are you out here talking to me?"

"What do you think, genius?" she said. "I escaped."

The backdoor was left open, she told me, so she made a run for it. She didn't know if any of the others got away, but she couldn't wait around to find out. It seems she'd only been out a few hours when she happened upon Lemon Drop Sunshine. She'd heard rumors about me but was never certain I was real.

"But, if you were real," she said, "I knew I needed to meet you."

"And why's that?"

"I want you to kill Golden Showers."

"Is that right?"

"You bet your ass it is."

"Well, you're in luck," I said, "because that makes two of us, sweetheart."

I'm sitting poolside, naked but for a pair of Speedos and a slick of suntan oil, soaking in rays while Pink Gash enjoys a swim. Joe brings out a Caesar salad and a piña colada on a silver tray, setting it down beside me. I tell him we have a guest and he's being rude.

"I don't see a guest, Master Dolph."

"In the pool."

"In the pool?"

"Pink Gash."

"Pink Gash?"

"She's a unicorn."

"She's a unicorn?"

"Would you stop adding a fucking question mark to everything I goddamn I say, Joe?"

"Sorry, Master Dolph," he says. "I just, well—"

"Yeah, yeah, I know, you can't see her," I say. "Obviously."

I call out to Pink Gash and ask her to splash around. When she does, all Joe sees is the pool splashing water all by itself, which causes him to faint. Pink Gash swims up beside him, asking if he's all right.

"He's fine," I say. "When he wakes up, he'll bring you a salad and a piña colada."

"Are you sure he's all right?"

"The only thing I'm sure of is my hatred of Golden Showers," I say. "So, when will you take me to him?"

"I think we should take Joe inside."

"Fine."

We carry Joe into his bedroom in the basement. Pink Gash won't let me leave him there because she's concerned the lack of air conditioning, electricity, and a bed isn't conducive to his recovery. So, instead, we take him up to my bedroom. Pink Gash insists we stay until he wakes up, so I sit on my couch and turn on one of my ten televisions. Pink Gash stands at Joe's bedside, looking over him. When he finally wakes up he only sees me in the room.

"What happened?"

"You fainted by the pool."

"Yes, I remember," he says. "You said there was a unicorn splashing water."

"No," I say. "There *was* a unicorn splashing water. That's a fact. And that same unicorn is standing by my bed which you're laying in."

Joe looks to both sides of the bed, confused.

"You should be nice to him," Pink Gash says. "He's had a bad accident."

"Why don't *you* be nice to him?"

"Who are you talking to, Master Dolph?"

"The fucking *unicorn!*" I say. "Jesus, how hard did you hit your fucking head?"

"You know, this is all probably very confusing to him," Pink Gash says. "He hit his head, he's foggy, he's trying to process the reality of a unicorn being in the room. Maybe just give him a break."

"Oh, you want to be his best friend now?" I say. "Hey, Joe, guess what? You've got a best fucking friend. She's a unicorn that you can't see. Her name is Pink Gash."

"Dude," Pink Gash says, "chill out."

"No, this is great," I say. "You guys can be best friends. Hey Joe, tell Pink Gash your life story like best friends do."

"Master Dolph, I don't see anybody else in here."

"Well talk to the empty fucking room," I say, before storming out.

I go back to the pool, where I enjoy the salad and piña colada Joe prepared for me. As always, Joe's meals are reliably delicious.

I assumed Pink Gash would've followed me out of the room, but she doesn't. So, since I'm still mostly naked, I take a dip in the pool. Floating atop the surface, arms out, face towards the sky, I'm totally relaxed for the first time in a long time. For all the luxuries I have access to, I rarely take advantage of them, on account of being a superhero. Really, if it weren't for Pink Gash holding up my progress with Golden Showers, I'd be on the streets right this very moment doing what I do. So, in a roundabout way, I'm actually sort of grateful for the reprieve.

I close my eyes and drift off to a place not far from sleep. I think about being a boy, about having Mother and Father, about growing up in a candy store. I think about being surrounded by butlers and Joe and unicorns and the Superhuman Squad and how I've hardly taken a moment to stop and reflect on it all. I think about what it's all meant, how it's made me the man I am today. I'm sad Mother and Father aren't alive today, that they didn't have the opportunity to see me grow into a man. I'm sad also that they never saw me become a superhero, but I also know that were it not for their murders at the horn of Golden Showers, I never would've become Dolph the Unicorn Killer. On the other hand, I still would've gotten struck by lightning and I still would've gained the ability to see unicorns, so I can only imagine that would've manifested into something. Right?

I open my eyes and look around. For a moment I forget that I'm a grown man. I feel like the little boy who grew up with every material thing he could've ever wanted. But, just as it was when I was a boy, I'm alone. A wandering soul set loose in his vast inherited kingdom. But, even that's not true. There's always been Joe. Maybe Pink Gash is right. Maybe I do need to be nicer to Joe. I mean, I won't jump to any conclusions, because he's still Joe and all—but maybe I could remember from time to time that he's a person, like me. That once upon a time, he too was a little boy. Maybe he even had hopes and dreams.

I get out of the pool, towel off, and walk back up to my bedroom to see Joe. I don't know what I'll say, but I feel like I need to be there with him. As I get to the door, I hear Joe screaming in agony and in that moment I realize what a fool I've been. Pink Gash was always a fucking unicorn and I left Joe in there alone with her. I'm sure I'll probably never forgive myself for what I'm about to see on the other side of the door, but I have no choice but to go inside. I enter my bedroom—still wearing only Speedos, but ready to fight—and see something that I never imagined in a million billion years I'd ever see.

Pink Gash is giving Joe a blowjob.

From Joe's perspective, all he sees is his erect cock poking through his fly and being slobbered on by some invisible force. His eyes are bulged nearly out of his head and his arms extend at his sides, gripping the sheets in both hands. I walk in just at the moment of climax, Joe's back arching as he shoots a load into Pink Gash's long pink mouth. Joe melts into the bed, panting, as Pink Gash licks her lips and looks my way.

"I hope you weren't waiting for your turn," she says. "It's not that type of party."

"Sorry, I didn't mean to interrupt."

"You didn't interrupt," she says. "It's about to be my turn, so you can stay if you want to watch. It *is* that type of party."

"No, no," I say, "I'm fine. I'll leave you to it."

I close the door just as Pink Gash gingerly straddles Joe's face. I have no idea what to do with myself. I mean, what do you do after seeing the man who raised you sucked off by a unicorn? I take a shower, rubbing one out while I'm in there—*not* thinking about unicorns, mind you—put on my unicorn killing gear, and sit in the kitchen waiting for Joe to bring me something to eat. I'm in there a good half-hour before I hear footsteps moving down the stairs. By the time they hit the tile floor, I recognize them as hoof-steps and soon thereafter Pink Gash joins me in the kitchen. She takes a seat at the kitchen table with me, pulling a cigarette from her mane and setting it on her bottom lip.

"Light?" she asks.

I light her cigarette and she leans back, taking a drag before exhaling a long, satisfied breath.

"That man," she says. "Very, very talented."

"I take it he can call you Pinky."

"He can call me whatever he wants."

"Does he have any idea what happened?"

"How could he?" she asks. "He probably thinks he hallucinated the best fuck of his life. Doesn't mean he didn't enjoy it."

"I didn't realize unicorns liked fucking humans."

"There are a whole lot of things you probably don't know about unicorns," she says. "For instance, all unicorns aren't murderers. Hell, all unicorns aren't bad. In fact, most unicorns aren't bad at all. We're no more inherently evil than humans are.

"Bullshit," I say. "I've killed enough unicorns to know you guys are basically assholes."

"Am I an asshole?"

I pause.

Fuck.

"No," I say, "but that's different."

"What's different about me?"

"You're kind of pleasant," I say, "and you haven't tried killing me or Joe. That doesn't mean anything, though. You're the exception that proves the rule."

"Why is it that you seem to know me better than any other unicorn you've interacted with?"

"I don't know," I say. "I guess because we've spent time talking and I've gotten to know you."

She smiles.

Fuck.

"Doesn't mean the unicorns I killed weren't evil."

"Doesn't mean they *were*," she says. "And now you'll never know. You know, there are bad unicorns and they actually do harm humans, sometimes even killing them. I can't pretend to know all of their motives, but I've known more than a few unicorns that have used *you* as the example that represents all humans. So, in their minds, if one human kills unicorns, they *all* kill unicorns. How many human deaths do you suppose are *your* fault, Dolph?"

"Now that's a stretch."

"Is it?" she asks. "You don't think there could possibly be even *one* human life taken by a unicorn because they sought vengeance for *your* actions?"

I pause.

Fuck.

"And if there was even just *one* human life lost," she says, "would that not be one too many?"

Pink Gash takes a drag from her cigarette, exhaling towards the ceiling, never taking her eyes off me.

"What do you want me to say?"

"That I'm right," she says, "and you're wrong."

"Fuck that," I say. "Golden Showers killed my parents."

"Maybe he did," she says. "But, I didn't. Lemon Drop Sunshine didn't. Every unicorn you've ever killed didn't. You say you kill unicorns to avenge your parents, but some part of you has to know true justice wasn't being served. And you say you want to find Golden Showers, but what happens after you do?"

"I'll kill him."

"And then what?"

Silence.

"Once you kill Golden Showers, you'll have avenged your parents," she says. "Do you continue on as Dolph the Unicorn Killer? Or do you move on with your life? Who are you if you're not a unicorn killer? What purpose do you serve? What happens to your identity? And, the most important question of all, do you truly even wish to find Golden Showers?"

"Of course I do."

"Because, I can tell you, he's no more than fifteen minutes from where we sit right this very moment."

"He's elusive."

"Is that what it is, Dolph?"

"What else could it be?"

"Like I asked before," she says, "who does Dolph the Unicorn Killer become when Golden Showers is dead?"

"I have an ability," I say. "I was struck by lightning and it gave me the ability to see unicorns. If I take that ability and do nothing with it, then I'm the asshole."

Pink Gash chuckles.

"You think lightning did that to you?"

"I *know* it did."

"How do you know this?"

"Because I got struck by lightning," I say, "and after that I saw Golden Showers."

"Let me hip you to something, Killer," she says. "Lightning has nothing to do with unicorns or a human's ability to see them. There are things in the world that just don't make sense, because we don't know enough about the world to understand them. We unicorns simply accept that the world is big and mysterious and we don't have all the answers. But, you humans will dumb shit down and add the most elementary logic in order to make sense of the world. What if you got struck by lightning and the next day you had your first wet dream? Would you start applying you caveman math to work out that lightning gave you the ability to shoot a load in your sheets?"

"Here's the fallacy in that argument," I say. "I was always going to have the ability to shoot loads in my sheets. I was born with it. It was in me."

"And?"

"And seeing unicorns wasn't."

"Of course it was."

"I don't think so."

"Well, I *know* so," she says. "Whether that lightning hit you or not, you were born exactly the way you are. No outside force made you this way. It's just you."

"So, why didn't I see unicorns before?"

Pink Gash shrugs.

"Maybe they weren't hanging around your big mansion."

"But, Golden Showers broke in."

"Interesting, right?"

She smiles, taking a drag from her cigarette.

"Is there something you're not telling me?"

She exhales a plume of smoke.

"What do you know about Joe?" she asks.

"I've known Joe my whole life."

"Yeah, but what do you *really* know about him?"

I pause.

Fuck.

"That's what I figured," she says.

"What the fuck do you know about him?"

"I know he grew up an orphan," she says. "I know his dad wasn't around and his mom died from some disease she got fucking junkies for cash. I know he raised himself on the streets, digging through trashcans for food and mugging people so he could spend the night in a shitty motel once in a while. I know he tried to mug a boxing coach who took the time to talk to him and convinced him to show up to the gym the next day. I know he became Golden Gloves champion and very nearly qualified for the Olympics. I know he joined the army and went away to fight in whatever pointless human war was going on at the time, watching his friends die, while managing to save a few others on his way to earning a Medal of Honor. I know he couldn't find a job when he came home until he met your parents and they hired him as your caretaker. I know they faked the mugging in the alley when you were a kid, putting Joe up to it because they thought it'd be funny. I know Joe loves you dearly and beams with pride when he talks about you like you were his very own son. And I know he fucks like a stallion and eats pussy like he was born with three tongues."

"Where'd you learn all that?"

"Joe told it to me."

"When?"

"After you stormed out of the bedroom like a big baby," she says. "Before you left, I believe your words were, 'Hey Joe, tell Pink Gash your life story like best friends do.' And when Joe told you there was nobody in the room—because, obviously, he couldn't see me—you told him, 'Well talk to the empty fucking room.' So, he did."

"But, when Joe mugged us in the alley, he wanted Mother's pearl necklace," I say. "It was made of sugar. And after he started working for us, he accepted several of those pearl necklaces as payments for a year. So, if he was in on everything, why would he do that?"

"Well, honestly, I don't think Joe's very smart."

"No, he's not."

"But, what he lacks in brains, he makes up for in heart," she says. "I mean, you're a fucking maniac, Dolph. But, the fact that you have any ability at all to function as a semi-civilized human being is because of Joe. I shudder to think of the man you would've become if Joe weren't in your life."

I pause.

Fuck.

She's right and I know it. All these years, I was begging for a chance to avenge Mother and Father's murders, cursing the world for leaving me alone in the world. But, I was never really alone.

I feel a tap on my shoulder and instinctively turn around to slap Joe in the face. I don't even know how I knew it was him, but I guess that's just the sort of bond we have.

"Make me a sandwich."

"Really, Dolph?" Pink Gash says.

"You're right," I say. "Joe, make me a sandwich, *please*."

While Joe makes my sandwich, I tell him that he's fucked a unicorn named Pink Gash, but he can call her Pinky. I also tell him she's very impressed with his abilities as a lover and that she probably wouldn't mind another bounce on his pogo stick. He seems very confused, which I attribute to him hitting his head by the pool. I ask him what he thought was happening when he felt his cock getting slobbed on and he says he assumed it was all just a lucid dream. I assure him it was all very real and his conquest is hanging out in the kitchen with us. I also tell him that Pink Gash knows where Golden Showers is and she's agreed to take me to him.

"When?"

I look at Pink Gash for an answer.

"How about you finish your sandwich," she says, "then we'll go."

I fill Joe in on the timeline and he insists on going with me.

"I don't think it's a good idea," I say. "Plus, you won't really see what's going on when I'm killing Golden Showers."

"I may not be able to see it," Joe says, "but I still want to be there when he gets what's coming to him."

"Okay," I say. "And Joe?"

"Yes?"

"Too much mustard."

Pink Gash takes Joe and me to a quaint ice cream shop tucked between a thrift store and a dry cleaner. It's where Golden Showers profits from the sweet excrement of kidnapped unicorns. I see no unicorns inside the shop, but Pink Gash says they work in a warehouse around the back. So, that's where we go. The three of us walk back towards the door leading into the warehouse and I can't quite shake the feeling that something isn't right. It's all somehow too easy.

"So, what do we do?" I ask.

"Do whatever you want," Pink Gash says. "Golden Showers is behind that door."

"What are *you* going to do?"

"I'm going to watch."

"That's it?"

"This isn't my fight."

"It sort of is, don't you think?"

"Why do you say that?"

"He kidnapped you."

She hesitates.

"Right," she says. "He sure did. Good luck in there."

With Joe at my side, I kick the door in and enter the warehouse. I'm immediately overwhelmed by the sugary aromas in the air. There are unicorns everywhere—all different colors, sizes, and genders—working together to shit, piss, and ejaculate delicious ice cream ingredients. They all look at me, of course, on account of my dramatic entrance and the large sword I wield. To my surprise, none of them gives me a look of hope or gratitude like I'd just come to rescue them. They actually look sort of annoyed.

"I'm looking for Golden Showers."

"Who's looking for him?" one of the unicorns asks.

"The man who's going to kill him."

That statement—more than the sword and me kicking down the door—causes a panic and the unicorns start shouting and running around, knocking over buckets and trays, pushing each other into conveyor belts as they try to take cover. From all of the chaos, one unicorn calmly steps forward. I look him up and down, taking it all in.

Golden mane.

Pink wings.

Deadly fucking pink horn.

"Golden Showers."

"That's what they call me."

"Not for much longer."

"You shouldn't be here."

"Too late for that," I say. "You remember me?"

"I don't know," he says. "Should I?"

"You pissed on my every night for years when I was a kid."

"Listen, man," he says, "I pissed on a lot of people, so you're going to have to be more specific than that."

"You also killed my parents."

This brings a hush over every unicorn in the warehouse.

"Whoa, whoa, whoa," he says, "I've done a lot of things in my life, but murder is not one of them."

"Unfortunately for you," I say, "I don't believe you."

I lift my sword and begin running towards him. Despite his much larger size, Golden Showers actually recoils in fear. Before I can go through with killing him, Joe calls out to me.

"Dolph, wait!"

I stop running, sliding on my boots toward Golden Showers, stopping just as the tip of my sword is about to touch his throat.

"What is it?" I ask, keeping my eyes on Golden Showers.

"Your parents."

"What about them?"

"I'm looking at them."

"Joe," I say, "I think maybe you hit your head a little harder than we thought."

Golden Showers squints his eyes at me, giving me a good looking over.

"Wait a minute," he says. "Dolph? As in Adolph? Adolph König?"

He smiles.

"You guys," he says, turning to the other unicorns in the warehouse, "I used to piss on this dude every night when he was a kid."

"So, you *do* remember me."

"Yeah, of course," he says. "You know, your parents put me up to that, right?"

"Fuck you."

"Seriously," he says. "They're the ones who let me in the house. They wanted me to piss on you. Every night. They thought it would give you character."

"You're a fucking liar."

"Think so?" he says. "Why don't you ask them yourself?"

The unicorns in the warehouse part in unison, creating a chasm that reveals Mother and Father. I see them, but I know it can't be them. This is Golden Showers playing some devious trick. This is what evil super-villains do, they create holograms of a boy's murdered parents to disorient him, making him vulnerable to an attack. Mother and Father begin walking towards me. When they're standing right in front of me, I put my sword in its sheath and reach my hands out to touch them, fully expecting to pass through their extremely realistic images. But, my hands land firm on their shoulders.

"Mother?" I ask. "Father? Is it really you?"

"Yes, Adolph," Father says. "It's us."

"I don't understand," I say. "I saw you dead in our kitchen with holes through your chests."

"We were certainly close to death," Mother says, "there's no getting around that. But, thanks to the miracle of modern science and our endless supply of money, we managed to survive."

"But, we had a funeral," I say. "I was inconsolable."

"I'm sure you were quite inconsolable," Father says. "But, that's what we hired Joe for."

"You hired him to console me after you faked your murders?"

"No, we hired him to look after you so we could focus on König Kandy," Mother says. "And we didn't fake our murders, mind you. We just didn't tell you we survived."

"But, that's really fucked up."

"It was all for a good purpose," Father says. "Mother and I had been wanting to branch out and start an ice cream parlor. So, our supposed murders freed us up immensely to give all of our attention to it. And, we're happy to say the ice cream parlor is flourishing."

"This is *your* operation?"

They nod and smile, beaming with pride.

"Then what's Golden Showers doing here?"

"He's the foreman," Father says.

"We brought him over from König Kandy after our 'murders,'" Mother says, putting air quotes around "murders."

"So, you can see unicorns?"

Mother and Father look at each other and laugh.

"Why, yes, of course we can," Father says. "We see them and we've been working with them for decades. We couldn't have built König Kandy without unicorns, such as Golden Showers. He was always such a good boy. A real hard worker, full of character."

"But, you asked him to piss on me every night!"

"Yes and we hope you've developed some character because of it."

"Hey, Pinky!" Golden Showers says, looking past me. "Where the hell have you been?"

"I took a break."

"Yeah, a long fucking break," he says. "Get back to work."

"I don't want to."

"Tough shit."

She steps forward, standing at my side.

"I don't want to work for you anymore."

Golden Showers looks at me, then back at Pink Gash.

"Wait a minute," he says, "*you* brought him here?"

"Yup."

"Were you going to let him kill me?"

She shrugs.

"You bitch," he says, "you were going to let this asshole kill me! And all because you didn't want to work for me anymore?"

"Yup."

"Why didn't you just quit?"

She shrugs again.

"Come to think of it," Golden Showers says, "where's Lemon Drop Sunshine? Did he leave with you?"

"Sort of."

"So, where is he?"

"Dolph killed him."

A collective gasp sounds from the unicorns in the warehouse.

"Adolph," Mother says, "is this true? Did you kill Lemon Drop Sunshine?"

"Well, yeah," I say. "That's sort of what I do. I'm Dolph the Unicorn Killer."

"You kill unicorns?" Father asks.

"How did you two *not* know that?"

"We've been very busy with the ice cream parlor," Mother says. "We haven't had time to pay attention to you."

"You didn't pay any attention to me all these years?"

"Like we told you," Father says, "that's what Joe was for."

I turn to Joe, who's standing just behind me. For him, all he sees is an empty warehouse with Mother, Father, and me.

"Joe," I say, "did you know Mother and Father were alive?"

"No."

I look to Mother and Father.

"Is that true?"

"Yes," Mother says.

"So, our family fortune was built on unicorns," I say. "And my ability to see unicorns was passed onto me by you two and not a bolt of lightning. And you hired Joe to take care of me and asked Golden Showers to piss on me every night. And you almost died, but didn't, and you let me think you *had* died so you could focus on a new ice cream business. Is that about the long and the short of it?"

"Yes," Father says, "I'd say so."

"Then I have one more question," I say. "Who attacked you in our kitchen and left you for dead?"

Before they can answer, a loud crash sounds from the entrance of the warehouse. The unicorns begin scrambling again, causing a tremendous commotion as I turn to look behind me. The door has been knocked clean off its hinges and a large black unicorn, rippling with muscles and fury, charges towards me, leading with his big black horn. I unsheathe my sword and take a battle stance, ready to face whoever this big bastard is. But, just as he's within striking distance, Joe throws himself in front of me.

It all happens as if in slow motion, Joe flying through the air horizontally just as the big black horn bursts through his spine. Pink Gash screams while the other unicorns scramble out of the warehouse. The black unicorn whips his powerful neck around, thrashing Joe's body to and fro until he slides off his horn and crashes with a dull thud against the nearest wall. The unicorns continue stampeding out of the warehouse. There are so many of them, I can't even see the black unicorn anymore. And when all the unicorns have exited, the black unicorn has disappeared.

"There's your answer," Father says.

"Answer to what?" I ask.

"That's the unicorn that left us for dead."

"Licorice Knight Mare," Mother says. "He's quite the nuisance."

I don't care about Licorice Knight Mare—not yet anyway—so I run to check on Joe. His eyes are open and I hope against hope that maybe he's okay, that maybe the damage isn't as bad as it appears. But, the hole in his chest is wide and I can see clear through to the concrete floor on the other side. I kneel beside him, cradling his head in my lap. Here I am, fancying myself a superhero, but Joe, in the final moments of his life, sacrificed himself to save mine. He didn't even hesitate. He saw Licorice Knight Mare coming for me and—

Wait.

What?

"Joe sacrificed himself to save me."

"That's right," Father says. "Quite a tragedy."

"Quite a tragedy, indeed," Mother said. "We never paid him to die. Pity."

"That's not my point you fucking psychopaths," I say. "Joe could only do that if he saw Licorice Knight Mare charging at me. Is Licorice Knight Mare *not* a unicorn?"

"He most definitely is a unicorn," Father says.

"So, does that mean Joe had the ability to see unicorns?"

"No," Mother says.

"Then what the fuck?"

"Licorice Knight Mare is a peculiar beast," Father says. "For reasons that nobody understands, he's a unicorn that is visible to humans of all ages."

"What was he doing here?"

"He hates humans," Pink Gash says.

"You know him?"

"I don't know him personally," she says, "but I know *of* him. Every unicorn does. He's quite a polarizing figure in the unicorn community. Some see him as a Robin Hood type, but instead of stealing from the rich and giving to the poor, he kills humans. Others see him as a maniac tyrant who is only acting in his own self-interest."

"He *is* a tyrant," Father says. "He's tried often to take our lives."

"And he's come close to succeeding a few times," Mother says. "If it weren't for the miracles of modern medical science and our bottomless wealth, we would have been dead long ago."

"If he tried to kill you before and you survived," I ask, "does that mean you can save Joe?"

"I don't think so," Father says.

"I believe your father misspoke," Mother says. "It's a hard no."

"You won't even try?"

"What would be the point?" Father asks.

"He takes care of me."

"There are several other butlers we pay to do the same."

"But, he's my friend."

"It was never our intention for Joe to be your friend," Mother says. "At any rate, mourning his death will give you character."

"You're a monster," I say.

"Now, Adolph—" Father starts.

"No, you're both monsters," I say. "I can't believe how many years I wasted seeking vengeance for you assholes."

I turn my back to them, walking towards the busted entrance.

"Adolph, wait," Mother says.

I stop.

"What about Joe?" she asks.

"What about him?"

"You're not just going to leave him here, are you?"

I know the right thing to do is to take Joe's body with me so that I can give him a proper burial. But, I decide it's more fitting to leave his dead body for my parents to reckon with. It isn't much, but it makes me feel a little better. And I have to believe Joe would've been okay with that. I turn back and start walking. Pink Gash walks at my side. Mother and Father continue calling after me to take Joe. I ignore them and, as I exit the warehouse, I quietly wish to never see them again.

Vengeance, murder, and unicorns.

Though a few of the faces may have changed, I find myself exactly where I began. I will find Licorice Knight Mare and, when I do, I will kill him. Joe's death will not go unavenged, not while I'm breathing. Licorice Knight Mare is definitely not your average unicorn and not just because humans of all ages can see him. He's bigger and stronger than any unicorn I've ever seen—and he has a mean streak the likes of which I've never encountered. If I'm going to get vengeance for Joe, then I have to comes terms with the fact that I'm not invincible. I'm going to need help. A lot of it.

Pink Gash immediately offers her services. She's not a fighter, per se, but she knows the unicorn community, so she can be of major use in helping to locate Licorice Knight Mare. She makes it very clear to me that she's not helping just because it's the right thing to do. For Pink Gash, it's personal. "I never got to go back for seconds," she says, "and for that, Licorice Knight Mare deserves to die." Pink Gash is turning out to be quite ruthless, which is good because we'll need as much of that as we can get. But, no matter how much she wants to help, I know we'll need more than the two of us to bring down Licorice Knight Mare. We'll need a squad.

The Superhuman Squad.

Getting in touch with the Superhuman Squad is surprisingly easy, considering how often they've rejected my application to join their crew. I don't bother calling their toll-free number because I've been down that useless road before:

Press 1 if you're in danger.

Press 2 if you'd like an autographed photo.

Press 3 if you're an evil mastermind bent on world domination.

Press 4 if you need 9-1-1.

Press 5 to speak with an operator.

Don't bother pressing 5, because all you get is elevator music and a perpetual stream of advertisements for all of the products they endorse. Instead, I go straight to my pal Arnel. He designs superhero costumes. Any superhero who cares to be fashion-forward works with Arnel. He's the best in town. Ever since he designed my Unicorn Killer outfit, I don't go anywhere else. Before I met Arnel, I was constructing my own half-assed costumes with Joe's help. For the first few months of my career as Dolph the Unicorn Killer, I'd been wearing a cape, because I assumed capes were a superhero staple. Arnel, in his otherworldly wisdom, told me to ditch the cape. He then designed a cool and functional costume, including a badass emblem for my chest—a unicorn horn with a circle and slash over it. He also offered to design a mask, but I said no. I wasn't going to be a superhero that hid behind a mask and cowered around in a secret identity. Arnel respected that and we've been cool ever since.

I hit him up for the address to the Superhuman Squad's head-quarters, but he doesn't know where it's at. Instead, he gives me something almost as valuable: The Squad Signal. More specifically, he gives me the coordinates to where I'll find it. The Squad Signal is a giant spotlight that flashes into the sky whenever the Superhuman Squad needs to be quickly assembled. It doesn't do much good for the crime that occurs during the day, but it's useful if super villains are terrorizing you in the evening. Arnel and a few select members of the local law enforcement have access to it. And now, so do I.

The Squad Signal sits on the rooftop of a relatively anonymous building in an unsavory part of town, presumably the sort of place you'd imagine superheroes to be most necessary. Pink Gash invites me to saddle up on her back, before flying us there. I turn on the signal, then wait on the roof with Pink Gash for several hours because the sun hasn't set yet. But, as soon as night falls, Lima Lad shows up, huffing and puffing as he'd run all the way up the stairs to the rooftop. "The elevator's broke," he says, short of apologizing for his poor cardio. Turns out he lives in the building.

Lima Lad is now the first Superhuman Squad member I've ever seen in person and he's every bit as impressive as he looks on television—which is to say, not very. He's just a scrawny teenager in a lima outfit. He's timid, so he doesn't speak again until Courageous Man shows up, soaring through the air and landing on the rooftop beside the Squad Signal. He sees me first, then looks at Lima Lad. I detect a flash of jealousy in his eyes, as he tries to work out whether or not I've defiled his little lima buddy. Lima Lad takes a few moments to soothe Courageous Man with a flirtatious batting of his lima lashes.

Fantastic Femme shows up next, pulling up to the sidewalk on her invisible motorcycle, before climbing the fire escape to the rooftop. Book-Hockey Man is the last to arrive, parking his Book-Hockey Van behind Fantastic Femme's invisible motorcycle. He puts on a pair of suction cup gloves from his Book-Hockey pouch and scales the brick building all the way to the rooftop. Shoulder to shoulder, there they stand.

The Superhuman Squad.

"I take it you know who I am."

"Dolph the Unicorn Killer," Courageous Man says. "Who's your friend?"

"You can see me?" Pink Gash says.

"I can hear you, too," Courageous Man says. "What's your name?"

"Pink Gash."

"Who're you talking to C-Man?" Lima Lad asks.

"There's a unicorn standing beside Dolph."

"Did you bring us here to watch you kill it?" Book-Hockey Man asks.

"I'm not going to kill her," I say. "She's here to help."

"Help with what?" Fantastic Femme asks, holding her Whip of Integrity in her hands.

"She's helping me do what superheroes do," I say. "Kill bad guys."

"You know, that's exactly the sort of attitude that keeps you out of our group," Courageous Man says. "We don't kill. We bring evil to justice."

"And I bring justice to evil," I say, "which usually involves killing somebody who deserves it."

"What are you even doing here?" Book-Hockey Man asks.

"I've come here to ask for help."

"How did you find our Squad Signal?"

"Arnel."

"Oh, you know Arnel," he says. "How's he been? I haven't seen him in a while."

"He's good," I say. "Busy. Lots of superheroes discovering their abilities these days"

"It's that time of year, I suppose," Courageous Man says. "Who exactly do you need our help with?"

"Licorice Knight Mare."

"Never heard of him."

"He's a unicorn," I say. "A very bad unicorn."

"Unicorns are *your* business," Fantastic Femme says. "Besides, Courageous Man is the only one among us who can see them."

"This unicorn can be seen by everybody," I say. "And he's a killer.

I just found out that he's the unicorn who tried to kill my parents."

"Your parents *aren't* dead?" Lima Lad asks.

"No," I say. "I mean, I thought they were, but I saw them yesterday. Turns out they've been alive my whole life. But, Licorice Knight Mare *did* kill my butler."

"That's not quite as tragic as killing your parents," Book-Hockey Man says. "If he'd murdered your parents, you could make a much stronger case."

"Well, I basically figured out that my butler was also my best friend," I say, "only I didn't know it until it was too late. That's pretty tragic, right?"

"It's better," Courageous Man says, "but, still, if your ultimate goal is to kill Licorice Knight Mare, then we can't help you. The Superhero Squad are not killers."

"Maybe not," I say, "but aren't you heroes?"

"Well, duh," Lima Lad says.

Courageous Man presses his finger to Lima Lad's lips.

"Shhh," he says. "Let him finish."

"If I were anybody else," I say, "just some average person on the street coming to you to say my friend had been murdered and I wanted justice, would you turn me away?"

Book-Hockey Man speaks up.

"No," he says, turning to the rest of the Superhuman Squad. "He's right. If we don't help Dolph in his time of need, then what sort of superheroes are we?"

"He wants us to kill," Fantastic Femme says.

"We can bring Licorice Knight Mare to justice without killing him," Book-Hockey Man says. "My Book-Hockey intuition is spurting like a geyser, wetting my face with purpose. And if your faces aren't wet, then maybe I should wet them for you. This is the right thing to do."

"You're right," Courageous Man says. "Dolph loved a man and now that man is dead. He deserves justice. Lima Lad and I are in."

"We are?"

Captain Courageous cups the back of Lima Lad's head.

"Yes," he says, "we are."

"I'm in, too," Fantastic Femme says, cracking her whip. "But, on one condition. We alert the media so they can follow us and document the justice as it happens."

"Obviously, we'll alert the media," Courageous Man says.

"I just wanted to make sure he knew."

And just like that, I'm finally teaming up with the Superhuman Squad.

A week later, our mission was in full swing. Pink Gash had tapped into her network of unicorn connections, managing to track down a grassy hill where Licorice Knight Mare spends her evenings—yeah, turns out Licorice Knight Mare is a *her*. Apparently, "mare" is what you call a female horse. Who the fuck is supposed to know that? And since when do unicorns take on the same pronouns as horses? Turns out Pink Gash knew the whole time, but never corrected me, because she thought it was hilarious to hear me sound like an idiot. Anyway, that's neither here nor there. I'm still going to kill her, so that part hasn't changed.

The Superhuman Squad, Pink Gash, and I head out to the grassy hill to confront Licorice Knight Mare. Courageous Man flies with Lima Lad holding tightly to him, belly to belly, his legs and arms wrapped tightly around his waist. Pink Gash and I ride with Book-Hockey Man in his Book-Hockey van. I sit in front, while Pink Gash fills out the back. I'd asked if she wouldn't be more comfortable flying, but she said she wanted to drive. "I'm not your fucking Uber," she'd told me. Fantastic Femme follows behind us on her invisible motorcycle, while behind her is a throng of media with their cameras at the ready.

In the van, Book-Hockey Man and I make small talk.

"So, there's really a unicorn in the van?"

"Yup."

"That's wild."

"Yeah, it can be hard to believe at first," I say. "Speaking of hard to believe, what do you do?"

"What do you mean?"

"For the Superhuman Squad," I say, "what is it that you do?"

"I'm a detective, mainly," he says. "The Sullen Sleuth they call me."

"Who calls you that?"

"The media."

"Why?"

"I asked them to."

"Are you sullen?"

"I can be."

"You seem pretty good tempered to me."

"Well, you can't believe everything the media says."

As we reach the grassy hill, we see Licorice Knight Mare standing beneath an apple tree, feeding on its fruit. Courageous Man touches down, setting Lima Lad beside him. Fantastic Femme pulls up on her invisible motorcycle and Book-Hockey Man parks his van beside her. We get out of the van and, along with the others, walk towards Licorice Knight Mare. The media keeps a safe distance, snapping pictures and recording footage. Licorice Knight Mare looks confused for a moment, taking in her unexpected audience.

"What do you want?" she asks.

Courageous Man steps forward.

"We want justice for this poor suffering soul," he says, pointing at me. "This man loved another man and that man loved him back. He loved him hard, too, and when you love someone that hard, loving becomes who you are. You become more than human, you become a lover. You killed Dolph's lover and we're here to bring you to justice."

Licorice Knight Mare looks at me.

"Do I know you?" she asks.

"When I was a child," I say, "you attempted to murder my parents."

"That's not ringing a bell."

"They make candy."

She shrugs.

"We lived in a mansion," I say. "They founded König Kandy."

"Oh, right!" she says. "I remember them. I try to kill them all the time."

"Why?"

"They exploit unicorns," she says, "and they're assholes besides. So, what's this guy talking about? I killed your boyfriend or something?"

"Indeed you did," Courageous Man says.

"No, you didn't," I say. "You killed my butler, Joe."

"I did?"

"Yes, about a week ago at the warehouse where my parents had unicorns producing ice cream sundaes."

"Oh, sure," she says. "I remember killing that guy. He was your *butler*?"

"He was also my friend."

"And lover," Courageous Man says.

"If it makes you feel better," Licorice Knight Mare says, "I was trying to kill *you*."

"It doesn't," I say. "But, I'll feel much better if you try again."

"No, no," Courageous Man says. "He doesn't mean that."

"Oh, yes I do," I say, pulling out my sword. "Let's go, Licorice Knight Mare. You and me."

Courageous Man steps in front of me, blocking Licorice Knight Mare from view.

"We talked about this," he says. "We didn't come here to kill Licorice Knight Mare."

"No, we didn't," I said. "But, I did."

"That's just semantics," he says. "I won't let you kill her."

"Try and stop me."

Lima Lad screams and the media begins to scramble. It's not clear what's happening, until I see Licorice Knight Mare's horn pierce through Courageous Man's belly. He looks at me in disbelief, touching his fingers to the bloody tip of the horn. Here he is, the Man with Impenetrable Skin—as the media calls him—being penetrated from behind. Licorice Knight Mare slings Courageous Man off her horn, sending him crashing into the apple tree, uprooting it as it toppled to the grass. Fantastic Femme cracks her whip across Licorice Knight Mare's ass, getting her attention. She lassoes the whip around the unicorn's neck and tries to pull her to the ground, but Licorice Knight Mare is too strong. Pulling against the whip, she tosses Fantastic Femme across the grass. Book-Hockey Man, having seen enough, runs into the Book-Hockey Van and ducks out of sight.

Lima Lad kneels at Courageous Man's side, crying as he presses his dainty hands against the wound in his belly. Licorice Knight Mare charges towards him—head tilted, horn pointed straight ahead. Lima Lad jumps to his feet and shuffles around, trying to figure out where to go, but, while he struggles to make a decision, Licorice Knight Mare buries her horn into his chest, lifting him in the air and whipping him to the ground. She picks him up again, letting his limp body slide down her horn, until he rests across her forehead. I charge for her and, before she can whip Lima Lad back down to the grass, I slice my sword clean through Licorice Knight Mare's horn. Lima Lad falls to the ground with the horn still piercing in his belly.

"Fuck!" Licorice Knight Mare screams. "Do you realize how long it's going to take me to grow another horn?"

I pull the horn out of Lima Lad and point it at Licorice Knight Mare.

"About half-past never."

"That doesn't make sense."

"Just give it a second."

"Is that a catchphrase?"

"No."

"Because if it's a catchphrase, it should resonate as soon as you say it."

"It's not a catchphrase."

"Well, it's gimmicky like a catchphrase."

"Shut up and let me murder you."

"That's an improvement."

"I'm telling you, I don't use catchphrases."

"That's for the best if I'm being honest," she says. "Not that it matters since I'll be murdering you in a bit."

"Why wait."

"Maybe I want to savor the moment," she says. "You ever consider that?"

"Savor it all you want," I say, "because if I ever get murdered by a unicorn, I promise it won't be you."

"We'll see about that."

"Yes," I say, "we'll see who murders who."

"Is it *who* or *whom*?"

"What?"

"You said, 'We'll see who murders *who*,' but, as you said it, I found myself wondering if it's *who* or *whom*."

"I don't know," I say. "Come to think of it, Joe used to tell me if you can replace the word with 'he' or 'she,' then you should use 'who.' But, if you can replace it with 'him' or 'her,' use 'whom.'"

"That's clever," Licorice Knight Mare says, "let me try. We'll see who murders *he*. We'll see who murders *him*. I don't know, it's still kind of tricky, what if—"

"Dolph!" Pink Gash screams.

"What?"

"She's stalling!"

My god, Pink Gash is right. Licorice Nightmare *is* stalling. Cutting her horn off must've made her vulnerable. So, I charge at her with my sword in one hand and her horn in the other. And, perhaps because she knows no other way, she charges back towards me. As

I look into her eyes, I know I'm ready to do whatever is needed to kill her, even if it means dying in the process. Once she's one or two gallops away, I slide to a stop and steady myself, holding my sword at the ready. But, before Licorice Knight Mare can make contact, Pink Gash comes out of nowhere, tackling her to the ground. The black unicorn cries out as Pink Gash shoves her horn deep into her ribs. She pulls it out, before stabbing Licorice Knight Mare again and again, over and over, spilling her onyx blood all over the grass. The air fills with the scent of black jellybeans, as Licorice Knight Mare writhes in pain. I run to join Pink Gash, still holding the horn in my hand.

She looks at the horn.

"You know what to do."

"I sure do."

I get behind Licorice Knight Mare and, with all my strength, shove the horn up her ass, letting my fist disappear completely. The unicorn screams for mercy, but her cries fall on deaf ears. I pull my arm out of her ass and pick up my sword as the media crowds in around us. Licorice Knight Mare closes her eyes as I lift my sword with both hands over my head, swinging it down hard through her neck, chopping her head completely off.

"Whoa," Pink Gash says, "I didn't realize you were going there."

"It just seemed like the moment needed something dramatic to punctuate it."

"I think the horn in the ass kind of checked that box."

"Are you upset?"

"No," she says. "Things just got dark in a hurry."

"I wanted to make sure she was dead."

"Believe me, she wasn't coming back from the beating we put on her."

A voice sounds from the herd of media.

"Whom are you talking to?"

"I'm talking to a unicorn," I say. "Her name is Pink Gash."

She looks at me, smiling.

"You can call me Pinky."

I pose over Licorice Knight Mare's dead carcass as the media snaps photos, records video footage, and asks questions. Pinky stands at my side, smiling for the cameras, perhaps forgetting that they can't capture her image. It doesn't matter, though. She's earned this moment just as much as I have. I finally got my vengeance and I made a new friend along the way. All and all, I'd say things worked out pretty darn good—unless you're Lima Lad. That shit was fucked up.

In the immediate aftermath, I became the most famous superhero in the world thanks to the media's coverage of "The Battle on Apple Hill." That's what they were calling it. I thought it was a terrible title, but nobody seemed to care. My face was all over every newspaper and newscast. Footage of me killing Licorice Knight Mare captured the world's imagination as it proved to millions on a global scale that unicorns do in fact exist. And it also showed the world how dangerous they can be and how important it is to have a superhero fighting on their behalf, protecting them from evil unicorns.

Courageous Man healed up inside of a day, after learning the hard way that that his weakness is unicorn horns. He mourned the loss of Lima Lad for several heartbreaking hours, before replacing him with a healthy eighteen-year-old boy who agreed to take on the mantle of Lima Lad. Even with their numbers in tow, the Superhuman Squad finally extended me the invitation I had long waited for. My answer was a no-brainer.

"No thanks."

"But, why?" Courageous Man asked.

"I've decided to start a team of my own."

Me and Pinky. The first order of business was burning Mother and Father's ice cream parlor to the ground. It wasn't exactly superhero business, but they had it coming. Besides, it would help them develop character. Pinky moved into my mansion and we talked about the future. We talked about hunting down evil unicorns wherever they were, but we also talked about advocating for those unicorns who wanted nothing more than to live in harmony with humanity. And we talked about Joe. A lot. I miss him a whole bunch. I hope he's minding his own business in a better place. And I look forward to slapping him across the cheek again some day. But, until then I'll be here, hunting down evil unicorns with my trusty sidekick, Pinky, making the world a safer place.

You know, superhero shit.

Sin City

"You know why they call it Sin City?" the woman asks.

The professor shakes his head, no.

"The whole city of Las Vegas lives off of sin," she says. "All of the lights and the money, the very energy you feel when you walk down the Strip, is all fueled by sin. Literally."

"You mean *figuratively.*"

"Pardon?"

"You *said* literally, but you meant figuratively," the professor says. "It's a common mistake."

"Is that so?"

"Literally means that what you say happens exactly as you say it, down to the letter," he says. "For example, you can see I wear glasses, so if I tell you that I literally can't see without my glasses, that would be incorrect. I *can* see without my glasses, I just can't see *well.* I could say that the world literally looks blurry without my glasses and that would be a true statement."

"I see."

The woman grazes her perfectly manicured fingers across the crown of her cleavage, before taking hold of her martini. The professor watches the glass as it goes up to her mouth, her red lips balancing the rim so the alcohol could run down her tongue. He's never been in the company of a woman like this before. He's seen them in movies and heard about them in locker rooms, but he isn't the sort of man that a woman like this seems to pay attention to. But here he is sitting at a bar in Caesar's Palace with a beautiful woman who could've been pulled right from the pages of the several *Grunt* magazines that helped sooth his raging pubescent urges.

"Were you finished?" the woman asks.

"Pardon?"

"You were educating me on literally and figuratively," she says. "Were you finished?"

The professor feels shy all of a sudden and worries the next words out of his mouth might very well be nonsense. He's never been particularly at ease around beautiful women. He nonetheless accepts her invitation to continue, if only to steady his nerves by talking about something he literally gets paid to talk about.

"Where did I leave off?"

"Figuratively."

"Yes," he says. "Figuratively means you're speaking metaphorically, not exactly to the letter. So, when you say Las Vegas is fueled by sin, you don't mean that literally. Otherwise, what you're saying is Las Vegas somehow generates power and energy from acts of sin like a combustion engine. That would mean that somewhere in Las Vegas, perhaps deep in the bowels, there is an engine where the combustion of a sin occurs with some sort of oxidizer in a chamber facilitating energy into the city."

The woman touches her fingertips to the professor's temple, letting them slip ever so slightly into his hair.

"I like your brain," she says. "I bet it's delicious."

"Figuratively speaking?"

The woman shrugs, smiling.

The professor laughs.

"I'm sure you're familiar with the idiom, 'What happens in Vegas, stays in Vegas.'"

"Of course."

"That would also be figurative," he says. "The idea that we can act out of character in Las Vegas, that we can do things we otherwise wouldn't do—perhaps things we *shouldn't* do—and somehow the very nature of the city absolves us is a fallacy."

"So, does that mean you don't want to do anything sinful while you're here?"

The professor's heart quickens and his cheeks blush. He is a teenager all over again, filled with desire and awkwardness. The woman slides her hand across the bar, bringing her fingers to rest on his hand. With her thumb and forefinger, she pinches his wedding ring, pressing the cool silver between her fingertips. She looks at the ring, then brings her eyes back up to his, smiling.

"You're a married man."

The professor nods, yes.

"I could care less," the woman says. "Literally."

The professor vibrates, his body shaking like the first time he'd kneeled before a naked woman.

"What you mean is you *couldn't* care less."

The woman smiles, silently inviting him to go on.

"If you *could* care less, it means that you *care* and, therefore, have room to care *less*," he says, "at least a little bit. But, if you *couldn't* care less, it means you care so little that you have no room to care any less than you already do."

"In that case," she says, resting her fingers on his thigh, "I couldn't care less about that ring on your finger."

The professor grows hard in his pants, immediately feeling shame. As much as he wants to feel the woman touch it, he hopes she won't notice. He's never cheated on his wife, not once, not ever. He's thought about it before, but only in the context of fantasy. The professor's wife is at home, somewhere in the Midwest, probably watching the evening news and drinking tea. If he were home, that's what he'd be doing with her. It's what they'd done together for over two decades, occasionally shaking things up with a dinner date or lovemaking. As much as he loves his wife, the professor has come to accept that the white-hot flame of passion is no longer part of his marriage.

Relationships can be fortified with that sort of passion, but it's not meant to last. And he's okay with that—at least that's what he tells himself. It doesn't stop him from fantasizing about the pretty student who sent him an email offering him a blowjob or the sexy divorcée who always squeezes his arm when they exchanged small talk in the break room. He knows those flirtations would never lead to anything because he's not the sort of man who does those things. The professor loves his wife and never planned on engaging in any sort of infidelity. Even when he told his wife he was going to a conference on rhetoric in Las Vegas, she didn't so much as blink. It would never occur to her that her husband might find himself at a bar in Caesar's Palace sharing a drink with a beautiful woman.

"You're a smart man," the woman says. "You like to analyze. I enjoy a man who takes the time to see what's beneath the surface."

She takes his hand and places it on her naked thigh, guiding it up her leg until his ring is concealed beneath the hem of her dress.

"Do you know about the tunnels?" the woman asks.

"What tunnels?"

"The tunnels beneath Las Vegas."

The professor shakes his head, no.

"I think you would appreciate them," the woman says. "Beneath Las Vegas—below where we sit at this very moment—is an underground series of tunnels. They're dark and private, home to scorpions and junkies and the homeless men and women who Las Vegas chooses to ignore. That's a metaphor, yes? You and I sitting here in this luxurious hotel meant to represent a time and place of over-the-top wealth and prosperity, while below us is the epitome of darkness and despair."

"Yes," the professor says, "I can see the metaphor."

"Would you like to go there?"

"Where?"

"The tunnels."

She guides his hand further up her leg until his fingertips can feel the heat generating between her thighs.

"I can take you inside," the woman says. "Would you like that?"

The professor nods, yes.

He takes the woman to his rental car in the parking garage and she slides into the passenger seat. The sound of the engine echoes against the concrete walls as the professor pulls out, driving onto the Las Vegas Strip. The woman directs him down Las Vegas Boulevard, past the resorts and casinos, past the expensive restaurants, past the tourists and locals alike who derive so much joy from this seemingly inexhaustible city. She guides the professor off of the Strip and onto some local streets, telling him to turn and turn again, until the familiar lights are out in the distance, pebbles crunching beneath his tires.

When they arrive, the woman steps out of the car and walks around to the front, waiting for the professor to do the same. He takes a deep breath, trying his best to weigh what he is actually doing.

"Are you going to come?" the woman asks.

"Yes," the professor says, stepping out.

She takes his hand.

"It's dark," the woman says. "Stay close."

In the darkness, the professor can just make out the entrance to the tunnels as they enter. He removes his phone from his pocket, using it as a flashlight. For the first few minutes it's mostly concrete and graffiti, but soon he sees beds and teddy bears and curtains fashioned out of blankets. Further still, he sees men and women. Some are sleeping, some stick needles in their veins, and some warm hotdogs over fires built inside of tomato cans.

"Where are we going?" the professor asks.

"Just a little further," the woman says.

They're deep enough now that the entrance where the professor left his rental car seems a distant memory. The woman walks in front of him, taking the phone, before placing the professor's hands on the curve of her hips. She lights the tunnel ahead of them as they continue to walk. Twenty minutes pass before the professor is fully aware of how absurd this is—being in Las Vegas in an underground tunnel with a beautiful stranger. For all of the absurdity, he hasn't yet done anything to feel regret over, nothing he can't comfortably keep secret from his wife for the rest of his life.

Then the woman stops walking.

"Here we are," she says.

"Where are we?"

The woman aims his phone at a wooden door built into the concrete.

"Why is there a door?"

The woman smiles.

Placing the phone back into the professor's hand, she presses her breasts into him, whispering in his ear.

"If you want to fuck me," she says, "you will literally have to walk through that door."

The woman removes her dress and stands naked before the professor, allowing him to hold his light on her, taking her in. Wrapping her fingers around the knob, the woman turns it and pushes, opening the door. A slight breeze exhales from the entrance.

"Come," the woman says, stepping through the doorway. "Come with me."

The professor aims his light inside, but it's swallowed by the darkness. He knows that what he's doing is wrong and he knows he'll likely regret it for the rest of his life, but at that moment, overcome with lust and desire, the professor gives in to sin. He steps inside and the door closes behind him. There are a few moments of silence, followed by the professor's loud and violent screams. He begs for mercy, pleading for his life, until the sound of his screams are cut off, like a needle being lifted from a record player—and, in that moment, the lights on the Strip shine just a little bit brighter, the booze tastes just a little bit better, and the money flows just a little bit easier.

All is right in Sin City.

As for the woman, she never does come back through that wooden door.

She simply appears in another bar on the Strip, sitting alone, waiting for someone to buy her a drink.

NOW WHAT?

Thanks so much for reading *Dolph the Unicorn Killer and Other Stories*. If you enjoyed your reading experience I hope you might leave a short review. Reader reviews from good folks like yourself are like gold for authors, so it'd mean a whole lot to me if you could.

Buy My Books

Looking for a fast and convenient spot to shop for all of my books? Well, all you have to do is go to the shop page of my official website here:

MartinLastrapes.com/shop

Podcast

Be sure to listen to *The Martin Lastrapes Show Podcast Hour* on iTunes or on the official website:

MartinLastrapesShow.com

The Martin Lastrapes Show Podcast Hour is the show that may or may not be an hour long, based on your perception of time and how much I've got to say! It's both a silly and earnest look into my mind as I talk about writing, publishing, and most anything else I find interesting.

Social Media

Keep in touch with me at any of the following outlets:

- Twitter: @MartinLastrapes
- Facebook: Facebook.com/MartinLastrapes
- Goodreads: Goodreads.com/MartinLastrapes
- Instagram: Instagram.com/MartinLastrapes

DEDICATION

This book came about almost entirely by accident, so the fact that you're holding it in your hands (at least that's where I assume you're holding it) could be considered a minor miracle. Truly, this book is a microcosm of my writing career, in so far as it was never anything I expected or planned on—yet, here it is. The same people who played a significant role in my writing are also (unwittingly) the same people who played a significant role in this collection of short stories.

Teachers.

I've always associated short stories with teachers, because writing them is how I first began learning the craft of storytelling. At the beginning of this book, you'll find I dedicated these stories to Kay and Jim—as in S. Kay Murphy and James Brown. I wouldn't expect anybody who doesn't know me to understand how impactful they've been on my life and I certainly can't do justice to their impact here. But, as I sit here in my office preparing this book for publication, I realize it wouldn't be complete without at least a few words about the two teachers who changed my life.

Kay was my first English professor. I was 18 years old, fresh out of high school, and desperately afraid my life wouldn't amount to anything. The first essay I wrote for Kay was an autobiographical essay about the time I worked as an ice cream scooper at Thrifty's and got interrogated in a dark room for four hours after stealing candy and money. Kay loved the essay so much that she read it out loud to the class. When she gave it back, she'd left a simple note on the last page that I should consider being a writer.

So, I did.

James Brown was my third creative writing professor. By the time I met him, I'd already made the decision to quit writing. I just didn't think I was any good at it. I enrolled in his class as a last-ditch effort, almost for confirmation that I should quit. Jim is an acclaimed novelist and memoirist, so if he said I was no good then I'd believe him. The story I wrote for his class was a first draft of what would eventually become "The Baldies." In response to my story, Jim was incredibly encouraging, kind, and thoughtful, which meant all the more to me because he had no idea I was trying to quit.

So, I didn't.

I could say more—lots more—but for now I'd just like to say thank you.

Thank you, Kay.

Thank you, Jim.

And thank you to all the teachers in the world who provide hope, guidance, and inspiration in the lives of folks who really and truly need it.

Martin Lastrapes
Las Vegas, NV
July 21, 2017

ABOUT THE AUTHOR

MARTIN LASTRAPES is a bestselling and award-winning novelist. He is also the host of *The Martin Lastrapes Show Podcast Hour.* He studied at Cal State San Bernardino, where he earned a Bachelor's Degree in English and a Master's Degree in Composition. This is his fifth book (and his first short-story collection).